also by
Peter Conners

Cornell '77
Growing Up Dead
JAMerica
White Hand Society
The Crows Were Laughing in Their Trees
Beyond the Edge of Suffering

MERCH TABLE BLUES

A NOVEL

PETER CONNERS

MANIC D PRESS
SAN FRANCISCO

Merch Table Blues ©2022 by Peter Conners. All rights reserved. Published by Manic D Press, Inc. No part of this book may be used or reproduced in any manner whatsoever without written permission from author or publisher except in the case of brief quotations embodied in critical articles or reviews. For information, address Manic D Press, PO Box 410804, San Francisco, California 94141. www.manicdpress.com   Printed in Canada on recycled paper
ISBN 978-1-945665-31-8 (print)
        978-1-945665-32-5 (ebook)

Cover art by Ajaibs/Shutterstock.com
Back cover author photo by Natalie Sinisgalli

This is a work of fiction. The characters and their names, the places or events, the incidents and actual people, are used fictiously, or they are the product of the author's imagination. Any resemblance to reality, including names of characters, is entirely coincidental.

Cataloging-in-Publication data is available from the Library of Congress

CONTENTS

I

II

I

Forge the coin and lick the stamp
Little Jimmy's off to camp

—Tom Marshall, "The Squirming Coil"

OLD GOLD

The worn-out wipers smeared mist across the windshield blurring boundaries between the interstate, sky, and my own foggy mood. Industrial smokestacks rose like ancient Roman columns around the upstate city of Syracuse, New York. It was as if a gray veil had been pulled across the world. Within that veil lay the timeline of history: humankind's yearning for spiritual transcendence locked in struggle against our ceaseless cycles of birth, sex, death, and survival. I didn't know that murder lay ahead. I didn't know that reuniting with my old friend would rescue me from isolation, but cost the last vestiges of my youth. As I drove through dark stretches of bleak October earth, there were ghosts in every dip of featureless landscape between Ithaca, New York and Burlington, Vermont. The sky bled with moisture that was neither snow, rain, or sleet, but some mixture of all three.

This was all familiar territory.

By the time Richard and I were young boys growing up in Utica in the late 1980s, the former industrial city was already a husk: hollowed out, abandoned, a concrete skeleton stripped of flesh. It was then that we came to understand that in a world of shadows, two boys' comings and goings were of little importance to most. It was there that I learned how to be an observer, then a writer. It was there that Richard came to understand that he was an artist, then a musician.

In Utica, Richard was always leaving or arriving. He was never truly there. There was the anticipation of Richard, the echo of Richard, the thought of Richard; those sensations overwhelm the physical memory of Richard.

Richard's father died when a bulldozer he was driving flipped over an embankment at the site of the new Price Chopper grocery store, killing him instantly. Richard was nine years old. His mother was crazy. Not crazy in the way that all kids think of their parents as crazy, but truly sick. I couldn't define it at the time, but I suspect now that Richard's mother had a severe personality disorder. Possibly even schizophrenia, or bipolar on top of that. Who knows? It doesn't matter at this point. She is merely another cocktail of destabilized human consciousness, and I have seen more than I can take. In a more thriving environment, maybe she would have been managed, overseen, properly treated, and medicated. But not in Utica. Not then. Instead, Mrs. Knight was a woman left to her own devices — caring for a young boy, no less — until some public incident would force her to be hospitalized, and then Richard would be shipped off to his aunt's house in Troy.

Poof! My best friend would be gone.

Poof! My best friend would return.

The phone would ring: "Hey, Virgil, come on over." There would be no preamble, no explanation, no "Hey, buddy, I've been in Troy for a while, what's happening?" He'd just reenter my life, in medias res. "Okay, I'll ride over now," I'd answer. And just like that — a ten-minute bike ride, up the driveway, and in through the garage door — I would walk back into Richard Payne Knight's world.

To understand my friendship with Richard Payne Knight, it helps to imagine growing up, going through school, sitting in homeroom beside a full-grown Jim Morrison. Say, Morrison after he moved to Paris. Say, you are twelve, and he is Jim Morrison, the Lizard King: dark, mystical, the intensity of holy rivers coursing through his veins in ways you'll never comprehend; a mysterious presence; a magnet with sliding glass doors pulling you in until you can taste the magic, then slamming you back out onto the concrete threshold.

As I escaped graduate school and made my way toward him, this was the image of Richard that I held. It was clear there was nothing left for me as a creative writing student. All I did in Ithaca was smoke too much, think too much, and sink deeper into self-pitying loneliness and depression. My writing paled in comparison to my excuses for not writing. It was during a particularly hopeless night of staring at the blank page that I called Richard on the phone to complain about my life. His response was simple, direct: "Screw that place, man. What the hell are you doing there anyway?" I had no answer. "We're taking off for another East Coast tour in two weeks. We still need a roadie: someone to haul equipment, work CD and t-shirt sales, mailing list, shit like that. You make it to Burlington and you're on it."

Richard's words were a siren's song. I could not resist diving off the safe, predictable shores of graduate school into the choppy, dark waters of a touring rock band. I was in my truck the next day. It had been a week since the sun shone, and even the vibrant autumn leaves looked monochromatic through the chilly drizzle. I didn't even bother letting my two roommates know I was leaving. We had met through an English department message board that connected students with potential roommates. Mike and Dave, both second-year students in the PhD in English Language & Literature program, had lived for two years on the right side of a beat-up duplex on Linden Avenue in Collegetown. The exterior of the house was slathered in thick yellow paint, and the entire structure leaned left as if it were trying to escape. It appeared intentionally built for grad students to neglect — and Dave and Mike were doing their part. Their last roommate had abruptly decided that working fishing boats in Alaska was a better fit than obsessing over Modernist poetry, so they brought me in to sublet his tiny corner room. It was about the size of a walk-in closet: just enough space for a mattress the fisherman had left and an end table cobbled together from crates scavenged from GreenStar Food Co-op.

Before classes began, I spent a couple of nights attempting to bond with Mike and Dave over cheap red wine and obscure literary references. But once the semester started, they had actual work to do — and I had work to pretend to do — so we retreated behind our respective bedroom doors to read, write, and endure anxiety attacks alone. Other than my designated refrigerator shelf being empty (which it usually was anyway), it's quite possible they would never even realize I was gone.

It took only minutes to shove all of my clothes into the green duffel bag my parents had given me for grad school. I decided to leave my books piled in the middle of the mattress. Who knew? Maybe I would be back. If I wasn't, they could be a welcome present to the next potential drop-out. I only knew that I was leaving now. I was still enrolled in the MFA program and my cheap rent was paid through the end of the semester, so I had a little time to figure it out. With less than two months elapsed in the semester, it would be easy enough to find an excuse for a formal leave later, if needed. Or not. Eventually, I would have to decide. But for now, I was just gone. I didn't bother making any phone calls, even the big one to my parents in Florida. I was in no mood for heavy discussions about enrollment, scholarship money, loans, commitments, or rash decision-making. I was in the mood to make rash decisions.

As I sped past Syracuse toward Rome, I pushed Laverna's new demo, *Aventine Hill*, into the CD player on my dashboard. I immediately recognized Richard's musical fingerprint in the first crunchy guitar riff. Even with the heavier, darker sound that Laverna was developing, Richard's guitar playing was as vivid and unique as ever. His college bands, even the first Laverna CD, were more jam band style: sandy islands of structured music surrounded by the roiling, uncertain riptides of improvisational playing. It was largely upbeat — perfect for the kind of loose, floppy dancing the college kids, hippies, and college-kid hippies who populated Richard's shows enjoyed. But this new music had a moodier, heavier tone. The songs were more formally structured, and the solos lurked in an atonal, almost menacing, territory. Still, Richard's fingerprints were all over them. While I listened to his dexterous left hand lock into a repeating pattern, my thoughts drifted back to the very first time I heard him play.

It was an afternoon after middle school, and, as was often the case,

I'd let myself into his house and wandered down the hall to find him in his bedroom. Richard's house was perpetually drenched in the odor of dead flowers mingled with herbs, which I now know to be frankincense and myrrh. The walls, shelves, and every spare corner of the house were filled with heavy crucifixes. There were iron crucifixes, wooden crucifixes, twine crucifixes; there were crucifixes spotted with fake rubies, emeralds, and gold encrusted leaves; there were primitive carved wooden images of Jesus, and folk art depictions of Golgotha that looked as if they'd been scribbled by a four-year-old in a trance. There were also miniature altars to the Virgin Mary glowing in prominent corners of the dining room, bathroom, master bedroom, and kitchen. No matter what Mrs. Knight's state of mind, those candles were kept burning and the roses were replaced soon after their petals withered and crisped.

As I stood in the hallway surrounded by crucifixes and pungent smells, Richard played guitar on the other side of the thin white wall. The music I'd heard up to that point in my life was mainly 1980s radio hits. Most of it left the impression of cotton candy: sweet going in, dissolving immediately. But Richard's music was different. Soulful. Pained.

Richard had just run away from home again. He'd slept on my bedroom floor for three days. My window was on the first floor, so it didn't take much for him to sneak out in the morning before my mother woke me for school, and then come back in around dinnertime. I'd smuggle him extra food. Deny knowledge of his whereabouts. At night, I listened raptly to his tales of afternoon ramblings through the woods beside the blue water tower where he'd spend hours, leaning back against the encircling chain-link fence, watching deer, rabbits, foxes, grackles, clouds, dirt, the sky. But mostly, for those three days, Richard just wandered around smoking stolen Old Gold cigarettes and bouncing rocks off the tower to hear the echoing, metallic ping.

I realize now that my mother could've done more to figure out where Richard was hiding. She never pressed the matter too hard. I've never asked, but I imagine she knew he was staying with us all along. There was no true look of surprise on her face as she opened my bedroom door at 11 p.m., staggered just in front of Mrs. Knight, to discover

Richard and I huddled in dense conversation. No earnest disappointment as she half-heartedly punished me for my deceptions. It wasn't pleasant or satisfying for either of us to see Richard hauled outside by his elbow; an elbow I knew from experience would soon be wrenched hard behind his back. My mother's gentle scolding and soft punishment (no television for one week), along with a warm palm nestled between my shoulder blades as she escorted me back down the hall to bed, told me these things.

It took two days before I got the courage to check on Richard. He'd missed an entire week of school by then. Although I knew Mrs. Knight was at work, I tucked a sheath of his back homework papers under my arm for protection. I came in through their garage. Mrs. Knight's Duster was gone. I didn't bother knocking — cracked open the door, slid off my Timberlands, and padded on moist socks through the herb and rose-scented kitchen, down the narrow hallway toward the sound of Richard's guitar. It was the first time I'd really heard him play. I knew he owned the guitar, but many twelve-year-olds own guitars, trombones, hockey skates, and lacrosse sticks that seem like good ideas until the hard work of mastering them becomes a reality. Richard's guitar was white with a black pick-guard, I remember that. The amplifier had a small gorilla emblazoned on the upper right corner. It was turned up loud. I listened outside the door as his late night confessions, bruises, teary admissions, and stiff-jawed bravery became music too knowing for twelve. Too hurt, sad, revealing. Richard's guitar sobbed. He'd thought he was alone. I nudged open the door. Richard's cheeks were swollen, purple, his bare torso showing a right arm bruised from shoulder to wrist. I glanced from bruises to guitar cradled on his lap to the amplifier that had already answered the only question I needed to ask: "Does it hurt?"

And I will always see Richard Payne Knight's twelve-year-old face nodding back at me. "Yes, Virgil," he is saying. "It does."

In that barren life and landscape, the seminal myths of Laverna came into focus. Not the band, but the Roman goddess that the band is named after. Most people have never heard of her. She was no Minerva or Jupiter or Poseidon or Venus. Laverna was for the losers. She was the goddess of cheaters, thieves, con artists, scumbags, and anyone else skulking around the proverbial edge.

Richard said that he loved the goddess Laverna because she represented his audience. He said those were the people he made music for: the dregs, the outlaws, castaways on the fringes of society. But there was another part of the Laverna mythology, too. The part I think truly attracted Richard to the goddess.

Laverna harbored unwanted children: if a woman found herself unhappily with child, she could supplicate to Laverna, and the goddess would cast a spell on the woman, allowing her without regret to relinquish the child to the goddess's care. The child would simply be gone, and the woman would be free of parenting responsibilities. But, as with all mythology, there was a twist: the goddess could also return the child. Change the past. Because Laverna loved miscreants, she understood unfortunate behavior as well as remorse. If the desire was to have an abandoned child returned, a woman would visit Laverna's temple, and perform rituals with herbs, dance, drumming, prayers and incantations.

If these rites pleased the goddess, the child would be returned. Mother and child united. The child now enfolded in warm maternal embrace, without memory of anything else.

How much is such a fantasy worth to an unloved child? To what lengths would they go to make it a reality?

In a strange way, it's easier to think about the brutality connected with the Laverna band deaths than to peel back the top layer of those tender, raw, painful childhood memories.

The question looms large: Do I love Richard Payne Knight? Did I ever love Richard? The answer is yes. I do, and I did. Never romantically, because that is not my orientation, but like a brother, in a way that has made me want to protect him from all the destructive things the world has thrown his way. A dead father. A mentally ill mother. A culture that treats sensitive boys like broken toys. I saw all the cards that Richard had been dealt, and I wanted to keep him from folding. Through the years, I have asked myself over and over: Why, as a child, did they keep returning Richard to his mother's house after her hospitalizations? It seems important to understand; a key to the eventual death and destruction surrounding Laverna. I know that every time she was released, Mrs. Knight petitioned everyone from the courts to the Holy Ghost to get her son back. I was too young to see or understand those machinations, but her efforts still lead me to believe that she loved Richard. At the very least, she wanted to be with him. I am aware that the protocol at the time was that it was considered always in the child's best interest to be kept with his mother, too. But what about when the mother holds the power to destroy the boy's spirit? His soul? What about when the mother's illness defines the boy's psyche? What if her sickness mutates into inspiration for the boy? What if (to quote an early lyric of Richard's) "insanity and inspiration feed each other's flames"?

We were only kids — Richard, 9; me, 8 — when his father died. What did we know about life, much less death and loss? About despair and madness? To console his mother, Richard wanted to bring fresh roses to replenish her altars. Even in his own suffering, he was obsessed with mitigating hers. Mrs. Brown, a nearby neighbor, had a carefully tended rose garden, so we decided to steal the roses from there. With no money and no transportation, what else could we do? The method was wrong, but the sentiment was pure, and the yellow roses we brought radiated vibrancy and life into the gloom of the mourning Knight household. They worked. The offerings were accepted. Until one August afternoon, when the kitchen phone rang and Mrs. Brown told Mrs. Knight what had been happening: her rose garden had been pillaged, two thieving boys were to blame. One minute, Richard's arm was reaching, thin fingers pinched between budding thorns, and the next it was pushed up behind his neck, making its way toward the ceiling. Mrs. Knight snapped. Richard screamed. Mrs. Knight screamed. Her home perm shook, vibrating like coils of wicked electricity, threatening to shoot down over her pouched gray eyes, thin nose, razor lips, and wiry limbs to zap young Richard's torso through the wall. To mount him beside the Virgin Mary.

Before Mrs. Knight could target me, I ran.

Fourteen years later, I was leaving graduate school and running back to Richard. To help him. Or maybe to accept help from him. Or maybe just to help myself.

When the sun broke through the clouds on the outskirts of Lake Pleasant, it startled and disoriented me. I'd forgotten sunshine was a possibility. The direct light was immediately splintered by tree limbs overhead as the last vestiges of city gave way to the wilderness leading into Vermont. In some ways, it was strange that Richard had chosen Burlington as home base for his musical efforts. Why not one of the larger cities that would allow access to more opportunities? I had never been there, but in my mind Burlington conjured images of dirty cows chewing their cud in dung-filled pastures, and prep school skiers with expensive sunglasses and cocaine habits. But Richard had a larger plan. He always did. His goal was to develop material in Vermont, tour the East Coast, build an audience of loyal followers, and then use that base to launch into larger venues, tours, albums — all the accomplishments ambitious rock musicians admit to wanting when they are being honest with themselves. He was doing it, too. In terms of artistic drive and output, Richard had always buried me. I simultaneously admired and envied his ambition. In fact, my entire friendship with Richard had been peppered with admiration and envy. But I also knew that Richard's talent was large and undeniable. I was not so sure about myself. Leaving Ithaca, I rationalized that if I couldn't get my own artistic career going, at least I could help him with his. It was that idea — that insecurity-laced admiration — that propelled me toward Richard, Burlington, and Laverna.

GO BIG OR GO HOME

The house looked like such houses do. A dump. Anyone who is familiar with the scenario of a group of young men — musicians, no less — living together for the sake of cheap rent, communal food, and camaraderie has seen how decrepit such places can become. In addition to the daily wear and tear, they've usually housed years, decades, of these kinds of tenants, often with minimal landlord upkeep. And who can blame the landlords? Why fix a suspiciously boot-shaped hole in the dining room plaster when a fist-shaped one will only appear to take its place? Why install a new stove in the kitchen when its main function is to hold the dirty dishes that can no longer fit in the sink? Why bother with storm windows, fresh paint, sturdy railings — you name it — when you can collect the same rent regardless, and suffer less heartbreak at security deposit inspection time? The band's house was rough even by slum rental standards though. It made my place back in Ithaca seem tastefully shabby by comparison.

I knocked on the front door and waited. Nothing. I knocked again, took a step back and looked up at the second floor balcony. Still nothing. I wiggled the door handle. Locked, strange. There was a scuffed folding table and chairs in one corner of the first floor porch, obviously a curb-score, and a Folgers can filled with sludge water and cigarette butts. I banged a few more times, and then finally gave up. I took a chair, lit a Camel, spit into the can, and kicked my feet up on the table. The yard was speckled with cigarette butts, empty beer bottles, old gig fly-ers, and festive bits of metal and glass. Across the street was the Burl-ington Auditorium. To the left was a row of bars, small shops, a Mobil station. To the right, houses, stoplight, a hill. Two three-speed bicycles were leaned up against the lower porch railing, victims of a multi-col-ored spray-paint assault that actually looked pretty cool. One of the bikes had a wicker basket strapped to the rear fender. One cigarette, I thought, then take that bike for beer. It'd feel good to stretch my legs anyway.

It took me about six hours to get from Ithaca to Burlington. It was a relatively short distance, but it felt like traveling through more than just state lines. Leaving Ithaca meant more to me than just leav-ing school. It meant, for the first time, going completely off-program. At my core, I was a rule-bound person. I did what I was supposed to do, when I was supposed to do it, including marching from elementary school through high school, into college, and on to grad school. Even my creative writing focus was predicated on the belief that an MFA de-gree would eventually lead to a plum teaching gig. Did I want to write breathtaking works of fiction? Of course. What author doesn't? But my artistic ambitions were largely viewed as stepping stones down a career path from publication, to rave New York Times reviews, to the National Book Award, to an endowed chair on an Ivy League campus, the obliga-tory Paris Review interview, and on to canonization in American (may-be International?) letters. There was a track for everything — even art — and whatever I was doing, my wheels stayed firmly aligned in those ruts. Until now. Richard's willingness to forge his own path through the world had always terrified and fascinated me, but now I would need to draw heavily on his bold spirit to break me out of my own well-worn path and into the world of Laverna.

I dunked my Camel in the ashes, rain, and spit. It sizzled appealing-ly. I stretched my legs, cracked my back, and made for the three-speed bikes. Time for a beer run. I didn't get very far.

"Hey, what's up, man? You must be Richard's friend, right? The new roadie? Right on, man!"

This was Sam "Coolie" Brooks. The drummer.

"Yeah, right. That's me. Virgil. Hey, why don't you let me carry one of those bags? It's my job now anyway, right?"

"Right on, right on!" Coolie slapped my back and handed me a bundle of plastic grocery bags. I peeked inside the bags as he fumbled with the front door: frozen pizzas, iceberg lettuce, cheese, bread, lots of beer. "What the hell's this locked for? This is never locked." Coolie turned to me looking confused, somewhat sad. I shrugged. "Well, I don't even... I don't even have a key, man. It's just — it's never been locked before. I've got a key somewhere, I think, but I don't even know where it is."

I set the bags down beside the door, fished out a cold six-pack. "But you do have beer, and that's a start." I nodded toward the folding table. "How about drinking a few of these till someone shows up? There's a bunch of guys living here, right? Someone's bound to come home eventually."

Coolie looked up at the sky, found the sun. I knew it was a little after four p.m., but perhaps he knew more. A smile spread across his lips. "Sounds like a plan. Drink beers and eat the cheese till they show!"

I handed Coolie a beer. As far as the cheese — it was all him. The beer definitely looked tasty though. We toasted cans.

Coolie's feathery blond hair framed his face in slick, low-slung ringlets. My first impression was of a fallen cherub; a cherub who now savored the taste of beer, cigarettes, women, loud drum kits, and, apparently, cheese, more than his angel gig. The onset of lines bracketing his nose and mouth, a slice of scar on his forehead, and a cautious pause before speaking were the first chinks in an otherwise celestial beauty. Life on earth was starting to take its toll; around his edges of loose laughter, deep swigs of beer, cocky exhalations of Marlboro and pot smoke, the first signs of strain were showing. But you had to search to find them. And to do that, you had to care.

"So, you just split school to come on tour with us?"

"Basically, yeah."

"Wild, man! That's wild."

"Yeah, pretty crazy, huh? Richard sent me your demos though, they sound really good. I'm psyched to check you guys out live."

"Oh, yeah, he sent you the demos? Both of them?"

"Yeah, both. I especially dug the last one, the CD, *Aventine Hill*. That's got some cool shit on it, man. Really intense."

"Right on, right on. Thanks, man. We have a good time playing." Coolie drained his beer and tossed the can over the side railing into the yard. Instead of the expected dull thud, it clanked against metal. I tipped my chair back, glanced over the railing and saw a pile of roughly two hundred cans sprinkled across the narrow muddy strip. "The dump," Coolie chuckled. He inhaled, belched loudly. "We're supposed to take 'em back before tour. Gas money to the first gig and all that... we'll see though."

I nodded, crushed my can and added it to the pile. All for a good cause. "So how long you been drumming for?"

"Long as I can remember." Coolie lit up a Marlboro, allowing it to dangle from his lips. He took a drag, turned it and blew on the cherry until it glowed fiercely. "My dad was a drummer too, so we always had shit around the house: congas, cowbells, broken heads, and sticks and shit everywhere. I'd be picking 'em up, banging everything around. My mom plays, too. She's a music teacher, so she didn't care. I'd be beating the dog's ass, flower pots, whatever made noise. I didn't get my own kit until I was nine, but I already knew a lot of stuff by then."

"It must've been cool growing up with all that music around. My parents never listened to shit. My dad was into classical, I guess, but he worked a lot, wasn't around as much, so..."

"Right on, right on, same here. When I look back on it, my parents actually had a ton of cool albums. Captain Beefheart, Quicksilver Messenger Service, Velvet Underground, all kinds of weird stuff. But my dad was usually out touring — he drummed for a bunch of people in the seventies and early eighties when he was really peaking. Stevie Wonder, Pat Methany. He gigged with Clapton on the Slowhand tour, all kinds of shit. But my mom was pretty much into classical, and she's the one who was around most. So that's what I remember hearing around the house."

"Are you fucking serious?" I asked, awed. "Your dad played with Eric Clapton and Stevie Wonder?" He nodded, obviously familiar with this reaction. "That's so fuckin' cool, man! Did you meet them and everything?"

Coolie flicked ash into the Folgers can, tucking stray blond locks behind his ear. "I met some people, you know, some famous people. Mostly it was just musicians crashing with us for a few days though, jamming in our basement and stuff. Just regular guys, gigging and playing, paying the bills." He waved toward the house. "Just like us, really. There were definitely parties and everything when the old man was home though. Then my mom kicked him out when I was thirteen, so I didn't see him much after that."

"Do you still... I mean, he must be into you playing and everything, following in his footsteps. Do you still see him much?"

"He pops up now and then." Coolie lifted one shoe and began absentmindedly picking at some dirt caked into the tread. "He's got a steady gig at a jazz club in Chicago. The Blue Room. He's house drummer. He comes around sometimes, usually when he's on tour with someone." He dropped the shoe, rolled it back and forth, pivoting on the heel. "When you least expect him to show up, he does. It's kind of his specialty."

"Jesus, man," I sighed. "My father was a fucking sales rep for a plastics company. Selling tubing and PVC and shit. I had to hide my *Slowhand* CD because of the song 'Cocaine,' and here your old man's touring with Clapton. That's wild, man."

Coolie belched, loogied into the can. "Yeah, well, like I say, my mom was the one who was around most. I pretty much lived the quiet way, too, you know. Then all of a sudden a tornado would hit, the old man would be in town, and it'd be like living..." Coolie thought for a second, then snickered. "Shit, like living here, man. Fun and games, right? Eric Clapton snorting lines off your third grade picture." He shook his head. "Too bad Moms didn't think so."

"How about her? What's she think of you being a musician like your dad?"

Coolie's eyes got alert. His voice tightened, "I'm not like him and she knows it." He dropped his Marlboro into the Folgers can and settled back. "It's cool though," he said, reassuring himself. "It's all good. Besides, I'm not a musician," he snickered. "I'm a drummer."

I chuckled along with him, but I couldn't help wondering who he was trying to fool: me, his mother, or himself. Parental acceptance, in both directions, is never easy. Richard struggled to accept his mother, I struggled for acceptance from my father, and Coolie clearly struggled with it all. It's like that sometimes, especially around divorce. Whatever our circumstances, parents become the shadows that stalk us through the world.

"She's into me playing and all. She lives in Chicago, too, so I don't see her much. We talk. I sent her our demos and she dug 'em. Shit, man, I been playing in bands since I was a little pisser. I was playing with high school kids when I was in sixth, seventh grade, and shit. 'Cause I started so young, you know? I'd play with kids my own age and it'd be like… I couldn't take it, you know? They sucked. Even the high school guys, but at least they knew the basic chords."

He killed another beer, launched it over the railing. "If she ain't used to it by now, she never will be anyway." He cracked another beer.

"She's cool. They both are. Just different. They weren't too surprised or pissed when I didn't go to college or anything. They pretty much knew it was coming. That's how I ended up here. My buddy, Reggie, from my high school band got into Middlebury, so I tagged along when he came up. He plays keys. We hooked up with another guitar player and bassist up here and played out while he was in school. Monk's Eye. It was cool, we played frat parties, bars and stuff. But then they all graduated and that was it, you know? Can't be wasting Mommy and Daddy's money at a private school for four years and then tell 'em you're gonna be a rocker." Coolie laughed, shook out another smoke. "So I bounced around here for a while, then hooked up with Richard." He lit the butt, smoke streaming from his lips. "It's cool playing with some serious cats finally, you know? Live or die, man, we're all totally down for Laverna."

A strange, sly grin crossed Coolie's mouth as he said that. Before I had time to respond, two arms grabbed me from behind and a booming voice yelled out, "Live or die, man! Live or die!" Then I was ass-down on the porch, staring up into Richard Payne Knight's sharply slanted grin.

By the time dinner was ready, Richard, Coolie, and I had already killed a case of beer and started in on the wine. We sat in a circle on the concrete basement floor surrounded by acoustic, electric, and bass guitars, amps, tambourines, gourd shakers, empty bottles, filled ashtrays, and stained set-lists. Broken guitar strings, drum sticks and picks, torn-open string packages, and paper wads hastily scribbled on with chord changes then quickly discarded, littered the floor around us, attesting to the frantic lifecycle of the implements of creativity. Upstairs, the sound of women's wine-soaked laughter warmed the kitchen, an occasional crescendo penetrating our nest in the basement practice space below.

The house was full and bustling. Julie, girlfriend of bassist Steve "Papa" Reynolds, was running the kitchen: delegating the chopping, mixing, and stirring duties in between testing her special psilocybin mushroom spaghetti sauce, adding seasonings as necessary. Papa glowed in the center of the linoleum floor, surrounded by Julie's cute girlfriends. He glanced around furtively, winking playfully at the tipsy girls, pulling off a water glass filled with cheap Chardonnay and following Julie's instructions for cross-sectioning tomatoes, green pepper, and onions for the salad until the urge to steal a kiss overtook him, and he'd grab Julie by the waist, pull her to his side, and work his way from her flushed ear down to dipping cleavage.

In the family room off the kitchen, a handful of high school stoners whooped and jeered, passing around joysticks for Coolie's ancient Atari game, staring in amazement at the primitive graphics of video games like Pitfall, Asteroids, and Donkey Kong. A fat Bootsy Collins P-Funk bass-line vibrated the floor. The phone rang; no one answered it. It was a Wednesday night in Burlington, a kick-off party for Laverna's new tour, and spirits were high.

"So, you sure you're ready for rock-n-roll life on the road, buddy?" joked Richard, playfully pinching my arm. "The bars? The traveling? Fighting off groupies with a mike stand? You'll see it all this time."

"Yeah, man," sighed Coolie philosophically. "Groupies. I dig girls, man. I dig 'em." He bobbed his head, looking from Richard to myself. "You like girls, man? I mean, really like 'em?"

"Yeah, I — "

Coolie cut me off. "You got a girl? I don't know, maybe you got a girl already." He looked from me to Richard. "He got a girl? At home, or something, a girl?"

Richard shook his head. "I don't know, man. Why don't you ask him?"

Coolie bobbed again, thinking this over, rotating his gaze to me. In addition to many beers, he'd smoked two joints the size of hot dogs while Richard and I caught up. We'd actually started this conversation in Coolie's bedroom on the third floor — Richard and I sharing in his first rolled bomber. But thirty minutes later, Coolie's urge to show me his new conga and the band's practice space drove him to gather us, the beers, and buds together, and take us into the basement. That was Coolie: impulsive, direct, guided by forces so primitive and pure, it was best to just watch and follow along. I actually liked this better though. The house was enormous, three floors with five or six bedrooms, from what I could tell. By the sound coming from upstairs, it was filling up fast, too. I was ready for a party, but not quite yet. One more beer, maybe two, and let the pot wear off some, then I'd be ready for upstairs.

"No, I don't have a girlfriend anywhere. And yes, I do like girls."

"No, no, no. I wasn't saying anything like that, man. That's not what I'm saying. I'm cool with whatever, you know. I'm not saying you're gay, or anything. I'm just seeing what's up, that's all."

Richard and I exchanged quick, knowing glances in a shorthand developed during years of friendship: this was Coolie's way. Coolie was wasted. Coolie was an idiot. Just shrug it off, and tell yourself it's just Coolie being Coolie.

"I hear you, man. I know what you're saying. No, I don't have a girl-friend. Things have been kind of fucked-up in that department, a little slow lately. Let's just say, it's been a while. Who knows though —"

"Who knows?" Coolie interrupted, contemplating this idea. "Who knows? Who knows?"

"I do," declared Richard. "I know you're fucked up," he pointed to Coolie. "I know I'm getting fucked up. I know Virgil's gonna get laid tonight. And I know that whatever those girls are cooking upstairs is starting to smell real fucking good." He lifted his nose, sampling the food-fragrant air. "Shit, I'm getting hungry, man. How about you?"

I rubbed my stomach, nodded. The last thing I'd eaten was a luke-warm Big Mac, cold french fries, and a strawberry shake at a McDonalds in Minoa, just outside of Syracuse. The beers had filled me up, but I was hungry again for solids. And the smells from upstairs were tantaliz-ing. Unidentifiable, as I'd been living exclusively on microwaved food, but tantalizing nonetheless.

"I could definitely eat, man," I grinned. "What are they making up there anyway?"

"Who fucking knows?" slurred Coolie, popping another beer.

"I don't know," shrugged Richard. "Some rice and beans stuff, may-be. Julie was talking about all kinds of food. She gets into these big fam-ily dinners. It's the Polish in her, I guess."

"I thought Papa was the Polish in her," said Coolie, already laughing at his own joke. "He puts the Polish in her anyway. The Polish sausage!"

"Papa's not Polish, you dumbass," sneered Richard. "He's Dutch, or something. Shit, he's nothing. He's American. Like you."

"Papa ain't like me," said Coolie, shaking his head.

"And thank god for that," shot Richard.

I waited for the retort, but Coolie just sipped his beer and stared into the corner. Apparently, he was one of the few people in this world unconcerned with getting in the last word.

Richard tugged my arm. "By the way, Julie tends to put hallucino-gens into whatever she makes at these dinners, so… just something to keep in mind." He cocked his ear at the ceiling. "Ah, I think the girls are all here, too. At least I know I heard Megan's laugh."

"Fuck Megan!" Coolie sparked back to life. "Fuck her."

"Shut up, Coolie," chided Richard. "Megan's cool. You're just pissed 'cause she won't let you get in her pants. Can't blame a girl for being smart. Who knows what you got crawling on that dick?"

"I got nothin'," shot Coolie.

"No dick?" jeered Richard, obviously toying with the drummer's drunken state and fragile male ego. "What do you mean, you got nothing?"

Coolie flipped him off, reclining, and slowly unzipping his pants. He took out his flaccid penis and shook it at Richard.

Richard reached over and flicked the tip with his middle finger.

Coolie howled in pain.

"Shut up, and put that thing away." Richard laughed, watching Coolie struggle to sit up and zip up all at the same time. "Take that out again, and I'll sic Julius on it. He'll know what to do with it."

"Fuck you, man," snarled Coolie. "And I'm not getting stuck sleeping with him this tour either. I had to crash with him when we sprung for hotel rooms last tour, and I'm not doing it again."

"What's wrong with Julius?" I asked cautiously.

I knew Julius Edson was the keyboard player, and from the band photo on the *Aventine Hill* CD, an intense-looking young man: dark, thick-lidded eyes, obscured by black tousled hair, a dead-on stare wanting to penetrate past the constraints of photography into the eyes, the mind, the thoughts of the observer. Even at first glance, Julius looked to be the perfect companion to Richard's new earthy, yet ephemeral sounds.

"Where is he anyway?" I asked. "He lives here, too, doesn't he?"

"Yeah, he lives here," answered Richard. "Julius is a different kind of dude though. You'll see. He just kind of comes and goes, like a cloud. A big, dark cloud. He's into some different shit."

"Look who's talking," hissed Coolie under his breath. "What type of shit are you into, Richard?"

For a sudden unexpected moment, Richard's eyes flashed with anger. An anger tinged with fear. A defensiveness I'd never seen in him before. Even through the masking layers of alcohol and pot, his reaction to the seemingly innocuous jibe unnerved me. After years of knowing someone — especially through the heady, charged times Richard Payne Knight and I had shared — one assumes to have seen all the other person's layers of emotion, expression, and reaction. To know and be able to interpret and react to them in an instant is, in large part, the definition of friendship. Until that moment, Richard and I had shared that type of bond for years. But his look, reaction, his sudden fugitive defensiveness, unsettled that foundation.

And what's worse, I didn't even understand the question. Into? What was Richard into? What was Julius into? What was anyone into? Hell, what was I into? The truth is, from that point on, I was unsure what anyone in Laverna — Julius Edson, Coolie Brooks, Papa Reynolds, and even Richard Payne Knight — was into. In fact, I was sure of only one thing: We were all into it, and in it, together.

"Shit, man, I was wondering where you guys were at." Papa crossed the threshold of the practice space, cutting through the tension that still hung in the air. As he walked towards us, the long wisps of his hair hanging down his chest and back feathered out lightly on either side. He was an imposing man at 6'3", and well over 220 lbs., with the disposition of a once abused, now rescued and treasured family dog. A relaxed air of security shielded whatever pain lurked below. And whatever lurked below, just barely below, wasn't to be mentioned, probed, or engaged any longer. He was Papa now. That was all.

"Come on upstairs. The food's all done, we're all ready to eat." His eyes shined with the wine and buzz of human contact, his skin healthy and flushed. Papa had the sort of honest face and non-threatening good looks that draw wallflowers from their corners, wondering if this might be the man to understand them. And he was. Papa was that sort of man. But he had Julie now. And, what was more obvious, Julie had Papa. His safe haven, his new home.

"Alright, man, alright," nodded Richard, breaking his funk. "Who's up there anyway?"

Papa threw out his arms. "Everyone's up there, man! Julie, Megan, Tara, Jill, Maya, the skate rats, Flora, the guys from Dino Bones and Flatfoot, some of their buddies. Everyone's been wondering where you guys are at. A couple of the girls have been asking where the new guy is, too." Papa nudged me with his toe, winking. He reached out a hand, gripping mine in his own huge paw, pulling me to my feet. "Come on, stoners! Time to leave the jam temple and meet society! That food's not getting any warmer either."

I reached out a hand and pulled Richard to his feet. Richard extended a hand to Coolie.

"Naw, man, I'm not going up there." Coolie batted the hand away and swigged from his beer. "I'm staying down here."

Richard cocked his hip, staring down at Coolie. "What do you mean you're staying down here? Don't be anti-social, Coolie. We've talked about this before."

Coolie flipped Richard off without looking up. He leaned over to one side, reached into his jeans pocket, and pulled out a plastic bag with pot and some rolling papers. He unrolled the bag and began sorting buds.

After a few seconds, all three of us waiting in silence for something to happen, Richard spoke up. "Fine, stay here. Who cares?"

Julie appeared in the doorway and quickly glided over to Papa's side. She barely even noticed us, wrapping both arms around his one bulky left arm, then tugging him toward the door. Her purple flowered hippie skirt was brand new, hanging just above a matching pair of purple Converse. Her hair was long, straight, and chestnut brown, matching Papa's in every way, but thicker, cleaner, more nurtured. This was no raggedy hippie chick. This was a wealthy daughter, slumming for a few years with bohemians and musicians before gravitating back to whatever suburb she'd grown up in and currently rejected. But who was I to criticize, anyway?

"You coming, baby?" she asked.

Julie was high. The kind of giddy edginess that precedes a solid mushroom trip. There was a breathlessness to her voice that showed her body to be out of sync with her mind; different parts operating at mismatched tempos. The tension that Papa had broken with his entrance returned, and was heightened by Julie's face flickering through emotions like a deck of cards being shuffled. She fingered her hair, touched her lips, massaged her neck, her fingers in constant motion across her face and scalp.

Papa pulled Julie tight against his side, but didn't look down at her. His eyes were on Coolie. "Don't you think Coolie should come up with us, baby?"

"What?" Julie exhaled a fluttering, breathy laugh, and then pushed her body tight against Papa's and back out again, over and over, back and forth. The tips of her ears were flushed beet red.

Richard smiled at her. "Jesus Christ, look at this one."

Julie started to say something, but then just swallowed hard and began tugging at her hands instead. She pulled up and down on her fingers, twisting at the silver rings adorning all but her left thumb.

Richard looked slowly between Julie's face and her fingers, grinning smugly, studying the widening cracks in her persona. "A little high, Julie?"

Julie nodded fast, looking down at the ground. The comment had obviously flustered her even more. She dropped her own fingers and began playing with Papa's.

"Come on, baby," she said, gripping Papa's forearm now, leaning toward the door.

"Bring me down some food!" bellowed Coolie, still on the floor playing with his weed.

"Come upstairs and get it yourself!" Julie shot back. She obviously felt more comfortable bantering with Coolie than with Richard. In fact, his obnoxiousness seemed to embolden her. "Everyone's up there. There's a big pot of shroom spaghetti. Dinner's ready. No one's waiting for you."

"Megan up there?" asked Coolie.

"Yeah," Julie shrugged. "Why?"

"Cause he wants to dance with her, Julie," jabbed Richard.

I watched Julie, but she obviously wasn't going to defend herself against Richard. Papa was quick to respond though. "Easy, man," he warned. "Take it easy." His eyes widened. He squared his shoulders toward Richard, but didn't step forward.

"Fuck Megan," mumbled Coolie.

Richard kept smiling, but didn't say anything else. Julie resumed tugging at Papa's arm until she finally got his legs moving toward the door. Papa eyed Richard all the way out. As I watched this uncomfortable interaction, I realized it was just another level of inter-band tension and weirdness. Perhaps even the lowest level.

Once Papa and Julie were gone, Richard glanced at me and shrugged a little bit. He seemed embarrassed by what I'd just witnessed, by what they'd just revealed. But that quickly dissipated as he nodded toward our last hurdle: Coolie seated cross-legged on the basement floor, cupping a pile of pot grains, and a rolling paper in one hand, while with the other hand he sifted and dropped pot into the paper at random intervals. Coolie had beer, pot, a nice buzz on already, and was surrounded by drums and various other instruments. It was obvious that he had no need for the rest. At least, not yet.

"Whatever, Coolie," sighed Richard, bouncing back into action, obviously no stranger to this antisocial side of Coolie's personality. "Stay down here, but I'm not saving any food for you if it's all getting eaten. And don't complain about it later either." He paused a moment. Nothing from Coolie. "And I'm jumping Megan's bones, too."

Coolie lifted his head and stopped sifting. He thought for a second, then proffered Richard an exaggerated salute, and calmly resumed handling his marijuana.

Richard gave me the nod, time to head upstairs. He took the lead out the door.

Before we left I couldn't resist one final, deep-grained glance back: our empty beer bottles surrounded Coolie like pawns in a game of chess, get through them and you might reach the king. It was a cold, damp basement floor — nothing much to love — but easily recognizable as Coolie's comfort zone. I opened my mouth to say that, but thought better of it, and simply left.

WELCOME

Upstairs, the party was in full swing. I emerged from the basement to find Richard surrounded in the hallway by numerous friends and admirers. They spoke loudly, males and females topping each other's volume, maneuvering to keep eye contact with Richard as he rocked slowly left to right while talking. I watched silently from the basement doorway.

In Ithaca, I'd been all alone and, frankly, on the edge of a breakdown. It wasn't the first time I'd observed the symptoms I now suffered from; but it was the first time they had happened to me. There's a panic that grips American men and women in their mid-twenties: a life-shaking collision that occurs as what was expected grinds hard against what's fast approaching, like stock car drivers nudging each other out on a steep bank turn. From birth through early twenties, we swallow ambitious images fast and digest them thoroughly: bright smiles, new cars, briefcases slapping against pressed suit pants, trim lovers on vacation, horoscopes, lottery, dating services, employment services, promising that life can — and will — improve with their help, if only you help yourself, if only you find the perfect mate, the job to elevate you beyond the rest. And then it hits: you are the rest. Now what?

Maybe this is an exaggeration. Maybe most people coast through these stages with little more than a nod of recognition to past, present, and future. But I did not, was not, coasting. And I was searching hard for hints of others struggling with the same fear and disillusionment. The same mid-twenties life crisis.

"Virgil, I'd like you to meet our number one fan." Richard pushed a young girl, twenty at most, into my arms. I felt the bones in her thin back as she leaned into my chest. Her red hair was braided into a thick knot, her clothes loose, handwoven from somewhere in Central America. She wore blue eyeshadow, no other makeup, and had a string of wooden beads hanging down her flat chest. She smiled at me.

"Tara, Virgil. Virgil, Tara." Richard reached out, tenderly stroking Tara's cheek. "Tara handles our mailing list and database. I told her you're a writer, Virgil. She's a writer, too. Right, Tara? Poetry. She's gonna write us a song one of these days."

Richard winked at me. Tara beamed at this, laughing at Richard, then staring evenly into my eyes. I shifted uncomfortably, her diminutive weight still pressing firmly against my chest. Richard clapped my shoulder, then pecked Tara on the cheek.

"Bring him in for dinner when you guys are finished, okay?"

Tara nodded, never taking her eyes off me.

Richard walked away through the crowded hallway.

So there I was — Tara and me — and she's looking at me like I just split the atom or predicted her future in exceedingly optimistic terms. But I didn't. I'd been driving for hours, eating crap, chain-smoking cigarettes, and contemplating the minutiae of my life and future until my brain threatened to ooze out of my ears. And now I was slightly drunk, somewhat stoned, and a little nervous about what would happen next. I hadn't so much as kissed a girl in more than a year, a fumbling mess with the daughter of my mother's bridge partner in Florida. It was a blind date during a visit to their new condo ("Mary says Claire is a wonderful girl, just a little shy..."). Claire and I ended up doing tequila shots at a country music bar, then smoking a joint and sloppily making out in my father's Buick in the back parking lot. There, under a buzzing halogen, she winked at me and unhooked her bra beneath her sheer blouse. Then she leaned over and threw up out the car window. We proceeded to consummate our six-hour long relationship with me patting her knee and reassuring her that I wouldn't tell my parents (who would then tell her parents, who would send her back to rehab in Minnesota). After that, I called her a cab and cleaned her vomit off the Buick's door.

While my sexual history in general was not pathetic, it was undoubtedly spotty: brief flashes of activity, followed by doldrums filled with fantasizing about girls I'd meet while wallowing in the belief they'd never want me back. These doldrums were usually preceded by the fruitless infatuations of an overly romantic imagination: the checkout girl with the diamond nose ring; the dental hygienist with the adorable laugh; the still-life painter in the corner booth at the public market. Each crush a roller coaster of hormonal hope and disappointment. I did have one ten-month long relationship with a girl named Joanne Turner in college. She looked a little like Tara: small, wispish, thick hair, narrow eyes, long nose. Joanne was more athletic than hippie-ish though. In the middle of junior year, she broke up with me to, as she put it, "explore the boundaries of my freedom." She proceeded to explore them with a lacrosse player named Chester "Chest" Houseman.

Tara seemed more familiar with freedom than boundaries. Given my state of mind — tired, high, loitering on the fringes of depression, and coming off a two-year sexual cold streak — her forwardness was appreciated, but also a little nerve-wracking.

Tara, already pressed against my chest, edged even closer. Our noses almost touched; I felt her breath hot against my lips. All around us people were mingling, talking loudly, smoking, laughing, and not noticing us at all. Her gaze was solid, unwavering, as if she was trying to penetrate deep into my thoughts.

"So you're a writer, huh?" A small grin crossed her lips. She wedged her leg between my thighs and placed her hand on my waist. "What do you write?"

I was frozen solid, no idea what to say. I looked straight into Tara's eyes, but somehow not at her at all. It was pure sensation: her hand, my nerves, loud voices, numbing substances, a collage of sound and sensation.

"Not sure, huh?" she said, teasingly. Her hand moved to the small of my back, slowly rubbing up and down. Her confidence was terrifying. "Come on," she said, nudging me back down the stairs. "I bet you haven't seen this room yet."

With Tara's palm guiding my shoulder, we descended into the basement. She took the lead at the bottom of the stairs, turning right where Coolie, Richard and I had gone left. It was pure black. The only light came from the practice space where Coolie sat smoking. Tara took my hand, drew me forward. The basement smelled of mold, stale beer, and cigarettes. Upstairs, thumping footsteps, laughter, and music rattled the ceiling. Tara squeezed my hand. I heard a handle turning. We entered a new shade of black, the sound of metal scratching over flint as Tara sparked a lighter. Shadows loomed deep. I saw crimson scribbling over white plaster, letters and crude drawings I couldn't quite make out.

Tara lit one tapered candle, then another, until an entire candelabra burned. She pushed my chest. I fell backwards onto a velour sofa. Tara sat down next to me still holding the candelabra, her brown eyes locked onto my own. Each inch she lowered onto the couch threw more light against the wall behind her back, revealing another word written in red. *SACRIFICE* — her head passed mine — *TO* — she touched down beside me — *LAVERNA*. She set the candelabra down on a low table in front of us, and moved forward to kiss me. As she did, something inside of me twitched, snapped. I leaned back and studied her face.

"What are you doing here, anyway?" I asked.

The question shook her out of it. Tara leaned to one side, sizing me up in the dim light. "What do you mean?" She settled back a little farther. I could tell she was really thinking about the question. Then she reached into a billowy front pocket that'd been hidden by the folds of her pants.

"I don't know," I said. I chortled a little bit, but it was a pressure release; there was nothing particularly funny going on. "I mean, how'd you hook up with these guys? How did you come into this whole scene?"

Tara pulled a tiny zip-lock bag out of her pocket. It was too dark to tell exactly what was in it, but it was obviously a powder compressed by the small baggie and too much handling.

"Coke?" I asked.

Tara smiled demurely, and shook her head. "No," she said. "Not coke."

But that was all she said. As I sat there waiting for her to add more information, the sounds of the party above grew louder. My heartbeat grew louder. My pulse. The flickering of the candles. Total silence seemed an impossibility, even as it filled the room more than ever.

"Well," Tara finally replied. "Here's what I'll tell you." She moved the candelabra to a side table, and dusted off the tabletop in front of the couch. It was covered with mounds of old candle wax blackened with dust, ashes, and who knew what else, not to mention stray burns and sticky patches of dried fluid. Still, she dusted. Then she reached into her front pocket again, and pulled out a piece of foil, and another piece rolled into a tube. She unfolded the first piece of foil, and began tapping the powder onto it. "I'm a townie."

"From here?" I asked.

She looked at me pityingly. "Everyone's a townie from somewhere," she said. "But it's not really worth mentioning unless you're..." She drifted off, glancing around the tabletop until she spotted an empty pack of matches.

"Yeah," she finally said. "From here." She turned the pack of matches on its side, and used the stiff edge to nudge the powder closer together on a pinched corner of the foil.

"Do you go to school here?" I asked.

She nodded. "Yeah, me and my twin sister Marge both go here. My mother's a secretary in the Philosophy department, so we get cheap tuition. Otherwise..." She let this sentence fly away, too. Instead, she reached back into her pocket and pulled out a white plastic lighter with a picture of a hummingbird on the side.

"Twins, huh?" I was trying to be cool. What I really wanted to say was, 'If that's not coke, what the hell are you — and, most likely, me — about to do?' But instead I focused on the normal progression of conversation; the progression you'd have with a stranger on a bus, instead of the one you'd have with a troublingly alluring girl in the eerie basement of a rock-n-roll party house.

"You wouldn't know it though," she said. "I mean, we look alike and everything, but we're not … You know, we don't have much in common besides that. We dress different, talk different, look different…"

"Hang with different crowds?" I offered.

She liked this; liked the fact that I was finally getting with the program. She gave me a small, seductive smile that worked, bringing my libido back into play, then reached up and squeezed my knee.

"You got it, Virgil," she said. She picked up the foil and the lighter, and handed them to me.

"Careful now," she instructed. "Just move the flame back and forth under the foil. Hot enough to get it smoking, but don't burn it all up."

She studied my expression as I narrowed my eyes, taking in her instructions. She snickered a little. "It's easy. Just keep it down here," she rubbed the inside of my thigh to show the height she wanted the foil held at.

I did as instructed. Sure enough, once the flame heated the powder, it began to almost wriggle, momentarily alive, then turned into a small bead that melted into vapor. Tara leaned over my lap with the foil straw and inhaled the white smoke as it twisted up. She'd matched the powder well to her lung capacity, so as the smoke tapered out, she leaned back and placed her hand over her mouth to hold in the hit. I watched her carefully, wondering what would happen next. When she finally exhaled, her eyes rolled back under her eyelids. It was like puncturing a balloon; her entire body seemed to deflate. She softened everywhere, and her neck went limp, drawing her head back even farther.

I had never actually been around it before, but I'd heard about smoking foils, chasing the dragon. I had some idea what was involved. I was pretty sure I'd just helped her smoke heroin.

"Good?" I asked, my voice deepening and instinctively softening to match her new mood.

Her head eased slowly, very slowly, back up, and her eyes took their time bringing my face into focus. "Oh, yeah," she sighed.

"Wanna talk about your family any more?" I asked.

She shook her head slowly, sighing again. "Not at all."

She leaned forward, raising up onto her knees, and placing her hands on my thighs. She took the foil and lighter out of my hands, set them on the table beside the foil straw, then slid her hands forward and brought her face closer to mine. Tara's chest was now wedged tight against my shoulder, her breath hot against my ear. I could feel the broiling energy emanating from her. She leaned in and kissed me.

After a few seconds, she looked into my eyes. "Want some?"

She was not talking about dope.

I nodded slowly, moving in for another kiss. She leaned back and eyed me, teasing me, testing me, before accepting. Her lips were soft, dry, and cool. I could feel her smile as our mouths parted and our tongues met.

"Hello, Virgil Frey," she purred, climbing onto my lap. She inched forward until I could feel her rubbing against me in a gentle rhythmic motion. As we continued kissing, feeling the contours of each other's bodies, she rocked back and forth, getting us both hotter. For the first time in months, my mind quieted. She slid her hand down my chest, reached into my pants and squeezed, as if testing my level of interest. I let out a low moan, moving my hands beneath the waistband of her panties, gently stroking her. Now we both moved back and forth, grinding, fully clothed, our breath fast against each other's skin.

"Fuck this," Tara finally blurted out, breaking away. For a moment, I thought it was over. The bubble had burst. She didn't want me after all.

My hopes plummeted even while another part of me was throbbing. Then Tara climbed off my lap and, in two fluid motions, stripped off her clothes. My breath caught — it wasn't over after all. In the candlelight, I could see a delicate trail of fine hairs leading from just below her belly button to a small patch of soft curly red hair. Her legs were thin and well shaped, tapering down to long, narrow toes. She placed one hand on her waist, and cocked her narrow hips to the left.

"Well?" she said, feigning impatience.

I began to say something about her sexiness — which was true, and also what I thought she wanted to hear — but she shushed me.

"Your clothes, Virgil," she said. "You gonna keep those on, or...?"

Before she could finish, I stood up, kicked off my shoes, and pulled down my pants. I moved so quickly that I tipped over, falling backwards onto the couch with my pants around my ankles.

Tara raised one eyebrow. "Been a while?" she asked, grinning.

Looking down at myself, my clothing was half on, half off, but I was otherwise ready to go. I was like an overeager teenager getting his first shot with a real live girl. While that wasn't technically true, after two years without a girlfriend, I certainly felt a strong connection to those days.

"Sorry," I said, releasing a nervous laugh. I pulled off my shirt, and shimmied my pants down over my ankles and onto the floor. As an afterthought, I took my socks off, too.

"Virgil, Virgil, Virgil," Tara sighed, moving closer. She reached out and slowly ran her hands up my thighs. "Whatever will happen to you with Laverna?"

She straddled me and slowly lowered herself onto me. At that moment, my entire world — all the worry, anxiety, exhaustion, even my significant buzz — focused into a single tingling point. Tara moved up and down a few times. The agonizing sweetness of her body was almost too much. I quickly realized I had to do something to slow myself down. For both our sakes, I wanted to last at least a couple minutes, if possible. I picked a spot on the wall behind her — a red paint splotch beside the word Sacrifice — and focused my attention there. Anything to distract myself.

Tara took my face in her hands and stared sweetly into my eyes.

"It's okay," she said, leaning over and nuzzling my neck. She moved up and down faster, pressing harder on the downstroke. "Just let go, Virgil," she whispered over and over. "Just let go, just let go..."

Within seconds, I exploded. It was my first time with anyone in a long time, and the power overwhelmed me. My heart pounded and my limbs trembled, quaking uncontrollably. I remained inside of her as the tremors subsided. Tara studied my face with a mix of pride and amusement. Finally, I leaned back, my breath slowing to regular intervals.

Tara laughed at me, but tenderly. She seemed to almost appreciate my ineptitude. Perhaps she even felt flattered by my eagerness. In any event, she didn't complain, which was generous.

"Don't you want to know if I'm on the pill?" she asked, grinning down at me. I was still inside of her. It was far too late.

I'd been so caught up in the moment — and, frankly, lacking any confidence that sex would actually happen — a condom hadn't even occurred to me. Not that I had one anyway.

"Oh, shit," I said, starting to pull out. "I'm so sorry." She pressed down harder, forcing me back inside. "I mean," I sputtered, "are you?"

Tara smiled, taking my nipples between her fingers and lightly squeezing. "Don't worry, Virgil. You won't be a daddy yet."

She leaned down and kissed me deeply again. "I'm on the pill. I also get tested all the time. I'm safe." She started to slide her hips back and forth again, slowly but insistently. "I'm gonna go ahead and guess you are, too." She laughed a little, increasing the pressure of her hips.

"Yeah, that's a safe bet," I said, flashing from worry to embarrassment, and then quickly back to lust. "It's been a while, in case you didn't notice."

Apparently, there was a bright side to waiting so long to get laid. I was already getting hard again. I could sense Tara knew that would happen, too. Perhaps it even helped her acceptance of my lackluster first performance; she knew an encore would follow soon.

She took my hand in hers, and straightened my index finger. She slid it into her mouth, keeping her eyes pinned on mine.

"Like I said, Virgil," she said, taking it out and letting a long moan escape from her lips, "it's okay."

She grabbed my shoulders and rocked back and forth with more focus and intention. "We've got time."

She held the back of my head and pulled me closer.

"Just do me a favor," she whispered. "This time let me finish, too."

PLAYING OUT

The house woke with a growl. I jerked up, tilted my head towards the door. There was a crackle of snare drum followed by double bass kicks; a smooth, cruising bass line; a wandering guitar lead, going nowhere, shifting immediately into harmonics tuning. The house fell silent. I lowered my head to the floor, closed my eyes. Five seconds passed, then eight, ten, twelve. I drifted off, merging back into the dreamworld I'd just come from, the one that had danced through my brain all night merging guitars and crucifixes, naked women, squatting drummers, mysterious portals, beckoning fingers... I drifted gently, gently, until Coolie's drumsticks clicked three times and the band kicked into a jam twice as powerful as the early flourishes, pounding through the floor vent by my head like gunshots through a barrel. I lifted my head high enough to read Richard's alarm clock. 11:05 a.m.

Last night had ended with Tara going home, and Richard and I tipped back in our chairs, smoking one last cigarette on the upstairs balcony at 3 a.m. The house was quiet. The band asleep. The guests all gone home or crawled off to some corner to trip quietly or pass out. No cars drove by on the street; the blinking yellow traffic lights were the only sign of activity in the Burlington night.

"Have a good time with Tara?" Richard asked, grinning.

I nodded my head, still a little dazed.

"I did," I said. "Yeah, definitely."

Richard gave me a wry smile. "Right on, man. She's a cool chick." He looked over and studied my face. "But, hey," he added, "don't get too attached, okay, Virgil?" He was still smiling, but more earnest now. "I know how you are, man. You fall easily. But not with Tara, okay? She's not like that. Just enjoy it for what it was."

"And what was it?" I asked, truly curious.

"Your 'Welcome to Laverna,'" he said, reaching over to pat my knee. "That's all, man. Just letting you know we're glad you're here." Before I could respond, Richard changed the subject, no doubt heading off the questions he knew were coming. "So you ready for the kick-off show tomorrow?" he asked. "Your first roadie gig? We're playing right there," Richard pointed across the street and left to a two-story building; the neon orange sign in front read "Tangerine's," with a picture of the fruit on top. "A hometown gig to get us off right. Should be a good one."

I nodded, exhaling into the cool evening air. The smoke wrapped backwards around my head, drifting into the screen door leading to Richard's room. His room was sparsely adorned: a picture of Hendrix torn from Guitar magazine, bits of lyrics scrawled on notebook paper stuck to the wall. There were a few clothes on the ground, soda cans used as ashtrays, songbooks, postcards, pen and ink drawings of Richard onstage drawn by some fan — but the room wasn't messy. In fact, it looked barely lived in. A temporary abode. A place for Richard to hang the only physical reminder he kept of home: the enormous crucifix he'd slammed through his mother's television set so many years ago.

"Yeah, I'm looking forward to it, man. I'm curious about the whole scene, too, you know?" I paused, allowing an easy silence to fill the space before venturing into headier territory. "So how's your mom these days anyway? You talk to her lately?"

It was a topic we seldom discussed on the phone, but was often on my mind with Richard.

I didn't bother turning to look; I could feel him shaking his head next to me.

"Christmas, man. I called last Christmas, my once-a-year routine."

I waited, but Richard didn't say anything else.

"How was she?"

Richard shrugged, took a drag off his smoke. "I don't know; she wasn't there. The nurse on duty said they were letting her stay in the chapel all day. Christmas and all that. Same old same though. She's still locked up in the loony bin, crazy as a shithouse rat. She's never getting out of there, man. Least I hope not. She's fucking nuts. She belongs there." I held my tongue, sensing that he wasn't finished yet. "Stabbing that cop was the best thing that ever happened to her, man. People like that shouldn't be allowed to..." Richard trailed off, taking a last heavy drag off his smoke before flicking it over the railing. "I was thinking I might stop in at the psych center when we play Utica, see how she's doing. It's been..." he paused, counting years, memories. "I don't know. It's been a long time. I might as well see if they've made any progress with her at all."

"I'll go with you, if you want," I said quickly. "I mean..." I paused. "Only if you want. I'm sure it'll be weird; it's been so long since you've seen her."

Richard chuckled mournfully. "Always was weird, don't see why it'd be any different now." He turned to me. "Thanks though, man. I might take you up on that."

I finished my smoke and launched it into the air following the arc Richard had set. We watched it go, then stood and headed for the door. Richard held it open as I passed through.

I crawled into my sleeping bag on his floor and stared at the shadows out Richard's window, thinking about the truth of his statement: "She belongs there." He was right, of course, his mother did need full-time psychiatric care. But mainly I thought about the emotional distance Richard had traveled to arrive at that statement. As children, the farther his mother slipped into mental illness, the harder he worked to present her as normal. Richard became such a master of rationalization that even I believed her hoarding of religious objects, or yanking him out of school to pray on his knees all day, or getting caught for shoplifting baby clothes despite the fact that she didn't have — or even know

— a baby, were just things that some moms do. I looked up to Richard so much that I even spent time wishing my own mother was less "normal" in order to emulate him more.

But things changed in high school. Richard stayed away from his house as much as possible, and I rarely ever entered it myself. I might spot his mom filling her Duster at a gas pump, or glimpse her through the blinds while waiting in the driveway for Richard to come out, but he'd just pile into the car with his guitar and start talking about the next gig, or a song he was working on, or a girl he was into, or a school assignment he needed help with. There was rarely any commentary or discussion about what was happening at home. For all intents and purposes, Richard's mother no longer existed to me. He did his best to create the same situation for himself.

I believe that Richard's mystique, his persona, his charisma, blossomed in direct proportion to his mother's mental illness. Around middle school, as kids became more aware of social status and norms, and more ruthlessly judgmental, there was a period when Richard could've easily become a social outcast. He teetered on the brink: didn't have the trendy clothes, didn't play sports, and there was a buzz in the hallways, undoubtedly stoked by disapproving parents who wanted their kids to stay away from him, that his mother was in and out of psychiatric institutions.

That was when Richard the artist was born.

Rather than fold up and endure being ostracized until graduation, Richard plowed straight into his outcast status, embraced it, presenting it as a worldliness that his sheltered peers could never understand. First, he learned to own his circumstances, and then he learned to wield them like a battle-axe and shield. Once he strapped on his guitar and began playing in front of people, that worldliness was accentuated by natural magnetism and repackaged as untouchable cool. By sophomore year of high school, Richard inhabited his own singular stratosphere in the social structure. There were the nerds, the preps, the metal heads, the jocks — all the usual adolescent groupings — and then there was Richard.

And if you looked closely, just behind Richard, there was me; warming my hands in his aura, drafting off his celebrity. That became my currency. Virgil Frey was Richard Payne Knight's best friend. In some ways, despite the fact that we went to different colleges (encouraged by my parents, who hoped to see me blossom outside of Richard's oversized shadow), it was an identity I never escaped. There was a familiar warmth to being back in his aura once again.

When I woke the next day, early afternoon light glinted off the porch table and chairs, falling in a bright diagonal halfway across the floorboards, spreading toward Richard's bedroom. I scratched my head, propped my back against the bed frame, and scanned his bedroom in this new light. Richard was not at home in this place. I'd been to several of his apartments over the past seven years and had yet to see one he felt at home in. Henry Miller once wrote of returning to the home in Brooklyn that he'd grown up in, that it felt like "a monument to twenty years ago… like a polished mausoleum in which their [his parents'] misery and suffering had been kept brightly burning." Richard Payne Knight carried that mausoleum in his heart, mind, and memory, constantly recreating it, not in the homes he set up for himself, but in the way he refused to set them up. This was a place to crash, not a bedroom. This was a rest area between tours, not a home.

I threw on some clothes, pissed, lit a cigarette, and ambled down to the basement.

It was my first experience listening to Laverna rehearse. As I stood in the doorway of the practice space, I was filled with a feeling of privilege. It was my own private concert, and these guys were good. Richard had finally tracked down players capable of taking his new songs where they belonged: murky places of muted light, filled with creeping, shrouded figures. Inside these new songs, intricate myths sprouted out of swirling melodies, and the band's moody playing guided listeners through this strange new world. With Laverna, Richard had moved beyond his jam band roots, but even in this truncated, rehearsal version, I could hear where the songs would still open out in exciting new directions each time they were played.

The band stopped.

"That sounds good, much better." Richard stood with his back to me, giving instructions to Papa and Coolie. "We've just got to make sure not to speed up in that middle section. Keep it even, just like you were doing, Coolie. We need to lay down an even groove for Julius to solo over, if…" he paused. "If he ever decides to fucking show up."

Coolie took a cigarette from the pack beside his stool and lit it. He nodded to me across the room. "Morning, Virgil. We wake you up, dude?"

I took a step back; Richard and Papa spotted me and turned. They were obviously between songs, but I still felt a bit intrusive. "Not at all, not at all. You guys sound great, really excellent, man."

"Cool, cool," nodded Coolie, exhaling past his splash cymbal. "It didn't sound too fucked up? Too thin or anything?"

The guys watched me. As I stood there, searching for a response, it hit me that not only was I expected to be a roadie, packhorse, strong back for them, but I was expected to be a sounding board, too. I suddenly felt nervous and half-important. I wanted to say something worthwhile, something significant yet not overbearing, to prove myself worthy.

"Well, you said Julius usually solos there, right?" Coolie nodded slowly. "Yeah, that would definitely fill in the sound more. The groove is solid; it just needs some kind of melody to stretch it out. I remember that song from the demo though. Right in the middle, I think. What's it called again?"

Richard placed his guitar in its stand and took a seat on his amp. "It's called 'Via Salaria.' Yeah, it's on the demo. It's a great tune really. Julius does some really cool shit on it when we play out. Hopefully, he'll show up tonight so you can hear it." He shook his head, perturbed, and lit a cigarette.

"If we're taking a break, I'm gonna call Julie real quick," said Papa, setting his bass on its stand.

Richard shot him a stern look: practice wasn't over yet.

"I'll be like two minutes, man," he reassured Richard, breezing past him. "She's at work so she can't talk anyway. I just want to tell her what's up with tonight." He squeezed my shoulder as he slid past, climbing the stairs two at a time.

"He's so fucking whipped," hissed Coolie.

"Whatever," sighed Richard. "At least he's here, man. What the fuck's up with Julius?"

I entered the room and took a seat on the only chair available: an old office chair on wheels, the padding torn from the vinyl seat and back. I rolled slowly back and forth as I spoke. "Have you heard from him at all? Did he come home last night?"

Richard flashed a quick glance at Coolie. Coolie shrugged.

"Who knows?" said Richard. "I don't think so though. If he did, he'd probably still be sleeping." Richard shook his head again, flicked ash on the concrete floor. "He does this sometimes, just disappears. It's not like it happens all the time or anything — it's just annoying as fuck when it does. Plus, it's been happening more often lately. As soon as we're back in Burlington, he's gone. Nobody's even sure where exactly. He just disappears."

"I've got a good guess," injected Coolie.

"I do, too," Richard said. "I just don't feel like getting into it right now."

I looked from one to the other, but kept my mouth shut. If Richard didn't want to get into it, I wasn't going to force him.

Richard searched my eyes. "He's just been partying on a different level lately. With some people none of us are really into. It's his life, so whatever. But none of us are down with it." I assumed he was talking about drugs. By his tone, and my experience last night, I imagined heroin, cocaine, some derivative of either, or a combination of both. "You'll see when he shows up tonight," continued Richard. "He hasn't missed a gig yet, so I'm sure he'll be there… in body anyway. He usually dries out into his own weird self after a couple of days on the road. But lately when he's in Burlington, he's been a whole different dude. Weird. Bad weird."

Papa came thumping down the stairs, beaming. "Alright, let's play! What's next?"

Richard ground his cigarette out on the floor, took up his guitar. "Let's go over 'Dear Thieves' first," he said, segueing seamlessly into practice mode. He placed the strap over his shoulder, adjusted the tone on his guitar, and clicked a few pedals on the floor with his toe. "I want to get that intro section really tight. We've got to hit those breaks crisp with nothing in between. It's got to be totally sharp, then dead." He turned to Coolie, started counting off, and then stopped and turned back to me. "Hey, man, we'll probably be down here at least a couple more hours. Go get yourself something to eat. We don't have shit here, but there's a great bagel place just across the street and up Main a little. You can walk there in two minutes. Pretty cheap, too."

I nodded and rolled toward the door, prepared to listen for a few more minutes before leaving. The guys just stared at me. My private concert had clearly ended.

Walking up the sunny streets of Burlington it felt like I'd never left Ithaca at all. The people I passed had that same healthy, youthful glow as the ones in the college town I'd just left. Even the older ones moved with the same easy purpose; not hurrying, but quickly on their way to a definite destination. I felt afloat in their vigor. The shops were unimpressive — drugstore, hair salon, restaurant, computer store — but there was that certain element: a record store window cluttered with gig flyers and band posters, a head shop with proud little bongs in the window, a woody used bookstore with rare editions of Bukowski/ Crumb collaborations and local broadsides that revealed this to be a town of liberal virtue and free experimentation. A college town that didn't forget its open-minded roots; home to the Brautigan Library, the only library dedicated solely to unpublished manuscripts. This was a place that accepted, forgave. I saw what Richard liked about the place.

I took a right through the glass doors of The Bagelry, and queued up behind two college-age girls in matching green Birkenstocks. They turned, deemed me insignificant, and continued discussing their weekend plans, oblivious to their surroundings. I carefully scanned the wall menu over the heads.

"I don't care what we do, I just don't want to go to Mickey's party." The shorter, stockier girl spoke authoritatively to her taller friend. "All those guys do is smoke bong hits till they can't walk, then sit around playing video games and talking about Widespread Panic." Both girls snickered. "I'm serious though. Sometimes it's cool to just hang out like that, but I want to do something different. We did that all last year and I'm sick of it. I don't want to spend my whole sophomore year waiting for Giggles Murphy to break his old record on Street Fighter or whatever."

Sharing a laugh at Giggles Murphy's expense, they stepped forward and placed their orders. For lack of better diversion, I decided to stay close to them. I got my food and took a table close enough to listen, but not so close as to spook. The taller, thinner one gave me the once-over as I sat down and took a bite into my turkey reuben bagel — thousand island dressing creaming down my chin — then turned back to her riffing friend. I put my head down and chewed in silence.

"Well, what are we gonna do then?" the taller one asked, a hint of desperation tainting her voice. "I mean, it's Thursday night. I'm not gonna do nothing!"

"I don't know. I'm sure there's something going on. I'm telling you, anything's better than going to Mickey's. Grab that Seven Days and see what's listed." The tall girl leaned over to the empty table beside them and snatched the free weekly paper that had been discarded there. She fanned rapidly through the pages while the short one devoured a tuna melt on an onion bagel, quickly swabbing her lips with a napkin in between bites. "Well?" she said, taking a juicy bite of pickle. "See anything good?"

The tall girl's head moved side to side just above the paper. "No, not really. Crop Duster is playing at The Black Hat, but I'm totally sick of seeing them. I'm sure Mark and Lionel and those guys will be there anyway, and I really don't want to see them either."

The short girl nodded, taking another bite of pickle. "Who's playing at Tangerine's?" she asked, smacking her lips together. "I didn't check when we passed."

The tall girl shook her head, skimming pages, until she found the listing. She immediately folded the paper in half and pushed it aside with a loud, dramatic groan.

"Oh, hell no!"

The short girl looked up mid-bite. "What? Who's playing?"

"Those freaks," the tall girl answered definitively. "Guess."

The short girl's mouth was full, but she stopped chewing. It hung open. "Laverna?" The tall one nodded slowly, meaningfully. "Oh god, I thought they'd be in Los Angeles or someplace creepy by now. What's that guy's name again?"

"Richard," the tall one answered with a shiver. My head raised instinctively, but I fought to lower it.

"Richard Payne Knight," she said. "But he wasn't even the creepiest. They're all creepy in that band. All those weird songs about worshipping gods and sacrifice and everything. I mean, I actually thought they were kind of cool when I first heard them. Kind of tribal and stuff. But then that night, in their basement, that little room with all the weird writing and candles and everything." The girl shivered again and composed herself.

"Those guys aren't just playing around. They really believe all that stuff. I swear I think that one guy, the leader, Richard, believes he's really a god, or really worships them, or something. I mean, he's really into it. What's even scarier is that I hear they've got a following now, too. Like in other places and stuff. People are starting to follow them and tape their concerts and all that. Marge's sister is really into them. I heard she even slept with all of them, or was in some weird orgy with them, or something."

"No way," exclaimed the short girl, obviously grossed out. "You mean Sybil?"

The tall girl shook her head. "No, Sybil's just friends with Marge. They totally look alike though, don't they?" The short one snorted her agreement. "They're not related though. Marge's sister is Tara; they're twins actually. She's really thin just like Marge, but she's got long red hair, kind of a hippie girl, always wears swirly skirts and this long bead necklace."

I couldn't keep my head down any longer. I caught the tall girl's eyes with a look of curiosity. She barely noticed, completely engrossed in her gossip. Her friend goosed her on. I edged my chair a bit closer.

"Anyway, I guess she's totally into them now. She goes to all their shows and will, like, travel to go see them. And apparently she does all this weird sex stuff with them, too. I haven't heard a lot about that, but from what I saw myself that night — I told you about that." The shorter girl nodded, absorbed. "I believe it. I'm telling you, I wouldn't go see those guys again if you paid me. They're fucking sickos. I mean, serious weirdos."

"Wow," said the short girl. She popped the last of her sandwich into her mouth, and licked her fingers. "It's scary that people are getting so into them, too, huh?"

"Oh, totally," nodded the tall girl. "It's not some gimmick with them. They're serious head-cases, those guys. Seriously into all that stuff." She broke an edge off her chocolate chip cookie and pushed it into her mouth. "Anyway, I've got to stop by the bookstore before Chem. I still haven't bought the book yet, and Stacey told me we have homework in it tonight."

The girls pushed out their chairs, dumped their trays into the garbage, and left. I lifted my head and watched them stroll up the sidewalk. Just as they reached the end of the restaurant's windows, the tall girl shot me a look — she'd busted me watching them. She scrunched up her face, scowling disapproval. I quickly dropped my head, embarrassed by everything that'd just taken place.

But who were these girls? What did they know, really? I mean, besides Tara's name and, apparently, her M.O. And Richard's full name. And the idea behind the band's songs and image. And ...

"Shit," I cursed into my sandwich. I lingered over my last couple of bites, allowing time for the girls to get well away. I dumped my tray and left, turning toward the band's house. After a few steps, I thought better of it and headed the opposite direction. They'd still be practicing anyway. I needed some time to walk and process everything.

I passed shop after shop on Main Street, glancing into windows but never stopping to go inside. My eyes took in details, but my thoughts were back at The Bagelry. It wasn't until I was standing in front of a small t-shirt store, reading the corny shirt slogans — "I'm Not As Think As You Drunk I Am" ... "I Do Whatever My Rice Krispies Tell Me To" — that I really came to terms with what I'd just heard. I mean, what was it really? So Tara slept with the entire band, if that was, in fact, true. Considering last night, was that any big surprise? (That said, given that assumption though, I did decide it would be wise to leave my encounter with her at a one night stand, as Richard suggested.) And people believed that Richard had a god complex, that the band worshipped Laverna, that they held orgies and practiced strange rituals — so what? What did they used to say about Led Zeppelin and the devil? Or Robert Johnson and the devil? Or almost any popular, edgy rock-n-roll band and the devil? So the band Laverna was linked to worship of the ancient pagan goddess Laverna, was that any big surprise? I had seen for myself that these guys were heavily committed and toting highly artistic personalities to boot. So two inexperienced college sophomores were shocked by what they'd seen and heard about a rock-n-roll band? Big surprise! Truth be told, it showed that the band was on the right track more than anything. At least people were talking about them.

I crossed the street and walked back toward the house, taking in the shops on this new stretch of sidewalk. I paused and read the words on Tangerine's marquee across the street: *TONIGHT – LAVERNA.*

Half a block away, their music leaked out into the street, but nobody seemed to notice.

TANGERINE'S

I stood in the practice space with my back against the wall, bobbing my head to *Electric Ladyland* as the guys packed up their gear. It was the warmest, most familial atmosphere I'd encountered in years. This was their terrain — cradling and packing away the gear that in hours would elevate them to a place of adventure, creativity, and in so doing, a measure of celebrity; the gear that buoyed them through hard times, offered the best times, and was closest to each since they first played it as children. They joked with each other more easily than I'd seen before, sharing this bond more than any other, like a grown family who'd put up with a crazy uncle for years but ultimately treasured him. Music, the processes and hassles as well as the playing, was their life: sometimes dizzyingly gratifying, sometimes damaged or insane.

Occasionally there were gripes, especially from Coolie whose job as drummer was considerably more involved: hardware to unscrew, break down, pack away, multiple drums of different sizes, weight and fragility to deal with. But the convivial atmosphere never subsided, their heads wagging soulfully to Hendrix, even while volleying jokes about whether Julius would even show for the gig.

It was my first realization that Laverna really didn't need a roadie at all. There was work to be done — cases, bags full of patch cords, microphones, electrical tape, tuners, effects pedals to be carried — but once the gear was packed away, a job methodically, almost soothingly, completed by each member, it was simply a matter of carrying it out, packing it away, and carrying it in again. A pain, yes. But worthy of a hired hand?

Richard ambled past my stand at the wall, a guitar case in each hand. He caught me watching them, waiting for a chance to be useful, and handed me the thinner electric guitar case.

"Come on, help me bring these out." He grabbed a tambourine by the doorway and thrust it into my empty hand. "Here, take this, too."

As we climbed the basement stairs, through the kitchen and out to their van in the parking lot, Richard laid out my job description. I followed behind, trying to silence the jangling tambourine in order to hear him.

"This gig is easy, obviously, 'cause we're just down the street and we've played tons of shows at Tangerine's. We know Sean, the sound guy, and we know they've got a good PA and Sean knows what he's doing. But once we get on the road, it's all different. We've played most of the places we're playing before, but there's always some hassle, something coming up at the last minute to fuck you up. So that's where you come in."

He opened the back of the van and packed the guitars inside against the foam padding they'd installed along the side panel.

"You'll pick up stuff as you go along, but eventually it'd be cool if you learned how to work the PA, break down Coolie's drums, deal with the sound guys and managers and that kind of shit. It's not big deal stuff really — like I said, just handling things as they come up. We might use our PA two gigs out of twenty, or we might use it every night. You just don't know what's going to happen, and either way we've got to play when we're supposed to play."

He closed the van door and clapped me on the back as we headed inside. The premature cold front that had chilled the whole Northeast was gone and a crisp autumnal breeze ruffled Richard's shaggy black hair. His torn jeans clung tightly to his legs and a crescent of skin on his lower back was visible through a hole in his Black Flag t-shirt. He'd worn that same t-shirt since high school. We saw Black Flag together at a shitty little dump in Utica our junior year and Richard immediately added hardcore to his list of musical influences. Aside from a little extra swagger on-stage, you'd be hard pressed to spot any obvious punk or hardcore DNA in Laverna's sound, but Richard was as non-judgmental a music fan as you'll meet. Regardless of what turned up in his playing, he was well-versed in everything from punk rock to reggae to be-bop to new wave to jam bands, and every riff in between. Everything except Country. For some reason — aside from legends like Willie Nelson, Kris Kristofferson, Johnny Cash, Gram Parsons, and a few others — Richard's musical open-mindedness ended there.

"There's the mailing list and merch table sales stuff, too," Richard said, standing back and holding open the kitchen door for me. "But for now, just watch, learn, check everything out, and be ready to pitch in."

We stood on the dingy green linoleum floor in the middle of the kitchen. A single bulb burned over the stove, but the sun coming in through the grease-smeared windows was more than enough to light the room.

"Just enjoy the ride, man," he said, pulling a pre-rolled joint out from behind his ear. "After all..." he flicked out a lighter, fired up the joint, took two hits, then handed it over. As I took my first hit, through the gush of his exhale I heard him moan, "...it's only rock-n-roll."

The bar was already packed when we arrived. I ducked through the crowd carrying equipment; it amazed me the way people moved aside when they saw us coming, even as waitresses struggled through the throng with trays of precious drinks. They searched my eyes, men and women both, trying to gauge my instrument, skill level, confidence. I watched the musicians and quickly learned what to do: move fast, head down, acknowledge greetings with a nod, smile, or backwards wave, but never stop moving. We piled the gear onstage and made return trips to the van until everything was inside. The guys started reassembling the equipment on-stage. Richard tossed me the van keys.

"Might as well just take the van home and walk back. Parking here sucks anyway, it'll be just as fast." I spun the keys on one finger and tucked them into my pocket. "You know where you're going, right?" Richard asked. I nodded, still stoned. You could hit the house with a champagne cork from where we stood. "Cool, just drop it off and come back. I'm sure we'll have something else for you to do," he smirked, "or drink, when you get here."

As I saluted and turned to leave, Coolie yelled, "Shit!" behind me. We all spun around to see him staring down at his gear, shaking his head. "I forgot my stick bag," he pouted. "I always fucking forget that thing. I don't know why. I can't even play without them, you'd think they'd be the first thing I'd remember." He shook his head looking from person to person. "I gotta go back and get them."

"You know where they are?" asked Richard. "Virgil's taking the van back right now. He can just grab them for you."

"Oh, you are?" Coolie looked at me excitedly. "Yeah, I know right where they are. They should be against the wall, right next to where my kit was set up." He thought for a second. "Either that, or on the kitchen counter next to the door." One more beat. "Or else in my bedroom, on the dresser next to my stash box." I smiled, Coolie snickered back. "One of those places, man," he insisted. "I swear it. They'll be there: a black nylon bag filled with Vic Firth sticks."

I flicked him a thumbs-up and turned to leave. As I entered the crowd I heard him yell, "If you don't find them, Virgil, call the bar and I'll tell you where else to look!" I shook my head, waved backwards, and merged into the masses.

I was high while driving back to the house, but not just from the pot. For the first time in weeks, I actually felt good. Lighter, more energized. It took everything I had to pull myself out of the funk I'd developed in Ithaca to come to Vermont. I'd felt lost there, struggling and — more terrifyingly — alone. As always, my mother seemed to be the one person who understood my situation, but they lived in Florida now, and as much as she cared, it was still my problem to resolve. I still hadn't worked up the courage to tell her I'd left school either. That would have to happen soon enough though. In the short term, I had a mission to focus on now, and that felt good, fulfilling, useful: return the van and find the sticks. If that small punch-list of purposefulness sounds pathetic, it's because it is. But that still doesn't make it any less revitalizing. I was involved in something, a part of something that felt special, burgeoning, exciting, mysterious. I was finally outside my own head, contributing to a larger cause: Find the drumsticks, drop the van off, find the drumsticks, drop the van off, find the drumsticks, drop the van off... That was my mantra, and, for now at least, it was enough.

Until Julius Edson dropped a dung beetle into my meager soothing balm.

The sticks weren't on the counter. That was my first problem. And they weren't by the stash box in Coolie's bedroom either, which, by the way, was as sparsely decorated as Richard's. Plus the stash box was empty. Problems two and three. I descended into the basement to encounter my fourth and final problem; the one that immediately eclipsed all others.

The stick bag was in the corner near Coolie's practice drum setup, hidden under the colorfully erotic Electric Ladyland album cover. It took some searching to find, but nothing too strenuous. That wasn't the problem. The problem was a moan coming down the basement hall; the same hall I'd navigated in awkward darkness, led by Tara, the night before. I tucked the stick bag under my arm, and moved silently towards the sound. It was a moan and a pulsing drum beat. Strange sounds, an unknown language, hypnotic percussion. I placed my hand on the door handle and listened; another moan, deeper and more guttural, joined the first. I turned the handle slowly, carefully, and peered through the crack.

Once again, only candles lit the space. This time there were twenty or more burning in every corner of the room. For the first time, I clearly made out the crimson paintings of Laverna on the walls. The paintings looked ancient, cracked and flaking, but timeless in their decrepitude. The drumming pulsed from speakers located in the corners of the room; a recording of hand percussion that sounded like ancient rhythms being beaten against the darkest edges of human history.

In the farthest corner of the room, a corner that had been obscured in shadow the previous night, stood a four-foot-tall stone statue of Laverna surrounded by small shrouded figures of men and women. One woman's left hand reached up to pour wine from a pitcher into the goddess's outstretched chalice. A mixture of fragrant dried herbs burned on a small stone tray built into the front of the statue. It layered the air with thick, dense, pungent smoke. In front of the statue, holding a cloak similar to the women surrounding Laverna, was a lithe person of undeterminable gender clad only in silk scarves. It took me a minute to realize they were neither a statue, nor an apparition. Definitely alive, human. The scarves draped across their shoulders and waist were adorned with images of Roman soldiers carrying knives, spears, and shields; the sheer material slid across pale white skin. The cloak swayed back and forth in their fingertips. A face, obscured by long, twisting black locks, revealed itself only in flashes as their head rolled back and forth in a combination of writhing, dancing, and prostration at Laverna's feet. On the velour couch closest to the door, sat Julius Edson — a syringe, spoon, and cotton balls lined up by the lit candelabra at his side — watching the frenzy, dressed in solid black clothing from head to toe. He rose languidly and came up behind the sylph, shadowing the movements with his own syrupy undulations. He unwound a length of nylon stocking from his bicep and wrapped it around the other's waist, pulling them against his body. Grinding back into Julius's hips in front of the stone statue, their voices were a cacophony of unintelligible noise that sent cold ripples down my spine. The other one bucked, the nylon band tightened, and the air hung thick with fragrant smoke and the scent of sweating bodies mingling in dank basement air.

I struggled to breathe, frozen in place. Deep in the throes of their writhing, Julius's gaze slid across the room, scanning the wall paintings through heavy drooping lids. His eyes widened, then narrowed, as he spotted me peering through the crack in the doorway. He was looking at me. I wasn't invisible. This wasn't a dream. Julius smiled, pulled the other one tighter, and licked his lips like a lion savoring fresh blood.

After trying to gather myself together by splashing cold water on my face in the upstairs bathroom, I finally walked back to Tangerine's in a daze. The mystery of the missing keyboard player had been replaced by a chilling tale of ritual deviation, pagan worship, and direct-delivery drugs. The van was parked, the sticks found, and, once again, I felt lost.

I yanked the door open at Tangerine's and, in my distracted state, slammed the edge into the tip of my nose. Dark blood gushed down my chin and shirt.

Holding my nose, trying to contain the blood, I stumbled into Richard just inside the front door. He waved off the approaching bouncer and ushered me against a wall, away from the bulk of the crowd. "Jesus, that looked painful, man. You okay?" He handed me a stack of napkins from the bar to press against my nose. I began to speak, but Richard had neither the time nor the inclination to hear it. The gig was starting any minute. They were just waiting for the drumsticks.

"Listen, man, just go home, take some aspirin and get some rest. You're going to be seeing us enough over the next few weeks, one gig doesn't make a difference." He looked around the room, as if scanning for a specific person, and then turned back to me.

"We'll take off around two tomorrow for Saratoga Springs, give or take. It's only a couple hours away, so it's no big deal." He pulled the drum sticks out of my hand. "It's our first gig at this club though — the Dark Star — so we want to do it right. We've played other places in Saratoga, but not the Dark Star. It's a good room, the owner knows lots of people, too, so we've gotta hit it hard." He stood back, taking in my bloody shirt and muddled expression. "You sure you're alright, man?"

I waved him off, "Yeah, just a little dizzy. I slammed my nose pretty hard."

Papa came up behind Richard. "Hey, man, we gotta start now if we're gonna do it." He saw my shirt, scanned my face for abrasions. "Jesus, Virgil, what the hell happened to you?"

Richard deftly deflected Papa's question. "He got in a fight with

Mike Tyson. And lost. Is Julius here yet?"

Papa pointed through the crowd to where Julius sat slouched against the bar by the back door flanked by Tara.

"Jesus Christ," sniffed Richard. "Go get him and let's do this."

He moved toward the stage, then turned back.

"You take it easy, Virgil. We'll see you tomorrow, man."

I bumped Richard's fist and made my way back through the bar along the wall opposite where Julius sat. I'd be on the road with him for weeks; I didn't want to deal with him again just yet.

As I reached the door, still cradling my nose, I noticed two distinct groups of people clustered together. The first was gathered near the three or four mike stands springing up out of the crowd, manned by serious-looking men in their late twenties or early thirties. These were tapers, a fringe yet established group ubiquitous around skilled improvisational players. Their appearance marked the emergence of a band into underground circulation. Their role was to record live shows and make them available for free to anyone obsessed enough with a band to want to hear every note of every gig they ever played.

The second group carried the same significance, but remained unnamed until the moment, two days later, when I christened them "Lavernites." They sat cross-legged in a circle at the back of the bar, passing around photocopied sheets riddled with words and symbols I couldn't quite make out. Their hair, males and females alike, was long and unkempt, some falling in dreadlocks around their faces. They looked young, late teens, early twenties, and carried the hungry, gaunt expression of kids without a permanent address. Their pants were baggy, patched, and hadn't been washed in a long while. They raised their heads only to scan the crowd with the suspicion of zealots searching out non-believers. It was my first encounter with Lavernites, but, unfortunately, not my last.

I made my way past them, past the thin stalks of mike stands, and out the door onto Main Street.

It took me hours to fall asleep that night. I scrubbed the blood off my face and threw my bloody t-shirt into the garbage. It was a lost cause. It was never going to get cleaned. It would be my first sacrifice to Laverna. Once I rolled my sleeping bag out across Richard's floor and settled in for the night, my mind automatically flipped through memories of all I'd encountered since landing in Burlington. In between every strange memory — the drugged-out ritual with Julius, the dazed groupies, the weird band members, the unexpected basement encounter with Tara — the thought, So what the hell do I do next? repeated in different variations. What do I do next? What do I do with all of this? More than once, I thought, Fuck it.

I resolved to just up and leave. This was clearly a weird scene. Did I really need to deal with this shit? I could just hop into my truck and drive back to school. I'd only been gone a few days. They probably hadn't even noticed yet. I could be back in my shitty little room writing first drafts of tedious short stories before I knew it; my time with Laverna nothing but a brief, strange memory.

As I lay there, shifting restlessly, I zipped and unzipped my sleeping bag as if preparing to open an escape hatch. At one point, I even got dressed and walked to Richard's bedroom door with car keys in hand. It was around midnight. No one was back yet. I could slink away undetected and make an explanatory phone call to Richard once I was back in Ithaca. I would be out clean, more or less. But every time I got close, I was drawn back by my own ambivalence. I just couldn't bring myself to hit eject. As much as I was yearning to flee, doing so would've also felt like just another failure. A loss of courage. Of conviction. A cop out. First grad school, now this. Or perhaps I was just exceedingly well trained when it came to being loyal to a friend I'd protected my whole life.

As anxious as I was about the situation, I must've drifted off, because at 4:15 a.m. I was startled out of a deep sleep. I didn't know where I was. I tottered around Richard's room like an astronaut taking his first steps in zero gravity. Outside, I heard men scream at each other. I tripped, fell against the wall, and landed on Richard's bed. He wasn't in it. His mother's crucifix fell off the wall next to me, bounced on the bed, and landed on my neck. It was cool and sharp. I rolled over and looked toward the window as the screams outside sounded again. I made out one of the voices. It was Coolie. Coolie was outside yelling. I grabbed the heavy crucifix, flung the screen door open, and stepped out onto the upstairs porch. A bottle smashed far up the driveway, then another. A man was running, dodging bottles, cursing over his shoulder. Coolie howled at him, insanely launching bottle after bottle. "Get out of here! Nobody wants you here anyway! Get the fuck out of here! You fucking dickhead asshole!"

The outbursts were punctuated by more smashing bottles. The man turned the corner and sprinted up Main Street. Coolie kept his tirade going, until finally — out of gas — he turned and slithered back inside. I slumped against the upstairs railing, dazed.

"You remember when I got that?"

I whipped around to find Richard seated in a dark corner, smoking. "Jesus, man, you scared the crap out of me!" I took a step toward him, then stopped."What the hell are you doing out here? What's going on down there?"

Richard took a deep drag off his cigarette. His eyes were locked on the ornate crucifix dangling from my right hand. "Do you remember?"

I looked down at the crucifix, then back at him. "Of course, I remember." I took the seat next to Richard and slid a cigarette out of the pack at his feet. "How could I forget?" I lit the smoke and exhaled a thick cloud into the cool fall air, shaking my head at the memory.

How could I ever forget the startling violence of Richard exploding in rage — smashing a crucifix through a television set?

It happened a couple of years after his father had died. His meltdown was triggered by an anti-abortion ad that, unbeknownst to him, Richard appeared in. As we sat together in front of the t.v. in his mother's living room, it was obvious that he had no recollection of filming the commercial. It was one of the first batch of strong pro-life propaganda to hit the airwaves. It was simple really: a fetus couched in amniotic fluid, the sound of a heartbeat, lots of gray and white. The first half was just fetus. Then the fetus faded to a wide-angle shot of a family standing in a grassy field, sun shining down. The initial shot showed the family deep in the field, too far back to make out any faces, just mother holding baby, father's arm hooked stiffly over mother's shoulders, and that was all. But as the camera came closer, more details came into view: mother's floral print dress, father's chino work pants, a glaze of pleasant bewilderment lighting the baby's face, until finally their faces filled the shot and the words, Choose Life, appeared over their heads. The camera moved tighter and tighter until only the baby's face remained, its pillowy cheeks filling the screen.

Did we understand the politics of abortion? Realize the implications of the slogan? The debates? The struggles? The history? We were kids. "Choose Life?" Okay. It could have said, "Choose Hershey's," or "Choose Cheerios," or "Choose Hot Wheels" — that we would have understood. But it didn't. It said, Choose Life. And Richard chose destruction.

His reaction was instant. Quicker than a payloader flips. Quicker than a heart stops. Richard grabbed the nearest, heaviest item within reach — one of the roughly two hundred crucifixes riddling Mrs. Knight's paneled walls — and hammered it, head first, through the television screen. He stood before the wretched mass — threadbare corduroys patched at the thigh, legs trembling — his face an obscene mass of popping nerves and trepidation. The crucifix — Jesus's slick black feet pocked with the nodules of a homespun paint job — extended past the control switches, into the family room. I sat cross-legged, stunned at the sudden outburst of violence. A few pieces of glass had landed in and around my lap, but most were directed back inside the smoking shell of the television set. Richard took a tentative step toward the set, then another. He placed a finger on the balls of Jesus' feet, then traced the arch up and over the crudely defined toes to the place where a Roman spike had nailed right foot and left foot together. He pressed on the spike and the wooden body dropped lower sending glass tinkling to the patchy, carpeted floor.

A figure appeared in the doorway. Mrs. Knight in her red polyester Price Chopper checkout apron and black plastic name tag: Ginny.

The apron strings dangled down her legs, swaying back and forth. I remained seated, focused on the sway. The apron strings, Richard, the entire room seemed to have come undone, swaying loosely back and forth in slow motion. I was sitting too close to the set. It occurred to me that if Mrs. Knight told my mother that, I would be in trouble, too.

I rose from my seat, quietly, and made my way past a trembling Richard. I willed myself to be a whisper of air, vapor, not there. I squeezed past Mrs. Knight and disappeared, barely brushing against her loose apron strings as I slid past. They dangled and swung. I biked home alone.

Richard stared into the Burlington night, speaking as much to the darkness as to me. "My mother made me keep that cross above my bed after that. She said I should never forget what I'd done. That I should keep it with me until the day I died as a reminder of how ungrateful I'd been. Of how Jesus died for my sins. How I'd slapped him across the face for his troubles. She told me if I did that, then maybe, maybe, I wouldn't burn in hell for what I'd done."

"Fuck," I whispered, rubbing my tired eyes. "You were only a kid, man. You didn't know what you were doing."

Richard nodded slowly. "Eleven years old, man," he said, grinning. "I was eleven years old." He chuckled softly. In almost a whisper, he said, "I knew what I was doing."

Then he said it again, this time louder. "I knew exactly what I was doing."

We looked at each other. "What did it feel like anyway?" I asked, hefting the crucifix in my hands, feeling its dense weight. "Launching this thing through a television set?"

Richard Payne Knight flicked his cigarette over the railing, and smiled. "It's just something you've got to know to love."

ON TOUR

This time, it was a light metallic crashing. The sounds came at uneven intervals, maintaining a persistently arrhythmic clatter. I raised my
head. Again, Richard was already gone. I heard voices outside on the
lawn: Coolie, Richard, two females. I looked at the clock, 10:23 a.m.
Damn, when do these guys sleep?

"Aw, sick, man!" I heard Coolie yell. "This shit is nasty. Look at
this!" There was a pause, then a hearty round of grossed-out laughter.

"Suck it up!" bellowed Richard. "We gotta get to Saratoga!"

I slid out of my sleeping bag and zipped it at the foot of Richard's
bed. This was it — the first day of tour. Fight or flight. Even after all
I'd seen and heard — the bagel girls' rumors, the infighting, the band's
collective moodiness and instability, Coolie's insanity last night, Julius's
habit and fetish — I was ready to go. The late-night conversation with
Richard had eased my nerves just enough to push me to the next stage.
Or perhaps he'd just set the hook a little deeper. He assured me that
Julius and Coolie would chill out once we got going. They always do,
he said. "People change when they're on tour, Virgil. Become tighter,
sharper. Some people snap shut like aspirin lids, some open out in ways
you could never predict. Coolie and Julius," he nodded reassuringly,
"they button down. Get more professional. You'll see. They'll be fine."

What I didn't bother telling Richard was how appealing the unpredictability of travel sounded to me right now. I craved the uncertainty of having to overcome challenges that never would've occurred simply marching from school to apartment and back again. How was I supposed to learn about writing just sitting in a classroom reading about the exploits of those who'd had the balls to live their lives? If I was going to get serious about my work, it was time to start living my own life. And if I was going to abandon it, I'd best not fuck up this shot at an interesting gig with Laverna.

Either way, it was time to leap.

I stuffed my sleeping bag into its sack, rummaged through my backpack, and pulled out some fresh clothes to start with: clean jeans, boxers, socks, t-shirt, sweatshirt. I didn't have to look outside to know what was happening: the band was collecting returnables off the aluminum can heap beside the porch for gas money. A noble undertaking, but not one for me. Mine was to shower, dress, eat breakfast — then begin.

As the jets of water hit my skin, three days of travel and partying slid off down the drain. A few days without showering and the human body creates a buffer against excessive body odor; a threshold is reached, maintainable for six or seven days. After that, successive thresholds are reached and surpassed until personal body odor gives way to the universal smells of poverty, desperation, gypsy travel or intensive naturalism. I was only at the first level, but who knew when my next shower would be?

I searched around for soap — found three small slivers in various corners of the tub basin, pressed them together as best I could, and worked up a thin coat of lather. This was the classic multiple male shower basin: gelatinous black film clung to the edges, down the side and onto the floor where a daily pressure of feet maintained a single clean strip down the center. And who would be the man to get down there with a sponge and cleanser to scrub? No one. That was the point.

I washed my hair using an enormous tub of generic green shampoo and shut down the water. A towel flew over and wrapped around the curtain rod above me.

"Who's that?" I asked, quickly pulling down the towel. "Richard?"

I peered out the side of the curtain; Julius Edson gave me a toodle-oo wave. "Oh, hey, man." I said, nodding quickly. "I'll be out of here in a minute. I just gotta dry off."

"No hurry." His words were languid, slow. "I showered this morning, last night, whatever — take your time." He lifted the toilet lid, unzipped. I ducked back in the shower to dry off. His urine stream hit the water. He spoke above the gush. "You didn't make it to the gig last night — I hope I didn't scare you off." I stopped drying, stood speechless. I hadn't told Richard or anyone what I'd seen. "I don't believe I'm mistaken — that was you in the basement last night, right? I didn't get a good look," his piss trickled off, "but I just assumed."

I heard him zip, wrapped the towel around my waist, and pulled back the curtain.

"Yeah, that was me. I actually slammed my nose into a door pretty hard last night." I touched it, testing for tenderness. It was still sore near the bridge. "I bled all over myself, my shirt and everything, so I just came back here. I'm, uh," my voice trailed off. I stepped out of the shower, eased past Julius, and rubbed a circle into the steamed mirror. I found his face in the reflection behind me. "I'm sorry about breaking in on you though. Just a wrong turn, I didn't mean to," I searched for the right words, "intrude or anything."

Julius chuckled, leaning against the bathroom wall. His clothes were neat, pressed: black denim jeans, black button-down shirt, black Doc Martins, his jet-black hair gelled into an updated version of the pompadour. I pictured his closet as a pit, a shadow, a brooding nest of dark fibers. I lathered and began shaving around my chin and neck.

"So you're Richard's boy from way back, right? Elementary school and all that?" He studied my razor's path through white foam. "Bosom buddies through the years?"

I stopped, rinsed the blade in the sink, found his eyes in the mirror. "Yeah, we go way back. Going on twenty years now." I resumed my shaving. "How about you guys? How'd you two hook up?"

"Oh us?" Julius took a step forward. "You missed a spot," he said, touching my neck lightly then stepping back. A shiver bristled across my scalp. "You know how it is with music; incestuous little business. This one plays with that one, that one plays with the other, and pretty soon we've all played together, haven't we?"

He seemed to be waiting for a reply.

"Yeah, it does seem that way," I answered, hesitantly. I rinsed off the blade, wiped down my face and packed the gear away in its travel case. "I'm just kind of learning as we go along, so..."

"Oh, we all do," interrupted Julius. "It's the only way, really." He leaned over my shoulder, checked and readjusted his hair methodically in the mirror.

"Right," I nodded. "The only way. Anyway, I should get dressed and go help out downstairs. We'll probably need to pack up soon."

I turned and made for the door, travel case in hand. Julius took my place at the mirror, more involved in his preening now. His next question stopped me cold on the hallway threshold.

"How well do you know Richard anyway?"

"Huh?" I turned back to him at the sink. "What's that?"

He looked back slowly. "I asked you how well you know Richard." He paused, allowing this to sink in. "I mean, you've known each other mostly over the phone for the past few years, right? An occasional visit here and there, but mostly long distance, no?"

His glare was amused, condescending. I fired a weak shot. "Who talks like that anyway? What are you — European or something?"

He snickered, "Sometimes, very," and went back to preening. "People change, Virgil, that's all I'm saying. Even islands unto themselves like Richard. Everybody, especially artists, need to find their creative wellsprings. New and greater sources of inspiration. Without vigilance, those wellsprings can become all that matters — feeding them, widening them, a lifetime pursuit. It's no different from the alcoholic moving from beer to whiskey or the drug addict —"

"Looking for a fix?"

He turned, smiled knowingly, then turned back. "Yes, exactly."

"Right," I nodded. "Thanks, Julius. Food for thought. I'll see you downstairs."

I turned to leave, but not before he got the last word.

"All I'm asking you, Virgil, is, as Richard's friend, where do you think his inspiration comes from?" He turned and fixed his stare on me now. "What are the great Richard Payne Knight's creative wellsprings? And how deeply do they flow?"

His stare was unnerving.

I stood in the middle of the bedroom pulling on my clothes. Julius's questions lodged like a bullet in my brain. How well did I know him? How well did I know Richard Payne Knight? Some of him I knew very well: his childhood, family history, place of birth, place of first kiss, first lay, first cigarette, first gig… I could tick off these ledger records like a friendship accountant; plain facts, a tally of events contributing to a shared history. Unfortunately, those records became fuzzy after high school, details clouded by first, sometimes even second or third person reportage. Did Richard really strut onstage naked at an Oneonta College homecoming dance his sophomore year? Did he refuse to come offstage or stop playing until the organizers, in desperation, cut the band's power? Probably. But after hearing this story re-told by Richard's friends, rivals, bandmates, casual observers, and assorted gossip mongers, where do you draw the line? How important are the details? Was he on acid at the time? Erect or flaccid? Did he do it to prove his love for, or to rebuke, a philosophy, music, or literature professor? Was he successful? Who was he seen with just before and after the gig? What did he really yell just before the power went down — and could he have meant it?

For my part, I took my limited information from what Richard offered to me in conversation, and simply enjoyed the rest. Richard seemed to pay little attention to such events or rumors after the fact, but to me they were magic: his existence away from physical presence. They contributed to a growing mystique and would make great true fan trivia one day: to know the most oft repeated versions would bring them closest to truth, mark those who knew them as the most devoted.

Julius Edson was a freak. But he had a point, too. Despite my intimate knowledge of Richard's youth, I didn't know a lot about him after that. I loved him, supported him, believed in him — but, in some ways, there was a lot I didn't know about Richard Payne Knight at this point.

I slung my backpack over my shoulder, checked the small bruise on the bridge of my nose in the mirror, and walked downstairs. I entered the kitchen to find Richard, Coolie, and two girls I'd never seen before sipping coffee in beer-and-mud-stained clothes. What the hell? I thought. I don't know any of these people. Hell, do I even know myself? And then, quickly, Fuck it. It's nothing that living out of a van together for a few weeks won't fix.

"Young Virgil!" Richard greeted, grinning. "How are you this morning?"

"I'm good," I said, stepping back as their stench reached my nose. "But you guys stink!"

"Fine, fine!" he replied, coming over to slap my back. "Then your nose is fixed! All the pieces have fallen into place!"

I couldn't help but laugh, even as Richard mimed wiping his filthy hands on my clean sweatshirt. They reeked of stale beer and sweat, but Richard was ecstatic. He was in a better mood than I'd seen in years; prepared to hit the road to do what he did best.

Richard reached into his jeans pocket and pulled out a crumpled wad of bills. "It took months of hard drinking, but we did it!" He pasted the bills into my hand. "Here you go, Mr. Roadie. Gas money to Saratoga Springs. This should do the trick. If not, we'll get out and walk the rest of the way." He squeezed my fingers shut around the smelly bills and clapped my hand between his two. "So what do you say, man? You ready to roll or what?"

"Hell yeah, I'm ready," I answered, buoyed by his enthusiasm. "Just tell me what to do while you guys are in the shower."

"Hey, man," sighed Coolie from the kitchen table, flashing an easy grin. "Who said anything about taking a shower?"

"You especially!" I said, pointing at him and laughing. "Either that or you're riding in the far back of the van — away from me."

"Actually, Coolie will probably start out driving," clarified Richard.

"We're taking his Subaru, too, since we can't all fit in the van, so we'll be convoying most of the time. Most of the equipment is still in the van from last night, so we've got it easy today. We'll take off as soon as Papa gets back from Julie's, and we shower and get ready," he nodded toward Coolie and the girls. "I think Julius is upstairs too, right?" He turned to Coolie, "Julius is here, isn't he?"

"Yeah," I jumped in. "He's here. I just talked to him upstairs."

"Good, good," nodded Richard, walking over to where the girls sat, taking each one by the hand. "Let's try and keep him here then," he said, pulling them to their feet. The girls — young, attractive, hippie-ish and slightly bashful — complied, trailing Richard down the hall. Coolie followed closely behind.

"Make yourself some breakfast, Virgil. We picked up some bagels at the store." He pointed to a bag on the counter. "There's some orange juice in the fridge, too. We'll take off in an hour or so, so just hang out till then." He flashed me a thumbs-up as the group disappeared down the hallway.

"Get psyched, man!" he called back, already out of sight. "It all starts today!"

And so it did.

Four weeks later, local newspapers reported that the bodies of Marisa Lowenguth and Tammy Sinclair were found buried in a cow pasture in St. Albans, Vermont. Their throats had been slashed. Strange symbols had been carved on their arms and legs.

MAGICAL THINKING

Why didn't I just get out of there? That would have made the most sense. I realize now I was living in a delusion. Magical thinking, I believe it's called. Somehow, things would get better. Julius would get less twisted. Coolie would get less aggressive. Richard and I would become as close as we used to be. My work with Laverna would turn me into a rock-n-roll power broker, or perhaps even the writer I had always wanted to become.

Not a journal keeper. Not a memoirist of sad stories, or worse, true crime: a person who can only write about tragedies that happened, rather than illuminating the myriad possibilities of our limitless human...

Jesus, what an asshole I am.

As much as I torture myself about my decisions now, I realize I still didn't have all the pieces of the puzzle before we went on tour. I knew enough to sense danger (which I stupidly ignored), but not enough to understand what was coming. How bad things could truly get.

The truth is, it felt good to be back in Richard's orbit. The fragmented pieces of my life were pulled together when I was with him. It also made me realize how lonely I had been before that. How uninspired. It's strange to think that an MFA student in one of the most prestigious writing programs in the country could feel so alone and stripped of creativity. But there you have it. The bottom line was that I had never met anyone like Richard. I had other friends, high school friends, college friends, but they all seemed patently uninteresting compared to Richard Payne Knight.

Even girls I dated. Yes, it's true. Perhaps that's why no romantic relationships ever stuck. I don't know. The world outside of Richard was just bland. At least, I felt bland. I felt like a black and white television stuck on a test pattern that never resolves to its regularly scheduled programming. I kept waiting for the show to begin, but it never did. No matter what I accomplished, where I went, who it was that I met along the way, I was always just waiting.

When I hooked up with Laverna, it felt like things were finally in motion. I was alive. I was a part of something… moving toward becoming the true Virgil Frey.

That's how it felt at the time anyway.

In all honesty, I probably would've given anything just to feel *more* than what I had been feeling. And Richard — and Laverna — made me feel *more*. So I wanted *more* of that feeling. I begged for *more*. And I was willing to ignore every signpost on the way to *more* that could've told me how dangerous things were about to become.

MAKING HISTORY

Thick slabs of sunlight soaked Richard in the driver's seat of the van. I rode shotgun. Coolie, Julius, and Papa followed behind us in the Subaru. The van was sluggish, weighed down with bulky speakers, amplifiers, and instruments. It was a whale to start with — a blue Ford Econoline, no frills, no style — and given the added cargo, it handled like a broken shopping cart through wet sand. Luckily I-87 was a straight shot through to Saratoga and weekend traffic was light.

Although I couldn't have pinpointed my feelings at the time, cruising along at a steady 65 mph I was glad to be out of the house. In the three days I'd been there, it seemed to have taken on almost human characteristics, revealing its darker nature only in flashes, keeping its accumulated crap out of sight, lighting up like a landing strip for casual guests and visitors. It seemed somehow complicit in all the strange things I'd seen the guys do and say. A partner in crime. The fifth member of Laverna. I was still feeling overwhelmed by the other four human members; being out of the house, on neutral ground, gave me some of the edge I needed to regain my delicate balance.

I broke a ten-minute gap in conversation. "So you said you guys have played here before?"

Richard shook his head, staring straight out the windshield. "No, we never played the Dark Star. We've played a couple smaller places nearby, but this is our first gig there."

"Nervous?" I asked, half playfully. Richard shot me a curious look, then snickered his answer: no. There are questions we ask in order to know the answers and questions we ask in order to know the person answering. In this case, I already knew the answer: in all the years I'd known Richard, I had no memory of him ever being nervous. But I was hoping for more insight into where his head was at now. I had known Richard through all the various stages of his life, and now I wanted to fully know Laverna Richard. "You never get nervous, do you?" I asked. He repeated the original look, then shook his head again: no. This time, his condescension struck a nerve. Perhaps it was the bland monotony of the drive, spaciness from the pot, or maybe preoccupation with the tour ahead, but Richard had transformed from the happy-go-lucky man from this morning into his clipped, brooding artist personality. I was sorry to see upbeat Richard go, but this was a version of him I knew well.

"So, whatever happened to those girls from this morning, anyway?" I asked. "Did you just leave them at the house or what?"

Richard tilted his head until he faced the roof, then focused back on the road. "Yeah, Virgil, we left them there." He spoke slowly, carefully. "Some guys are gonna come by to pick them up later." He turned, studied my face, then turned back to the windshield.

At some point after Richard, Coolie and the girls had gone upstairs, while I was still eating breakfast, I'd heard a patter of feet filing down to the basement. Although I heard no voices, I could tell there were at least three or four people by the sound. Time passed, no one emerged. Papa showed up, we talked some, I ate my bagel. It was Papa who urged me not to check on what was happening in the basement. A pre-gig ritual, he suggested. One the other guys believed in. Best not to interfere. Or ask too many questions.

Forty-five minutes later, I heard footsteps slapping — loud, quick — all the way upstairs. The shower started. One hour later, we were on the road.

I forged ahead, poking the tiger. "So what were you guys doing in the basement anyway?" Richard turned to eyeball me, but said nothing. I was getting frustrated. I'd restrained myself from saying anything to him about Julius, Coolie's weirdness, rumors about the band, anything at all. No questions, no comments, just acceptance. But now we were on the road and I knew that if I wanted to hold my own, I'd have to start speaking up. I decided to hit him full force. "So what's up with that little room in the basement?" He looked at me again, sizing me up. "The one with the statue and all the writing and stuff all over the walls." I waited. He remained silent. "Come on, Tara took me down there that first night — I'm assuming you told her to do it. You know I've seen it, Richard. So what's the story?"

"The story?"

"Yeah, the story," I said, flatly. "With the room. What's up?"

"You've been down there," he answered coolly. "You've seen the room. Why don't you tell me what's up? What did you see?"

Richard was pissing me off. The question posed earlier that morning — How well did I know Richard Payne Knight? — came scudding back slightly altered: how well did I want to know Richard Payne Knight?

"Well, the first time," I answered sharply, "all I saw was a bunch of candles and the top of Tara's head. But the second time —"

"You saw Julius," he finished matter-of-factly.

I was stunned. He'd sneaked a hook while I was busy jabbing.

"How did you know?"

"Julius implied that might be why you missed the gig." Richard shot me a weird, uneven smile. "A little freaked out, Virgil?"

I returned from shocked to pissed. Still, I tried keeping my cool. "Freaked out? Me? By walking in on your weirdo keyboard player shooting heroin and humping some strange scarf-draped teenager while worshipping a stone statue?" I shook my head. "No, not at all. Should I be?"

"What do you know about faith, Virgil?"

"What do you know about assholes, Richard?"

He chuckled calmly. "I know that sometimes things are exactly as they appear to be," he said, staring at me. "I know that faith is whatever you want it to be, and I know that eventually all things — good and bad — must end, and that when they do, only the stories, the mythologies, remain." He turned and stared out the windshield again. "That's why you're here."

"What's that supposed to mean, 'That's why you're here'?" I spat back, feeling angry, manipulated.

"To tell the stories, Virgil," he answered, calmly. "Don't you know that by now?"

"Is that what you need, Richard?" I sneered, stung by his cool detachment. "Is that what I am to you? Someone to testify to your ultimate over-the-edge rock-n-rollness? A human recording device to spread your badass legend?"

And I can still see Richard Payne Knight nodding back at me: Yes.

And there it was.

Richard's directness was an insult, but, in many ways, it was also a relief. Over the years, I had recognized a pragmatism to Richard that I'm convinced all artists must possess to succeed. It's not as sexy as words like "inspiration" or "fate" or even "talent," but it's always at the center of great artists' biographies. Richard's implication about my true role in Laverna — perhaps even his life — struck me like a crucifix thrown through a television set. But it was also obvious. Of course that's what he wanted from me. That had always been our dynamic. He was the artist; I was the best friend. I was Boswell; he was Johnson. I was Kerouac; he was Cassady.

I suppose I was the perfect person for the job.

I had been with Richard his whole life. I had seen him grow as an artist, all the while garnering a loyal following from the start. Ever since middle school, Richard had fronted a string of rock bands that could all be considered wildly successful in their own place and time. When you're in eighth grade and your band, Rough Diamonds, is asked to play the Activity Night dance, you've "made it" middle school style. When you lose your rhythm section because Mikey and Frank Shots are forced to move when their dad lands a job at the University of Rochester, but then quickly add a ninth grade transfer student/rock drummer and a jazz bass prodigy from the rival high school, and reconstitute as Soul Drops to play every major graduation party from sophomore through senior year... you've made it, high school style. The list goes on.

Over the years, Richard had written the music, the lyrics, sang the songs, and played lead guitar in five different bands, including Exit and Orphan Bags while attending Oneonta College. Five different bands, starting from age thirteen and culminating with the Burlington-based Laverna, guided by the unwavering creative powers of Richard Payne Knight. Throughout his life, those powers had garnered Richard praise from peers, suspicion from authority figures, and the adoration of countless young male and female fans. By the time he started Laverna at twenty-three, Richard was already uniquely capable of carrying off his role as guitarist, songwriter, and front man with startling authority.

And I knew that. I had witnessed it all.

Was I angry at being reduced to his chronicler? Yes. Was I surprised? No. And was I flattered? More than I should have been.

"Fine," I muttered under my breath.

"What?" Richard said, turning to study my profile. His trademark grin spread across his face. "What was that?"

"I said, 'Fine,' you asshole," I hissed, picking a piece of dried dirt off the tip of my Converse All-Star sneaker and flinging it onto the floor mat. "What the hell else am I going to write about anyway?"

"Exactly!" Richard proclaimed, clearly pleased that he had gotten his way. "What could be better? Rock-n-roll, debauchery, life on the road, shitty food, rest stops, a bunch of whacked-out musicians — it's the best stuff in the world, man!" He reached across the front seat and playfully slapped my leg. "Besides, your parents will be so proud, Virgil."

"Yeah, well," I said, finding a few more flecks of dirt to purge, "I'm afraid that ship has already sailed. They weren't exactly thrilled about this latest plot twist."

"Dropping out of school?"

I nodded, pulled a cigarette out of the pack on the dashboard, and lit up. "Yeah. They were pretty pissed when I talked to them this morning. I can't blame them, I guess."

While Richard had been occupied in the basement, I decided it was time to pull the trigger and tell my parents about leaving school. I had delayed as long as I could. I was clearly going on tour, which meant that at the very least I'd have to withdraw for the semester. As I stood at the payphone in front of the gas station across from the Laverna house, my parents' unbridled disappointment shrunk me back to feeling like a bashful eight-year-old. My offer to pay rent on the Ithaca apartment with my Laverna roadie earnings did little to soften the sting. There was no point in keeping it. It was a waste of money. And, besides, money wasn't the issue.

"What will you do, Virgil?" my mother asked.

Before I could answer, my father chimed in, "You're carrying their equipment? Like a sherpa?"

I chuckled, but he wasn't trying to be clever.

"I'm glad you think this is all a big joke, Virgil. Because I don't." He coughed nervously into the receiver, a habit that, according to my mom, predated my birth; a sound that immediately cued me in to his level of disappointment more than any words he could say.

"I've got to go, Virgil. Talk to your mother." He coughed again. "I'm done with this."

And with that, as with so many times before, my father was gone. He was done with this. Whatever "this" meant this time. It was the last conversation I would have with him until after the murders were discovered. As usual, my mother stepped in to smooth the ruffled air between us.

"He's upset, Virgil," she said, quietly.

"I know, Mom," I answered. "I understand. It's just…"

I stared at the house across the street. It was quiet on the outside, but seemed to almost throb in the sunlight.

"I just need to do this. Nothing was working for me in Ithaca. It was a waste of time, money, everything." I paused, allowing her to speak, but she stayed quiet. "I'm not saying I'll never go back, Mom. I might. I mean, I want to, I think." I shook my head, and toed the dirt at the base of the pay phone. "I'm actually hoping in some way this trip will help."

At the time, I wasn't exactly sure what I meant. I had some vague idea about adventure, experience, and travel being helpful to my creativity. But the idea of writing about Richard hadn't even crossed my mind.

Now it did. As I rolled down I-87 toward Saratoga, blowing cigarette smoke out the van window, the conversation with my mother intersected with the one with Richard, merging into some sort of direction. A way forward. Some strange kind of relief.

"You'll be fine, man," Richard said, reassuringly. He lit a cigarette and gestured out the windshield to the road being eaten beneath our wheels. "This is going to be good for you, trust me. It's the best thing, Virgil." He looked at me and smiled. "Richard and Virgil, on the road together!" He clapped my arm. "We'll make history."

DARK STAR

The third girl to disappear that tour approached me at the end of the Dark Star gig asking for the keys to the van. She was tall, 5'10" or so, with drab sand-colored hair dripping off her head in three separate sections, one down her back, one over each shoulder. Her nose swerved gently left — it'd been broken, but not reset — and, as she took the keys, I noticed a thin black line of filth pouched in her fingernails. Laverna's set was almost done. They'd been playing for three hours; the Dark Star was packed and rocking. I was behind the merch table off to one side of the stage; there had been some action before the band came on stage, and then interest stopped abruptly as soon as the music started. The Dark Star converted instantly into ceremonial grounds.

As many times as I'd seen Richard play over the years, it was clear he'd hit on something new with Laverna. It wasn't just the songs or even the individual musicians, all of which I'd heard by the time they took the stage, but the combination of those factors mixed with an energy that pushed the band to the next level. Quite simply, I'd never seen anything like it. The songs evoked dark myths that felt tapped into antiquity, but there was an edge to their live performance that was simultaneously compelling and terrifying. As I watched him onstage, Richard appeared transported, transcendent — his physical form, which I had been familiar with my whole life, shape-shifted to match the demands of each song. He was Richard, but he was also a changeling, conveying his inspired art with every fiber of his being.

The crowd fell under Laverna's spell, too. They swayed to the slower passages, and listened attentively while the band spun tales of worship, betrayal, sacrifice, and longing. Musical crescendos whipped them into a frenzy of gyrating bodies and flailing limbs. Along with applause and hoots, the ends of songs were accompanied by hugs, as if they had all just survived a journey and were transformed by the experience. Attendees arrived at the club as separate beings, but by the end of the night, the lines blurred, turning individuals into a collective mass of sweaty, moon-eyed Laverna converts. Not all, but a lot of them, anyway.

Apparently, sleeping arrangements on tour were made and broken from moment to moment. Richard had warned me something like this might happen. As Richard explained, "It's not like our big-shot manager is booking us a suite at the local Ritz-Carlton, you know? Every once in a while we spring for a motel room, but we pretty much make do with what we've got. Ninety percent of the time we'll end up crashing with locals or girls who offer or whatever — it usually works out that way. And if all else fails, there's always the Subaru and the van. Someone, usually Papa, ends up crashing there."

In other words, I'd been duly warned of the possible variations that might occur at night's end. It was band policy that no matter who you went home with or where you ended up though, everyone met in front of the club the next morning by noon — earlier or later depending on where the next gig was. There was a certain simple logic to all this, a loose yet effective arrangement. So I wasn't too surprised when this lanky hippie girl emerged from the middle of the packed dance floor and asked me for the keys to the van. Richard's wink from the stage just before the band broke into their final song, "Draping Garland," confirmed her purpose.

Telethusa came walking up from downtown
To the hills among the fig and olive trees nestled down

A free, free woman, Telethusa —
Free from the weight of man, Telethusa —
Behind her trailed a garland wreath lifted over sand
Dipped in the sweat of sex and man

It wasn't until after the gig that I knew where I would be staying though. I was still a novice, counting on Richard to show me the way. And he did.

That was my first night alone with Lavernites.

As the applause at the Dark Star died down and the tapers stashed their gear, Richard made his way through the thinning crowd towards me. A few drunken college kids clapped him on the back. I was putting the unsold merch back in boxes that had been stashed under the table. The rest of the band was packing their gear before drifting off to make their moves for the night.

"Hey, man, did you give that girl the keys to the van?"

"Yeah, yeah." I nodded, still not positive I'd done the right thing. "Is that cool?"

"Yeah, it's cool. That's what I wanted you to do." He looked around, surveying the late night bar scene. It was nearly two a.m. and only the drunkest or the most devoted remained. It was a scene I'd see repeated regularly over the next few weeks: girls and guys making their furtive last ditch efforts, deciding whether or not to take a chance on each other for the night; bedraggled waiters, waitresses and bartenders eager to clear out the bar so that they could head home or start drinking more heavily themselves; managers eyeing bar and door proceeds; bouncers wearing skintight t-shirts with bar logos on the chest, flexing their pecs to intimidate drunken frat boys. From Burlington to Saratoga to New York City, the scenes never changed; only the size of the crowd and the quality of the clubs shifted and, even then, only slightly.

I could see it in Richard's eyes, still glowing bright with the frantic energy of live performance: this was his world.

"So this is how we do it," he said, draping an arm across my shoulder, grinning broadly. "What do you think? Can you take this for a whole month?"

The bulk of my physical labor that night had taken about twenty minutes: help carry in the gear and contribute to setting up as best I could, which wasn't much. Other than that, I'd manned the merch and mailing list table, signing up about twenty new people whose information would then be sent back to Tara in Burlington to be added to the band's database. I'd also sold five Laverna bumper stickers (the band's name in Tempus Sans lettering, a picture of the goddess in the top right corner), six band t-shirts (basically the same as the bumper sticker, but with the goddess taking up the whole back), and one Aventine Hill CD. But basically I just stood around a lot, watching the crowd, listening to the music, occasionally chatting with patrons and fans. Between driving to gigs, waiting in-between gigs, and standing at gigs, my job offered a surplus of time to think and an opportunity to travel. It was perfect.

"Yeah, definitely," I said, clapping Richard on the back. "I can do this. So what happens next? What do we do now?"

"Well, that all depends," said Richard, winking at the waitress handing him a drink.

"Chuckie, the bar manager, said we can wait till tomorrow to move out our gear. That only happens at places like this that serve food during the day or places we're booked into for two nights, but it's cool when it does. Normally we're stuck packing up after the gig for at least an hour. So this means we're free to do whatever." He sized me up. "How about you? Did you meet anybody during the gig? Set up any place to crash?"

I shook my head. "No, I wasn't sure what the deal was, so..." I trailed off, feeling a bit lost.

"That's cool," he said, giving me an easy smile. "I had a feeling it'd be a slow night for you. First gig and all. Just remember, unless we make other plans, it's every man for himself after the gig. Don't worry though, we wouldn't leave you out in the cold, you'll always have someplace to stay." Richard clapped my back again. "We're playing Albany tomorrow so we don't have to go too far." He looked around, located the Lavernites standing in a cluster by the exit sign. "You see those people over there?"

I turned and saw the group. My stomach tightened in anticipation of Richard's next words. "One of them grew up here, so they're all going back to someone's house to crash. They said they'd put you up if you need a place."

Richard turned back to me, never acknowledging the Lavernites themselves directly. "Why don't you go with them? Normally you could crash in the van, but I'm using it tonight, and Coolie —" he searched for Coolie, but came up empty. "Well, it looks like Coolie split already."

"What about the other guys?" I asked, dreading the idea of throwing in my lot with the hippie pack. "What are Julius and Papa doing?" I looked around, but didn't see them either.

Richard's voice grew stern. "Listen, you want a place to sleep tonight, or what? Those guys are set already — everybody's set but you. It's either go with them," he nodded toward the Lavernites, "or find somewhere outside to sleep."

I took a step back, startled at Richard's irritation. I would need to develop a thicker skin to navigate his mood swings.

"Alright, man, alright," I said, backing off. "I was just checking my options. From now on, I'll make sure I set myself up during the gig — no problem." I motioned to the table with the boxes of bumper stickers, CDs, t-shirts, and the mailing list. "Do I just leave these here or what?"

Richard nodded, relaxing a bit. "Yeah, you can leave them, I'll take care of it. I've got to talk to the manager still, get our money and stuff. I'll just bring them out to the van when I go."

"Where'd that girl take the van anyway?"

Richard smiled. "Just running a quick errand for me before all the stores close. She'll be back." His confidence was astonishing. I was curious what the whole story with this girl was, but thought better of asking. No need to risk another outburst. "Listen, why don't you meet me back here tomorrow around eleven? I hear this place makes killer French toast. I'll buy you breakfast and we can talk some more." I smiled. This was the Richard I knew.

"Alright then," he nudged my shoulder, sending me on my way. "You should take off, those guys are waiting."

I looked over at the group: five men and three women dressed in similar loose, patched and dirty pants and t-shirts. They stood in a broken circle, speaking to each other, occasionally glancing our way. "You sure this is cool with them?" I asked, turning back to Richard. But he was already gone.

As I approached the group, the Lavernites began slipping out the door. Their sudden departure made me wonder if they even knew I was planning on tagging along, until the last one, a short, stocky guy sporting dreadlocks and a scraggly black beard, turned at the door and waved me on. I walked faster to meet him, extending a handshake, but something in his eyes told me to keep it to myself. I tucked my hand back down and allowed his subtle movements to guide me out the door. We fell into step ten yards behind the other Lavernites. They were walking in a silent group up the sidewalk; I could smell their patchouli and body odor wafting downwind.

"I'm Argute," my guide said, keeping his eyes straight ahead.

I waited, but that was all.

"Hey, I'm Virgil. Virgil Frey. I'm roadying for…"

"I know," he interrupted. "We're going up the street."

We kept the same pace, never gaining on the group ahead, the group ahead never turning to check back. It took all of my will not to give Argute a serious once-over: inspect his face, hair, clothing, ask about his name, life, but I decided to keep my cool. Bide my time. I suspected I'd have plenty of contact with Argute and the others over the next few weeks. For now, I'd keep my mouth shut and observe.

We hung a left onto a sleepy, suburban street called Pelham. The group turned left again, two houses ahead, and proceeded through an unlatched wooden fence, up a slate walkway, and through the front door of a modest, well-maintained Colonial style house. As Argute and I approached the gate, I glanced around the neighborhood. Not a single light burned in a window, only the little fake lanterns installed on the side of all suburban garages. A blast of wind carried the dusky odor of autumn's first dying leaves, rustling and dislodging the first to drop. Argute and I passed the gate. As we made our way up the slate sidewalk, I saw the house number mounted beside the door: 213.

Argute and I entered, and I spied our reflections in the front hall mirror. I looked tired. My hair swirled in opposing waves, half-moons blackened my eyes; I noticed traces of trepidation crowding the contours of my face and tried to ease them out, but was unsuccessful. Next to Argute, I looked like a narc.

The house was dark, silent. I wondered about the rest of the group. Where were they? Whose house was this? Why would they let this raggedy band of tripped-out kids into their home so late at night? I followed Argute through an orderly back hall, small, cozy kitchen, and into an open, spacious family room. A television, well-used sofa, and chairs formed a conversational area around a coffee table cluttered with fanned copies of Newsweek, National Geographic, and Time magazines. Several stout red candles burned beside the sofa. A man reclined there. No other Lavernites were visible. Argute led me to an easy chair beside the man's perch. When I sat down, I noticed another guy reclined on a sofa in the corner with a young girl lying back against his chest. The first man waved Argute out. I adjusted my chair so that my back was to the couple on the couch.

"My name is Felix." Despite his small stature, he had a surprisingly deep voice. "Are you shy?"

"Excuse me?" With everything going on, I wasn't prepared for this small man with delicate features to speak in such a direct way. "Did you just ask if I was shy?"

He stared intently, solemnly. "Shyness is a flaw," he said, deadly serious. "So is sarcasm."

I looked into his eyes to make sure he was for real. He was.

"Well then, I think I'm screwed," I deadpanned. "How about you? Anything make you feel shy?"

Felix responded without hesitation. "Faithlessness."

I checked the couple on the couch. The guy sat up straighter, watching me. I turned back to Felix. "Oh yeah? How's that?"

Felix stared hard. I was already frazzled by the late hour and weird scene, and his penetrating gaze seemed to find that hole and bore it even wider. Despite his diminutive size — 5'6" tops — and delicate features, his magnetism was impressive. He spoke with great authority, parting the dark hair that hung down his face, allowing each syllable to resonate from his chest in sonorous vibrations. He removed a long, fat joint from a pouch at his side, tucked it into a gap formed by a broken front tooth, and lit it. He took a few deep drags, then passed it over. I took a hit and held in the smoke, as he began unspooling a story. His story.

"When I was twelve years old my parents started worrying that all the beatings they'd given me were warping my brain. I was failing every subject, hardly talked at all, and when I did, it was just a whisper." He winced at the memory. "You could hardly even hear it. I'd ask for something — the salt, a pencil — and no one would respond. They couldn't hear me. Or they could, but the sound was too small to consider." He accepted the joint back, then held it in front of his face as the smoke curled up and around his head. "Either way, there was something wrong. The tests all said I was bright, exceptional even, but two minutes alone with me and you'd think I was slow-witted. I'd just stand there, staring at my feet, not saying anything at all."

He took another hit, leaned back in his seat, and exhaled up at the ceiling. "So my parents, understandably, began to worry that maybe over the years they'd unhinged my brain, knocked something forever out of whack." He handed the joint back to me. "I think, for the first time, they were concerned that they'd be held responsible for my stunted development. Questions were being asked at school. They knew they had to do something fast."

Felix turned to watch the other man who had returned to his reclining posture, running his fingertips methodically up and down the girl's forearm. Felix smiled and turned back to me.

"They decided the best solution was to send me to stay with my Uncle Martin in Gouverneur for a year. You know, life in the country: fresh air, new environment. I suppose they pictured me coming back with ruddy cheeks and some sort of woodsy swagger." He accepted the joint back. "My Uncle Martin was the town minister in Gouverneur, so, aside from taking the heat off of them back in Oneonta, they figured I would get some religion there, too. In their minds, they had it all: they could duck their culpability and get some god in me all at once."

I heard footsteps; a naked man and woman appeared at the edge of the room. The girl was curvy, large at the hips and chest, thick through the middle. The man was smaller, more hesitant, and quickly shrunk behind the girl in the doorway. Felix didn't even notice them until I gestured their way to get his attention. He seemed instantly disturbed by their interruption. A flick of his wrist sent them away. Another flick raised the couple on the couch to their feet and out of the room as well. The girl ran her fingers through my hair as she passed. A volley of shivers ran down my spine, dispersing like greasy, shocked eels. Felix waited until they'd left to continue.

"One might think that this new situation would be an improvement. An escape from an abusive home-life." He shook his head. "Unfortunately, Uncle Martin's house offered no such respite. I'd been there less than a week, when —"

"Why do they do whatever you say?" I interrupted Felix's story. I couldn't help it. It was all too bizarre. He stopped and fixed me with a curious stare, but I pushed on. Something weird was going on here, and I wanted to know what it was. "It's hard not to notice the way everyone does what you tell them to do. That couple," I gestured toward the doorway where the naked couple had appeared, "the guy who brought me here, those two on the couch in the corner. Everyone, they just seem to follow your orders without even thinking."

"That's because they know," Felix answered calmly.

I shook my head. "Know what?"

A tender smile severed Felix's didactic tone. He answered as simply as reciting his name. "They know that thought is the enemy of faith." I began to respond, but he silenced me. "Please," he said, lacing his fingers together in front of his face, moving them slowly back and forth, "allow me to finish, and then I will answer any questions that you have."

He waited for me to respond, but I conceded with a silent nod. He paused and smiled before continuing. He knew that he had me.

"As I was saying, it didn't take long for things to turn bad at Uncle Martin's." He took one last hit off the joint and then dropped it into a half-filled drinking glass on the coffee table. "As we are talking about faith," he exhaled down into the glass and coughed lightly into his fist, "I will explain it this way: Martin's faith was weak. Martin was weak. Martin's wife, Annie, lorded over their household with an iron fist. She was larger than him in every way — stature, strength, will, temperament — and used her advantage to abuse Martin, physically and mentally." His voice turned harsh. "It turned my stomach watching this weak, pathetic man preaching from his pulpit every Sunday. Fear of the Lord, wrath of God, judgment day, repentance, sin; the terms rolled off his tongue like the vacant, empty promises of lovers. And there we were, Aunt Annie and I, in the front pew, neat and folded, maintaining straight faces while listening to this man as if he deserved one ounce of respect or reverence from any member of that congregation." Felix paused for effect. "He did not."

"Was I abused physically or mentally in the traditional sense, as my mother and father had taught it, at Uncle Martin's? No. I was not. But seeing this man degraded so horrifically, so —" For the first time, Felix's face betrayed deep emotion. His mouth twisted, searching for the right word, but his brain came up short. He collected himself and continued.

"Uncle Martin went fishing on Sundays between service and dinner. There was a small stream with good hollows about a half-mile from their house where you could catch brook trout and sometimes rainbows. It was Uncle Martin's only escape, so he took it as often as he could, which wasn't often at all. Annie didn't like Martin being away from her, out from under her thumb. She'd complain about the smell he dragged home, but the truth was that she couldn't stand the thought of Martin enjoying himself. Eventually she figured out how to destroy even this last refuge.

"It was my first month staying with them, and Annie had decided that, due to my presence, hot water was suddenly a precious commodity. She said that their hot water heater was too small to handle both the water she needed to clean up from Sunday dinner and the bath she forced Uncle Martin to take after fishing. The idea was absurd, of course, water can always be heated, but this was their existence. So Aunt Annie gave Uncle Martin an ultimatum: stop fishing on Sundays, or eat dinner naked. After all, she insisted, there wasn't enough hot water to clean up pots and dishes after his bath, and she'd never allow him to put on clean clothes without bathing."

Felix shook his head, disgusted at the memory. "I'll never forget sitting at the kitchen table that first month, as Martin returned from fishing to learn of this new ultimatum. He actually looked relaxed, happy even, as he came in the door." He leaned forward, and narrowed his eyes. "It was the last time I'd see him that way. That one hour spent fishing that had buoyed his spirit each week was gone forever.

"Martin raised a pathetic struggle, but his arguments were dismissed. This first time was non-negotiable, Aunt Annie insisted, and after that he could decide what he'd rather do: fish on Sundays, or maintain his last shreds of dignity. It didn't matter though. Not really. I witnessed the last of Martin's self-respect fall to the ground that first Sunday beside his pants, shirt, socks and underwear. There we sat for dinner, Aunt Annie, myself, and Uncle Martin, his pathetic loose skin hanging in pouches across his bony torso. All through dinner, Aunt Annie looked back and forth between Martin and me, emitting a powerful, silent signal about who ran the house. All the beatings and berating I saw that man endure over the year — even all the beatings I myself have taken — have never come close to impacting me as much as having to eat dinner and look into the humiliated eyes of that broken man."

By the time Felix stopped speaking, he'd obviously been transported back to that troubled house in Gouverneur. And I was there with him. Something about his story had taken hold deep in my mind. I gazed into his eyes; they stared into the distance.

I was hesitant to break the silence that hung in the wake of his story. Still, I had to know, to understand. My words were hushed, reverent. "Why do they do what you tell them to?"

"Because they want to believe. To have faith."

"In you?"

Felix replied coolly. "In anything."

I looked down at my hands. They were clasped together, shaking in my lap. He rose and left the room. Seconds later, the curvy girl from earlier entered, still naked, and kneeled at my side. My mind whirled with the marijuana and Felix's story as she looked into my eyes.

"What's your name?" I asked, lifting her chin to face me.

She looked at me with lost, vacant eyes. I immediately understood that this girl was a gift from Felix. And then another, more troubling, thought came: maybe the girl was a gift from Richard. "I don't have one," she said, quietly. "I haven't earned it yet."

I looked past the girl, around the shadowy room, half-expecting to see the others watching from a corner, or blackened doorway. But they weren't. I was alone with this self-described nameless girl. I tilted my head back, and my eyes brushed across the room's middle-class décor: tables, chairs, brick fireplace, ceramic coasters, miniature figurines, and lastly, on the top shelf of the bookcase, a posed studio portrait of the girl I'd given the van keys to back at the bar.

The nameless girl leaned in and started kissing me. I tried kissing her back, but quickly stopped. There was no life, no spark to her kisses — they were cold, rote, disengaged. I looked down at her, trying to establish eye contact, but her eyes repeatedly slid away. She reached for my belt buckle and began to unfasten it. I placed my hand down to stop her.

"You don't have to do this," I said. "We don't have to do this. Do you want to just put some clothes on?"

The girl shook her head. Her blank expression was crowded with fear. "No, I… I can't," she said. "I mean, I want to do it. Please. I want to do this with you, Virgil."

I leaned back, surprised. "You know my name?"

Her eyes got wider, as if she'd spilled a secret. "I… I heard Felix say it," she quickly answered. "I mean, he told me your name."

I squinted into the darkness, studying her face. "But you don't have a name?"

She shook her head, no.

"And doing this ... being with me ... will get you one?"

She nodded. "I think so," she answered.

"And you want that?" I asked. "You want Felix to give you a new name? To be a part of," I waved my hand, "all this? Whatever this is? That means a lot to you?"

For the first time, the girl brightened, showing a spark of energy. She nodded, moving her hands up my chest and rubbing.

"Please, Virgil," she cooed. "Let me take care of you. Please just let me do this. For me." She put her hand back on my buckle and began to unfasten it. "And for you. You'll enjoy it, I promise."

Everything about the situation felt wrong, off. The night had been strange, too strange, like I'd fallen down the rabbit hole, and my previous conceptions of basic human behavior were grossly distorted. Even watching this young woman — this girl with no name, this girl trying to earn her name — as she unbuckled my belt, unzipped my pants, and reached in, was like gazing into a fun-house mirror. The movements were familiar, but the proportions — the intentions — were skewed. She took me inside her mouth. My body responded even as my brain shuffled questions, alternate scenarios, modes of response I knew I should be taking.

But I didn't. I just sat there.

The sensation of her warm, wet mouth overruled any common sense or hope of dignity — mine, or hers. She moved faster now, alternating with her hand and mouth, never looking up at me, diligently focused on her task. I knew it was just that, too. A task. For her, and, in some ways, for me, too. Within minutes, I reached out, grabbed the cushions on either side of me, and let go as she pumped me with her hand. By the time I opened my eyes and refocused, she was already standing up. The small spark I'd seen earlier was gone. I was in the room with a robotic stranger once again, one I couldn't even thank by name. One, it turns out, I would never see again.

"Goodbye, Virgil," she said, unceremoniously walking out.

The entire exchange took less than ten minutes.

I was alone. Nowhere to go until morning except a jizz-stained couch in some random suburban home. I grabbed a tissue from a box beside the lamp to clean myself off. Then I zipped my fly, buckled my belt, and looked around the family room. Nothing. Stillness. I walked into the kitchen, tossed out the tissue, filled up a glass with tap water, and stood at the sink sipping it. Part of me expected the lights to suddenly flick on and some middle-aged mother in curlers to walk in asking if I wanted a sandwich. Part of me wondered if another sex-robot sent by Felix would arrive on a crazy mission. Part of me worried that Felix himself would enter with yet more fascinating bullshit raps to scramble my brains.

As I rinsed my glass and placed it back in the cabinet, I realized none of those things would happen though. The stillness, the silence, told me the show was over for the night. For better or worse, I was alone. I walked back into the family room, pulled off my sneakers, and placed my head on the other side of the couch. Through a murky haze of weed, booze, bizarre monologues, and one quick, disembodied blowjob, I tried to quiet my mind, praying exhausted sleep would find its way.

This weirdness was getting to be a habit. And not one I particularly cared for. Then again, when it came to the Lavernites, I didn't mind waking up alone.

I swung my legs off the edge of the couch and glanced around. The house was silent. In the morning light, it looked even more docile, even more middle-of-the-road, middle class suburban, even more incongruous to the Lavernites' presence there. I quickly pulled on my sneakers. As I stood to leave, the picture of the girl on the bookcase sewed together the basic scenario for me: parents out of town, daughter sneaks off to see rock-n-roll band, allows her unsavory friends (whom the parents would never let in the door otherwise) to party and sleep there, meanwhile she's off screwing rock-n-roll musician in the back of the band's van. At the end of the story, the girl's parents return none the wiser and remark on how their little girl has matured and become so responsible.

In a way, it was as much American mythology as Johnny Appleseed or George Washington's cherry tree. Sure, it got less coverage. But it was still pure Americana.

I pulled myself together, and was through the house and to the front door in seconds. I glanced both ways before exiting, scanning for nosy neighbors or returning parents. Two houses down and to the left, a man was mowing his lawn; a little farther up, across the street, a boy shot baskets alone. If I went to the right, I only had two houses to get past before I made it to the street leading back to the Dark Star. I waited until the mower turned, making his diagonal back across the lawn, and scooted out the door, closing it gently behind me. I didn't look back until I hit the main drag; walking, waiting, feeling anxious. Finally it cleared, everything cleared. I was out safe. I lit a cigarette and walked along in the late morning light.

Of all the memories that blurred together from the night before, all the images I'd never be able to shake, one main thought stuck out like a thorn snagging my brain and bleeding out an idea I'd rather just forget: maybe the nameless girl was a gift from Richard. Maybe the nameless one, Felix, his story, the other Lavernites — maybe, in a way, they were all from Richard. But still, someone as powerful as Felix wasn't just a pawn… the others maybe, but not him. If that was the case, then how, and why, were Richard and Felix connected?

The Dark Star was transformed. It was still dimmer than your average Denny's or IHOP, but now families were seated at little tables on what had once been the dance floor, eating greasy tubular sausages, eggs, bacon, pancakes, and French toast. The bartender, dressed in a clean white oxford, poured only juice and the occasional Bloody Mary. The band's gear was hidden behind a cheesy, red velvet curtain. I allowed myself to be seated by the door so that I could see Richard when he came in. I checked my watch: 10:45. Richard had said 11:00.

I ordered coffee and sat back to wait. All around me were reminders of the American Dream I had scoffed at only minutes before. Men and women wiping the chins of boys and girls; scowling hopelessly at spilled orange juice and jelly-stained pants; kids and adults asking permission for more hot chocolate, more whipped cream, more syrup, more sausage, more French toast, more everything, more always, more this and more that. And where was I in this mix? I was smack dab in the center of the American Dream, touring with a band of rock-n-roll libertines down the tender edge of the country; skimming the scar tissue where land cuts into ocean, and gaining fast on something I didn't yet understand. Whatever I was after now had something to do with music and leaders and followers and where they start and where they end and what happens when they gain steam. Whatever it was, I wanted more. Needed more. And just like any good junkie: the more I got, the more I craved.

My thoughts were interrupted by a loud clatter behind the red curtain. All eyes turned toward the stage. There was a round of laughter followed by more clattering, and then loud thumps like sandbags being dropped from an airplane. Then came the sound I'd begun to associate with the cock's crow: Coolie's first loud curse of the day. "Shit!" I shook my head, laughing, and made for the stage.

"Jesus, Coolie," I said, popping my head through the curtain. "You trying to run away all this guy's business or what?"

The guys — Coolie, Papa, and Julius — all looked up.

"Gentlemen," I said, bowing slightly. "Good morning."

"Hey, what's up, Virgil?" greeted Coolie. "You have a good night last night?"

"Yeah, I guess so," I paused, considering. "It was... strange." I shook my head to clear the cobwebs. "You guys sounded amazing though."

Papa gave a thumbs-up and resumed packing his large bass rig. Coolie and Papa were dressed in the same rumpled clothes as the night before. Julius wore a new set of midnight blacks, his hair coiffed and perfect as always.

"So, where'd you guys crash last night?" I asked, beginning to gather and spool random cords and cables. "You disappeared right after the show."

A loud crash marked Coolie's hi-hat breakdown. He tucked the pieces away in a padded nylon case as he spoke. "We were gonna get you, but Richard said you had something all lined up. So what's up, dude?" He flashed me the winning Coolie grin. "You hook up last night or what?"

I paused, a quarter-inch cable wrapped halfway around my tricep and hand. I suppose Richard could've told them that after I'd left. Still, they'd all disappeared so fast, it seemed unlikely.

"No, I didn't hook up." It wasn't exactly the truth, but what had happened didn't feel like a hook-up anyway. How can you hook up with a girl who presents herself as a phantom, a specter, a non-entity? "Richard set me up with some people he knows, or something. I stayed right down the street. I think they were friends of that girl he was with."

"Could be anyone," muttered Papa.

They all exchanged looks.

"So how about you guys? Where'd you all stay?"

"Papa and I crashed with some dudes I met last time we played here," answered Coolie. "It was totally raging, man! You should've come. We were partying till like four or five in the morning."

"*You* were partying till like four or five in the morning," corrected Papa.

"Whatever," shot Coolie. "I was partying till like four or five in the morning with everyone else in the house, except Papa, who was probably on the phone with his girlfriend, crying like a baby while she told him how much she missed his pussy ass."

Papa shrugged. "So?"

Then in unison Coolie and Papa grabbed their crotches and yelled, "So this!"

Giddy with lack of sleep and various degrees of hangover, everyone laughed at some inside joke I'd yet to be invited into. Everyone except Julius. He continued packing, completely serious. I resumed winding cords and turned to him, curious. "How about you, Julius? Where'd you end up crashing?"

Julius looked up, studying my face. "Is this twenty questions? You want to know my favorite color, too?" Then he put his head down and continued packing.

Papa looked at Julius in disbelief, shaking his head. "I don't know," he muttered. "Could it be black?"

Coolie looked at me, and waved Julius off. His message was clear: don't worry about that asshole.

So I didn't.

"Sorry, man, didn't mean to be nosey," I said, trying to smooth things over a bit anyway. "Next time I won't ask." Julius only snorted. "Has anyone seen Richard yet?"

"He'll be rolling in soon," said Coolie.

"Yeah, as soon as we finish packing up," added Papa.

"He's got the van though, doesn't he?"

Coolie shook his head, remembering. "Yeah, that's right, he does."

On a hunch, I peeked my head through the curtain. There sat Richard Payne Knight alone at my table. He winked at me, and bit a greasy sausage in two. I shook my head at him in mock disgust, then pulled my head back inside the curtain and clued-in the rest of the band. We left the gear where it was to join Richard. On the table in front of him was his steaming cup of coffee and a plate with three sausages.

"Appetizers," he said, as we sat down. Coolie, Papa and I each grabbed one, clearing the plate. I don't think that's what he had in mind, but I could tell Richard was in a good mood anyway.

"What's going on?" he asked, sounding upbeat. "You guys finish packing up or what?"

"Yeah," shot Coolie. "Now you can carry it out to the van while we eat."

"Hey," Richard protested, "I didn't even order yet. Except the sausages, of which I ate one before you jackals swooped in and finished them off."

"Those things will you kill you anyway," said Papa.

"Death by sausage," sneered Julius. "Not very rock-n-roll."

"Hey, it worked for Elvis!" said Coolie.

Richard shook his head, focusing on Julius. "How're you feeling today, Julius? We haven't had a chance to catch up much since Burlington."

"Leaving or arriving?" muttered Papa.

Julius fixed a cold stare on Richard. He tried to hold it, but dropped it too quickly.

"I'm fine, Richard, thank you for asking. I know how concerned you are about the feelings of your players."

"What's that supposed to mean?"

Julius glared at him. "What do you think it means?"

Coolie and Papa exchanged insider glances. I began to get the picture.

A neat-looking young man approached. His hair was cut short, high above the ears, his pressed white oxford and black khakis indicative of a Dark Star server. He leaned over and planted a long, deep kiss on Julius's mouth.

"I'll probably get fired if my boss saw that," he said, brushing a hand over his lips. "But screw him, it was worth it."

I was glad to see Coolie and Papa looking as surprised as I felt. Even Julius seemed startled by the man's approach. A few diners glanced up, then back down at their plates, trying not to stare. That kiss was a fly in the American Dream syrup. Richard smiled, obviously enjoying the scene.

"Good morning, Philip," nodded Julius. "How are you?"

"I'd be better if you'd have been there when I woke up," pouted Philip, narrowing his eyes. "I didn't even hear you go."

"Practice," whispered Papa.

"Like I said, I had to come back and pack up. I didn't realize you were working this morning."

"Or you would have waited?" Philip asked hopefully.

Julius looked him up and down, nodded. "Sure."

Philip swatted Julius's arm. "Liar," he scolded. "But I don't care. Looks like I'll be bringing you breakfast after all. Just not in bed like I had hoped." Philip looked around at the rest of the band as if seeing us for the first time. He whipped out an order pad and smiled. "So what can I get for the boys in the band this morning?"

The rest of breakfast passed in relative silence. It's not the public demonstration that Julius was gay or bi or pan or whatever that quieted the scene; in the arts world, any form of sexuality is about as shocking as lactose intolerance, and everyone in the band already knew about Julius. What made things so awkward was Julius's own discomfort at our knowledge of his night with Philip. After all, what was the big deal? Why could he hardly make eye contact with Coolie, Papa, and me... and Richard not at all?

For once, I was on the same page as everyone else, and maybe even in front. Julius's avoidance of the band back in Burlington, his running with a different crowd, his escalating drug use: all these were merely buffers to his own overriding dilemma.

It appeared that Julius might be in love with Richard Payne Knight.

BREAK IT DOWN

After Saratoga Springs, we were off to Albany, then Kingston, New York City, New Paltz, Binghamton, Cortland, Ithaca, Rochester, Utica, Potsdam, and back to Burlington for a final show at Tangerine's. The idea was to build on the following the band was gaining in the college towns — keep selling CDs, t-shirts, bumper stickers, allow live tapes to circulate, do some college radio interviews, add to the mailing list — then slowly move the tours to larger circles, cities, venues. This was 'making it' the hard way: there would be no big-label million-dollar contract, overnight success, one-hit wonder, heavy rotation on album-oriented radio, then drop off the face of the earth cycle for Laverna. Too many bands had gone down too fast that way and the guys knew it. Laverna had incorporated the band to deal with taxes, they'd formed a payroll, put their CDs out on their own Lascivious label, booked their own shows, and boasted a current mailing list of over 15,000 people and growing. It wasn't easy. I was getting a firsthand taste of how difficult the process actually was: no representatives between the band and sketchy club owners or tyrannical booking agents or the fans themselves — often drunkenly overzealous — and no one but clueless me to help with set up, breakdown, merch sales, and moving from gig to gig.

But, despite all adversity, Laverna was doing it. The buzz on them was growing. Bumper stickers were pasted, t-shirts were worn, live shows were traded, their MySpace page was more and more active, their fan base was spreading, and Laverna was climbing the arc of musical success and longevity. By the time they were ready to deal with outside labels, they'd be more than just salivating dogs with billowing dreams and chipped equipment; they'd have bargaining power based on CD sales and fan base.

That was the thinking anyway. Maybe those things would help. Maybe they wouldn't. No one ever said rock-n-roll was easy. Or fair.

But there was also the beauty of autumn in upstate New York — the colors overhead exploding in spectrums of red, yellow, orange, and green, merging into a bold, intricate latticework of color and light — and we drove through that every day. We knew where we were going. What we had to do. What the mission was.

We passed minivans, compacts, pick-ups, eighteen-wheelers; we passed families visiting relatives for the weekend, traveling salesmen, truckers, drug dealers, lovers, losers, buyers and sellers. But we weren't them. That was the point. We were something different. We were a rock-n-roll band, making it the hard way: gigging, writing songs, radiating edgy mystique, and partying up and down the state of New York. We were the American Dream, hard at work.

Coolie took a huge hit off the joint and handed it to me. We were fifteen miles down I-87 out of Saratoga Springs.

"Here, man." He thrust the smoking bomber into my hand. "This thing's roasting! Take it!"

I turned my face toward the sun coming in through the windshield and took a long, slow drag. I held it, exhaled into the light beams, then took another.

Richard was at the wheel in the Subaru behind us, with Papa riding shotgun and Julius reclined across the back seat. I liked having Coolie in the van with me. He was lighthearted, still relatively sober, and in a good mood. As we passed the joint back and forth, I took the opportunity to get some information straight.

"So, does Julius have a thing for Richard, or what?"

Coolie half laughed, half coughed, spewing spittle and smoke all over the van windshield. He turned to me, his face red and grinning. "Gee, I don't know. You think?" His sarcasm was thick. "Yeah, I don't know when that started really. If you'd have asked me a year ago, I wouldn't have even known he was queer. All this stuff, his black clothes, being all moody, shooting dope, that's all happened within the last year or so."

"Why? I mean, what brought it all on?"

"I don't know really," Coolie shook his head, staring out the windshield. "Julius is just kind of like that, a different kind of dude. He's definitely the one I know least. At least I think he is. Shit, man," he took another hit and handed it over. "Who am I kidding? We're all fucking weird in this band."

"Is he from Burlington?"

"No, he moved there same as us." As Coolie spoke, he steered with his left hand while his right hand pulled a long blond curl down in front of his face, then let it spring back up, over and over. "He's a rich kid, man. His family's fucking loaded. That's where we got the money to make the CDs and do our first couple tours and everything. Studio time's not cheap, man. Neither is gas, a van, a PA. Shit, if it wasn't for Julius, we'd still be playing frat keggers at UVM."

I shook my head in disbelief. It's always surprising to find out someone you know comes from great wealth — like finding out they have a 160 IQ or a superfluous nipple.

"Well, where's he from? What's his deal?"

"I'm not sure exactly, but I know he went to school at one of those high class boarding schools. Essenger or Echinger or something," Coolie waved his hand, seemingly in the direction of the school, or whatever state it was in. "Somewhere in New Hampshire."

"Exeter?"

"Yeah, that's it," exclaimed Coolie, obviously impressed I knew the place. "Exeter! In New Hampshire. He went there. He was like one of those rich kids in the movies whose parents send him away to school so they don't have to deal with him or whatever, then they go off to Paris or Rome or wherever without him. His family has a sweet pad in New

York City. You'll see it when we play there. Just wait, man. It's intense. Like twenty rooms with huge bathtubs and maids and shit, right on the edge of Central Park. It's totally killer." I handed Coolie the joint, urging him on. "I only met his dad, like, once — last time we played Swampland — for, like, two minutes. I don't even know what he does, to tell you the truth. Something with banking, I think. Whatever it is, he makes a shitload of money. But they've got family money, too. One of those deals where his grandparents hooked up their kids to get married and doubled their money. So now they're mega-loaded, and Julius is all kinds of fucked up."

I nodded, vaguely familiar with this type of tale through the pages of John Cheever short stories and sensationalized magazine profiles. "So, how did Julius end up in Burlington?"

"He went to Middlebury. I met him when I was playing with Monk's Eye. He used to sell coke to my friend Reggie. Then one night we were playing this Earth Day gig for the school, and Reggie tells us he's got this guy, Julius, who's gonna sit in for a few tunes. We were all like, 'Whatever, as long as he can play and doesn't fuck up.' So Julius set up, rocked out hard, and ended up playing the whole show with us."

"And you just kept playing with him after that?"

Coolie shook his head. "No. We totally would have though. Julius has always been an amazing player. But he got busted for dealing right after that, so they kicked him out of school for a while. By the time he came back, Monk's Eye was done and I was just bouncing around, playing with different people. It wasn't until almost two years later that I jammed with him again. I had just started playing with Richard and Papa when I ran into Julius at a Black Hat gig. I basically grabbed his arm, dragged him over to Richard, and said he should play with us. He showed up at the house the next day, we jammed for like six hours straight, and that was it — he was in."

Coolie handed me the joint, but I was done. I was already baked to the brink of uselessness, and we still had a long day ahead. I declined. He took one last hit and let the wind whisk the roach out the window.

"So that's it, huh?"

"Pretty much," nodded Coolie. "Papa grew up in Bethel, the town where Woodstock was actually held. He came to Burlington 'cause he heard about the music scene and hooked up with Richard when he got there. Julius dropped out of Middlebury when he joined the band. And you already know the deal with Richard and me. So, yeah, that's it, man — the story of Laverna."

"Print it," I said, laughing.

"Yeah, man!" Coolie grinned. He seemed shocked that he'd been able to recreate the whole history so lucidly. It was probably his first time putting it all together that way. "Print it, man. Write it up, writer boy!"

"But what's the deal with Julius and Richard?" I asked. "When did all that stuff start?"

Coolie shook his head, baffled. "I really don't know, man. Like I said, until a year ago Julius was wearing Birkenstocks and tie-dyes. He smoked weed, did coke and all that stuff, but he was just your basic rich boy, Burlington trustafarian. Then, all of a sudden, all his clothes were black, he was making these midnight runs to who knows where, coming back all fucked up, and he started getting all —" Coolie faltered.

"Gay?"

"Yeah, that too, but that was no biggie. It was the other stuff that was mostly just weird, man. Different. All moody and shit. I mean, granted, we've all been getting into some pretty funky areas lately with the band, but—"

Coolie stopped, looked into my eyes, sizing me up. "Listen, man, I don't know what you know, and what you don't, and it's not my place to tell you. All I can say is, as Richard's friend, you should try and find out what his deal is. There's cool rock-n-roll kicks — I know that, man. I love it. Shit, I grew up with it! And then there's going way overboard into some kind of serious power trip, or whatever." Coolie could tell I wasn't following. He pressed on. "All I know is, I live with Julius and Richard, in Burlington and on the road, and even I don't know what those guys are fully into. To tell you the truth, I don't want to know. But I get the feeling lately..." Coolie shook his head, obviously disturbed. "I get the feeling things are getting kinda out of hand. Like we're rolling too fast or something… It's hard to describe."

What had started out as an interesting story about Julius and the origins of Laverna had taken a distinctly heavy turn. Then again, with these guys, I was getting used to stuff turning weird.

Coolie was obviously thinking hard about it though. Dead serious. And I wasn't sure what to do with what he was telling me.

"What are you saying, man? Are you afraid Richard or Julius are gonna get hurt or something?"

Coolie shook his head, looked out the windshield. "It's not them I'm worried about, man. Not really. It's everyone else. Everyone around us. Everyone getting swept up in this whole thing."

"You mean those kids? The spaced-out ones? The…" I struggled to find the word, blurting out a term that would end up being repeated hundreds of times in articles, stories, and news reports across the country. "Lavernites?"

Coolie turned, cracking a small grin through his visible dismay. "Lavernites, huh? You come up with that?" I nodded. "Yeah, I like it. Perfect."

"Is that who you mean though?" I pushed on. "Is that who you're talking about?"

Coolie kept his eyes on the road. "I really don't know what I mean, man," he said, shaking his head. "I really don't know, Virgil. Like I said, I don't know who's doing what to who anymore, things have gotten so weird so fast. There's things I like and there's things I don't. I like to play drums and party. Most of the time that's what this is all about. It's just sometimes, and definitely more lately, Richard's been taking things — the music, the band, himself — way too seriously. And I'm afraid people are getting hurt. Don't ask me why, that's just what I think."

I felt a tremendous surge of strange energy balling inside my chest; as if everything I was searching for, all the questions I'd been ruminating over, were being batted around inside my skull like a mangy kitten with a mouse corpse. I felt ready to pounce.

"But what are you —"

Coolie halted me with a raised hand. "Hey, Virgil, man, I don't have anything more I can tell you. I've already said more than I even know. For everything else, you gotta talk to Richard. Maybe Julius. Papa's just going along for the ride, like me. He's just happy to be playing, making money, and hanging out with Julie. Papa's good meat. No fucking around, no nothing. Tell you the truth, I don't even know why he's hanging around with us besides playing." He scratched his head, visibly agitated. "No, man, you just gotta talk to Richard. And when you do," he plucked a cigarette from the pack on the dashboard, placing it between his lips, "tell me what he says."

I reached over and took a smoke from his pack to calm myself. Coolie lit mine, then his own. We both smoked in silence. "One more question, man," I said, unable to resist. "And then we can talk about something else."

Coolie nodded.

"Before we left Burlington, that morning, you took those two girls into the basement. To that little room, down the hall from the jam room, with all the writing on the walls and the statue and everything?" Coolie took a drag, nodded. "Okay, so you three took them into that little room. Then what?"

Coolie turned away from me, stared out the windshield. He took a drag, held it, and answered through his exhalation. "What do you think?"

"Sex?" Coolie nodded his confirmation. "But is that, like, normal? I mean, were the girls into it and everything?"

Coolie shrugged. "Yeah, they were into it. Definitely. Let's just say, they knew what we were going down there for. They'd been there before."

That answered the first, most pressing part of my question. It was definitely consensual and they were game. But were the girls the same type as the ones back in Saratoga? The ones with Felix? Willing, but vacant. There, but not there. Who were they? Where did they come from?

I could have asked any number of questions at that point, but I knew that Coolie's patience was wearing thin. I took one last shot. "But why? I mean, why were they… Why would they do that?"

Coolie shook his head, obviously unsure himself. "That's what I've been trying to tell you, Virgil. I've been around rock-n-roll all my life. I've seen more groupies and wannabes than you could imagine. But I've never seen anything like this. I can't say I didn't dig it at first. Hell, no one forced me into the basement that day, or ever. I did it willingly. I do it willingly. But…" he paused here, pulling together memories, thoughts.

"Something's changed, man. Those girls, the other kids… What did you call them? Lavernites? All of them, man. This is more than just kids worshipping their favorite rock band. I've seen that, lived it. Something else is going on here, and I don't know what it is. I'm not even sure I want to know. I'm pretty sure if anyone has the answers though, it's your friend, Richard Payne Knight."

My friend, Richard Payne Knight.

At that point, we'd both had enough. Our mental exhaustion was apparent. We traveled the last forty miles into Albany in almost total silence: no radio, no chatter, and certainly no more talk about Richard Payne Knight, Julius Edson, or Lavernites. Our only accompaniment was the whisper of wind through lowered windows and our own dark thoughts.

It had been four days since I arrived in Burlington. Four days since I was a graduate student, plodding to campus and back to my tiny room with a stack of books under my arm, a series of vague ideas bouncing around my head regarding a plot for my next inconsequential, unpublished short story. And now I was in an Albany pizzeria, ten inches away from a glass mirror depicting a caricature of the chubby, red-faced owner in chef's hat, apron, and flour-dusted face. The entire band sat side-by-side, stool after stool, down one wall of Donny's Pizzeria. We ate in silence, occasionally staring at ourselves in the mirror, but never at each other. This was a trick I came to understand. It's the illusion of privacy, the implication of walls, a door to close, a room of your own, that helps maintain personal space on the road. Don't look at people and magically they're not there. I was starting to get a sense of how relationships on tour become strange, warped.

The band's instruments were already set up back at the club. It was 5:30 and they weren't going on for another four hours. Dinner lasted only twenty minutes.

This is how time also becomes warped on tour.

What to do? It's that question, that down-time, that instigates so much of the drug abuse, deviance, and mental instability in touring rock bands. It's traveling every day in total anonymity, sitting around strange cities for hours with nothing to do, feeling like you've examined your bandmates' every gesture, nuance, tic, and imperfection to a sickening degree, thus becoming utterly sick of yourself in the process, and then repeating it a couple hundred times a year for as many years as you can stand. And then all at once you find yourself on a Saturday night at Donny's Pizzeria in Albany, NY with nothing but time stretching out in either direction.

That is rock-n-roll.

Richard and Julius finished their pizza, and took the Subaru over to the SUNY Albany campus radio station to drop off the new CD and hopefully get on air for a few minutes to promote the gig. All through dinner I snuck glances at Richard in the pizzeria mirror, trying to recreate his path over the past two years; trying to put together the pieces, understand where he was now and how he'd gotten there. Even in his reflection, I was spotting changes I hadn't noticed before.

Laverna wasn't my first roadie gig. I'd schlepped equipment for Richard many times in high school. At a certain point, I realized it conferred some sort of secondhand authority onto me. Whether it was a house party, a talent show, whatever the occasion, there was deference given to the guy who helped the guy with talent entertain the room. I didn't mind being that guy, the other guy, and I genuinely liked helping my best friend, too.

By the time we were seniors, Richard was already moving through our high school like a rock star about to go onstage. It didn't matter if he was headed to Chemistry or to the cafeteria, the hallways seemed to clear as he made his way through the crowd to wherever he was going.

Even then, it amazed me. There were cliques of kids from all different strata of high school society — and then there was Richard. And, beside Richard, there was me. Our high school yearbook had one picture of us together: Richard onstage at the homecoming dance, howling into the microphone with a low-slung Stratocaster swinging at his waist, and me, on the side of the stage, looking up at him like a 14-year-old girl watching the Beatles debut on the Ed Sullivan show. My eyes were shining and my mouth hung open in bliss and fascination. In a way, it's embarrassing to even think about that picture. But in another way, I also dropped out of graduate school because of what it represents: my faith in Richard Payne Knight. It had always been there. I had always believed in Richard and admired him. With Laverna, there was a new pride accompanying my adult adoration: the pride of the early adopter. I knew long ago what the rest of the world — including the Lavernites — was only just discovering: Richard Payne Knight was a rare talent. A true rock star.

But there was another part of Richard now, too. I could label it aloofness, coarseness, ego, self-absorption, focus, intensity... I could call it a hundred different things. They all made me a little sad. The real problem was the glimpses I caught of the old Richard — the Richard who first fell in love with music and used it like a retreat from the horrors of his daily life, but who could also joke around, laugh at himself, and challenge the system without becoming bitter. It's those glimpses, those unguarded flashes, that made me sadder than anything else. The flashes that remind you of the person you used to know and love. Then they stop, click off, and you're left with someone new, someone previously unknown, and suddenly there are choices to be made that never existed when friendship was a given.

After Richard and Julius left, Coolie made a phone call to a local guy he knew who lived nearby, then moved Papa and me to a table near the window. Apparently, the guy usually had something interesting to sell. This time it was Ecstasy. So now we had something to do: wait for Coolie's dealer to show up with Ecstasy.

"This guy's always got the best shit, man. I'm telling you." Coolie craned his neck to see out the window and down the side of the building. Papa and I exchanged amused glances, fairly uninterested in the whole process. Still, it was something to do. "He's a pretty cool guy, too. A little paranoid, but whatever. He'll definitely come tonight, too. He didn't know we were playing, but he'll come." He leaned over the table and checked again. "Listen," he scanned between Papa and me, "when he gets here, just let me check out what the deal is, alright? You guys just hang here." Papa smirked at me, then gave Coolie a thumbs-up. "I'll come get you when I know the score. I just gotta make sure everything's cool first."

No sooner had Coolie given the instructions than a loud, grating sound came rumbling in from outside: wheels scraping over concrete, louder and faster as it came closer. I hated it. I knew what it was and I hated it. Coolie's dealer — a kid on a skateboard — came flying down in front of the store, spun around twice outside the window, then kicked the back of the board up and into his hand in one fluid motion. I've always hated skateboards. The whole idea of them annoys me. The kid cocked his hip and peered, searching, through the restaurant window. It was hard to tell through his dark Oakley sunglasses, but he seemed to be staring right past us. His hair was short, shaved on the sides, dyed blond, and intentionally disheveled. He was tall, gangly, limber, wearing a sharp-collared '50s-style shirt, wide-legged cargo pants, and Vans sneakers: a rolling Chester Cheetah, Generation Next, Mountain Dew poster boy for teenage rebellion. It wasn't until he flicked off the shades and I saw the crow's feet around his eyes that I realized he was no kid at all. He was mid-30s, at least. A man in kid's clothing.

Coolie went outside to meet him. They bumped fists and walked off up the street.

"Well, I guess that's Mr. X," I said. Papa looked at me and we both cracked up. I checked his soda cup. "I guess we should order something so Donny doesn't kick us out." I looked over my shoulder, scanning the wall menu. "They've got ice cream sandwiches. You want one? I'm buying."

Papa nodded. "Yeah, I'm just gonna leave a message at Julie's real quick, too." He looked a little sheepish. He'd taken a lot of shit from the band for his dedication to Julie. "She probably won't be home," he said, quickly. "I just want to let her know we're in Albany."

I waved off his concern — it was all good by me — and headed toward the counter.

"Hey, Virgil," he called out. I stopped, spun around. "Chocolate, if they've got it, please."

"Chocolate for Papa," I said, smiling. I enjoyed saying that so much, I said it again.

I queued up for ice cream behind a neo-Rasta white boy with dreadlocks, wearing a Jamaican soccer jersey and a nylon backpack that smelled suspiciously skunky. When he'd walked in five minutes earlier, I'd naturally assumed he was Coolie's connection.

Albany was full of surprises.

While I waited in line, I turned to watch Papa on the phone. He was glowing. Jesus, even talking to her answering machine made him smile. You had to wonder: maybe there was something to this love stuff after all?

My own experience with love had been substantially less inspiring. It consisted of a fleeting moment at a high school float-making party for our senior year homecoming parade. Our school symbol was a knight. The float theme: This Knight is Ours. However, the night was most certainly not mine. My own experience with love was an inches-away-from-victory collision of infatuation and reality that lasted four seconds — four seconds comprising my actual time in love — and ending in humiliating, heartbroken defeat.

In short: Kathy Baker, the girl I was obsessed with from tenth grade through twelfth, approached me in a way — perhaps it was the lighting, the convivial atmosphere, the mood of the barn, the scent of fresh hay, the feeling of reckless abandon accompanying one's senior year — that implied that she came with a purpose. I'd seen her in the corner talking to her friends by the cookie and juice table, pointing in my direction, giggling as high school girls are wont to do. We had spoken before. It wasn't as if I had no reason to think she might want to talk to me. It wasn't totally ludicrous or out of the question. She was simply a girl I was infatuated with, securely out of my league, whom I hoped to somehow get together with. And she was coming my way.

Had it been an after-school television special, the scene might've been shot in slow motion: her long auburn tresses bouncing and falling gently around her shoulders, her radiant smile growing larger with each step, and the soundtrack might've been my heartbeat, louder and louder, a muddle of laughter and kids in the background drowned out by the sheer romantic force of the moment. As it was, I happened to be standing by the stereo and it was cranked loud enough for the whole barn to rock out to Def Leppard's "Pour Some Sugar on Me." I tried to act busy, sorting tissue paper flowers into piles — blue in one pile, gold in another — beside my Chemistry teacher, Mr. DiPatrino. In truth, I was shaking in my Timberlands.

She spoke.

"What? Huh?" I couldn't hear her; the stereo was too loud.

She turned, giggled at her friends, then turned back. She spoke again.

I motioned to the speaker. "I still can't —" and stepped away from it. She leaned in towards my ear. All the way. Her lips brushed my lobe. True love flowered.

"Is it true you're…" She stopped speaking, looked into my eyes.

My mind screamed back: *What? Scared shitless? Going out of my mind right now? Completely and totally in love? Yes! Yes! Yes!*

"…going to the Pink Floyd concert with Richard?"

Her query wasn't about me at all. It was about my musician friend, the true target of her desire. Once again, I was only the friend. Richard was the man.

Richard and Kathy sat together in the back seat all the way up to Toronto to see Pink Floyd. He kissed her in the dark back seat all the way back home.

We were kids. Such things happen. One boy gets the girl that the other boy wanted; the same thing happens with boys to girls, girls to girls, boys to boys. It always has and it always will. But still.

As I watched Papa smile into the pay phone at Donny's Pizzeria, it made me wonder if I should put a little more effort into finding a girlfriend. Perhaps love was another way forward in my life. Another next step. It seemed to be working for Papa at least.

I paid for the ice cream sandwiches — one chocolate, one vanilla — and met Papa back at the table. "So, did you get Julie?"

"Thanks," Papa said, unwrapping his ice cream. "No, she wasn't home. I didn't think she would be, she's probably still at work. Saturdays are busy at the shoe store. I left a message on her machine though, just to let her know where we are." He looked at me, a little embarrassed. "She keeps track on a map with little colored pins."

Love.

"Wow, that's amazing." I shook my head. "It must be nice having someone so concerned about where you are and what you're doing and everything."

Papa nodded, licking between the edges of cookie and ice cream. "The guys bust my balls, but I don't give a shit. Julie's the goods, man. If all this stuff: the playing, CDs, the band, all of it, went away tomorrow, I'd still have her. That's a pretty cool feeling." He looked up, smiling. I wasn't going to shake him down about this and he knew it. "But enough about my love life. How about you? No girlfriend or anything?"

"Naw." I shook my head, blotting ice cream off my chin with a napkin. "Nothing at all. I'm starting to think it might be nice though."

Papa examined my expression. Perhaps he saw something there.

"It'll happen," he said, nodding reassuringly. "When you least expect it. It'll happen." He leaned back, smiling. "I don't recommend searching out true love this way or anything, but Julie and I actually met at a Laverna show."

Something about that surprised me, so I told him. He laughed.

"I know, I know. Like I said, I wouldn't recommend our shows as the place to look, but when it comes to love…" He shrugged his shoulders, let them drop. "Julie was on the Campus Events committee in charge of booking acts for Middlebury's parents' weekend. Can you imagine them wanting us to play for parents? Great way to make them feel safe about their kids being away from home, right?" He snickered. "Anyway, Richard was out of town when Julie called, so I ended up booking the gig for us, setting our fee and everything. We'd only played a handful of times at that point, but we were still pretty tight. So I talked to her over the phone a few times, getting all the details down, and that was that. We got along well, she seemed nice and everything, but we never met face to face."

Papa stopped, stared out the window. I turned to see what he was looking at, expecting to see Coolie and Mr. X, but there was no one there.

"I've never had that happen to me before," he continued slowly. "If anyone had told me they'd been through it, I would've thought they were full of shit. But I'm telling you, Virgil, it was like in the movies or something. I saw her, she saw me, and before we'd even said a word I knew exactly who she was." He shook his head, turning back. "So we started talking, ironing out all the details and everything, but all I could do was stare at her. We set up, played the gig, broke down, all I could think about was Julie. It wasn't even an option: I asked her out, she said yes, and that was it. We've been dating ever since. Almost two years now."

As Papa spoke, I got the feeling he'd been waiting to tell that story ever since the day he met Julie. I don't think the band offered a real sensitive ear for the retelling of love stories.

"That's really cool, Papa," I said, genuinely envious. "I wish you the best with all that, man. I mean it. I really hope it works out for you."

Papa pushed the last of his ice cream sandwich into his mouth. He licked his fingers, winking. "It will, man. It will."

I allowed his confidence to hang there for a moment, unencumbered, and then said, "Can I ask you a question?"

Papa shrugged indifferently. "Shoot."

"What do you think of all these guys? Partying, hanging out with different girls, doing whatever sex stuff they're into, and all that? Does it ever bother you?"

Papa shook his head. "I adopted an attitude a long time ago to get along in this band: play music with them but live my own life. It's all I can do. I mean, shit, I'm a musician and these guys are the best I've ever played with. That's nothing to laugh at. Aside from Julie, music is my life and I've got no intention of going back to selling CDs out of some hole-in-the-wall record store. If I'm ever gonna make it in the music business, Laverna is my best shot. And I'm not gonna blow that, no matter what.

"But to answer your question: No. I don't like most of what those guys do. Hey, man, I grew up in a little town in nowhere New York. I didn't see anything stronger than a can of Budweiser and a bag of seedy brick weed until I met these guys. My first night living in the house, Richard, Coolie, and Julius were down in that little room of theirs, chanting all kinds of weird crap with these freaky, whacked-out girls, and doing all kinds of crazy shit. This was before I even met Julie, and I wasn't into it then. I sure as hell ain't into it now."

Papa looked me in the eye. "Listen, I'm no angel, and neither is Julie. We do our share of partying. But for the most part, I don't have a goddamn idea what those guys do. I get on stage, play my parts, tour around for a few weeks, then go back home to Julie. I haven't told anyone yet — Richard will probably be really pissed — but we're moving in together after this tour, too." He shrugged. "Hell, I stay at her place most nights anyway. Only reason I haven't moved before is it's easier for practicing. But screw it, it's getting too weird over there. I'm moving. I'd tell you to take over my empty room, but —" he paused, measuring our trust, his disclosure. "Like I said, Virgil, I don't really know what those guys do. I mean, Coolie's obviously a drunk, but he's fairly harmless most of the time." He shook his head, discouraged. "But Julius and Richard, they're off in a whole different direction. I mean, Richard's taken this whole Laverna idea and blown it way out of proportion." He paused while I bit my ice cream sandwich, bracing myself.

"I don't know what Richard was like when you guys were growing up," he continued, "but I've seen him change a lot over the past couple years. He's taking this whole Laverna idea way over the edge. The songs are one thing. But now we've got these groupies — it's a whole fucking thing with them — and that little room in the basement. I don't even know what's going on in there anymore. I'm telling you, man, Richard's way into it all. If I were you," he said, patting my forearm across the table, "I'd think long and hard before I got too involved with this band. A tour is one thing, but after that," he looked right at me and lowered his voice, "I'd find something else to do, Virgil. You're too smart for all this shit."

First Julius and then Coolie had hinted that Richard was over the edge; two guys who, by any standards, shouldn't be pointing self-righteous fingers at anyone. But now Papa — good ol' Papa — was saying the same thing.

"Well, do you think I should say something to Richard? See what's going on with him? Maybe try to help him out or something?"

Papa looked away. "Virgil, I think you should finish this tour, take your pay, and get the hell out of Dodge. That's my best advice to you."

I searched his face for sarcasm, a hint of exaggeration. Nothing.

"Serious?" I asked, hoping he'd soften his message a touch.

Papa nodded to Coolie coming in through the pizzeria doorway, a huge grin across his face, blond locks hanging down over his eyes, one hand thrust inside his front pocket.

Papa turned back to me. "Serious."

DANCING ON A CLIFF

The first time I saw her was during the Albany gig. She was with the Lavernites, dancing at the fringe, casting sidelong glances my way at regular intervals. Felix was there. So was Argute, Fecunde, the two girls from back in Saratoga, and a few new arrivals. It was amazing how the new arrivals blended in. Aside from Felix's obvious dominance, the Lavernites were almost entirely interchangeable: same clothes, same blank expression, same random dance moves, and complete absorption in Richard's songs. As a group, they were easily identifiable. Unified. The Lavernites.

But this new one caught my eye. I found out much later that she had a name. A real name. Only then would I come to understand that her catching my eye was as intentional as my first meeting with Felix, all my talks with Richard, and truthfully, my entire presence on the tour. I was no more than a show poodle jumping through their hoops. Hoops I didn't even realize existed. Hoops that were about to be lit on fire.

Despite the fact that she wore the same clothes and danced the same way, this one stood out from the other Lavernite girls. It was how she carried herself. As if somewhere beneath the surface of her devotion lingered a headstrong person, unwilling to submit completely. She was not like the nameless girl. Not like Tara even. I couldn't help glancing back at her. As the night progressed, I found myself speculating about her, trying to unlock the gentle mysteries of her eyes, her wrists, the long, slow slope of her legs; wondering where she'd gone when she was out of my sight and if she'd be back.

I finally met the mystery girl, in a way, during set break. It'd been a busy night at the merch table. I'd signed up fifteen people, sold six CDs, eight t-shirts, four bumper stickers, and dispensed tour information to two separate groups of SUNY Albany students (a couple of them had heard Richard and Julius on the radio and brought their friends), and one grizzled taper attending his first show. I felt a part of the Laverna machine. And the band was rocking hard.

Between shows, it was easy to get lost in the fog of annoying interpersonal band dynamics and creepy Lavernites, and forget that Laverna was really an incredible musical group. When they were on, they were the best around. Each member was a skilled craftsman, so trained on his instrument and the band interplay that even the most improvisational passages interspersed throughout songs came across like choreographed ballet: Papa dipping down while Julius's organ soared above; Richard blasting little staccato rhythms across the crowd, stalking, taunting them with his guitar, while Coolie rode his bass drum and cymbals like a blissed-out dance instructor, arms and legs grooving in time.

It was a sight to behold and a wild garden of sound. Laverna could lean back on their jam skills to get a crowd dancing, or they could morph into that heavier new sound and get downright introspective and spooky. Their music defied easy categorization and was still very much evolving, but they had the range to take the songs and the crowd wherever they wanted. And they never forgot the main rule of rock music: support your front man. No matter what else happens, support your front man. He's the beacon, the one they'll talk about later. And Richard was a great front man, getting better with age, more confident in his physicality, using his movement, his body, his sensuality, as part of the show.

Dance with me on a cliffside, hold my hand, jump into the sea
Meet me in the springtime, the four winds carry our serenity
Dance with me on a cliffside, come all who wish to be free

As soon as Coolie came back to the table at set break, I knew he'd dipped into Mr. X's product. His eyes shone brighter than klieg lights, and his jaw did the back and forth slide. I reached into my pocket, handed him a piece of gum.

"Aw, Virgil, you're the best, man. The fucking best! Thanks, that's perfect. Gum, man. Yeah!"

It wasn't even my last piece, or anything.

"No problem," I said. "You guys are tearing it up, man. This place is rocking." As I spoke, he followed my mouth with his eyes, grinning broadly, working the gum hard. "I've been signing up people on the mailing list like crazy, too. Selling CDs and everything. You guys own this place!"

He grinned, nodding, making sounds like yeah, yeah.

"So how's that X treating you?" I finally asked. "Looks like you dipped in a little early."

Coolie held up a half-filled cup of water. "I've just been sipping a little as we go along. It's pretty strong stuff though. It's starting to kick my ass, man."

"Anybody else taking any?" I asked, searching the crowd for the other guys. I spotted Richard by the back of the club, near the soundboard, talking to a couple of tapers including the older one I'd noticed earlier. Papa was by the bar, gripping a pint of beer, and scanning the crowd with a wide grin. Julius was nowhere to be seen. Presumably he was in the dingy little dressing room behind the stage. Maybe alone. Maybe not.

Coolie nodded. "Papa's taken a few sips, not too much. Do not say anything to Richard though. He gets wicked pissed when we play fucked up."

Mr. X approached dressed in evening wear: black skinny jeans and a skintight silvery button-down shirt. He didn't look at me. He whispered in Coolie's ear, took a few steps away, then stopped and turned back.

"Alright, Virgil, I'll be back in like ten minutes," said Coolie. "If anyone asks, just tell them I went out to grab a smoke, alright?"

I waved Coolie on, slightly curious, but not too concerned. Coolie was the kind of guy who could ingest all sorts of chemicals and still play better than most drummers. No sooner had he left than Felix appeared. A school of greasy flutters swam through my intestines.

"Hello, Virgil," he greeted with a bow. "I trust you slept well last night?"

I nodded. "Yeah, just fine. You were all gone when I woke up though. Where'd everybody run off to so fast?"

Felix parted the dark hair on either side of his face. His small frame was clad in muted Guatemalan cloth patterns, a long necklace of wooden beads dangled down his chest.

"The early bird catches the grubs that live in the bark," he answered. He grinned slightly. "We had work to do, Virgil. Life isn't all sex and rock-n-roll, you know."

"Oh, yeah? And what kind of work is that?"

Felix glanced over at the Lavernites. They were gathered together in a corner of the club, talking and looking around, not mingling with anybody else. I noticed that girl again. She was talking to one of the Lavernites from last night. She looked up as I looked over. We locked eyes; she looked down.

"Life on the road isn't easy, Virgil. I suspect you're beginning to realize that by now. There are obstacles to overcome, hardships to be surpassed. It's best if you have a plan to function by, and a means of execution."

"Is that what they are?" I asked, nodding towards the Lavernites. "Your means of execution?"

Felix stroked his chin, his cracked tooth showed through a sliver grin.

"We help each other," he answered matter-of-factly. "I've been on the road a long time now, living by my wits, as they say. Some of them need more of my help, others I require more from."

"For sex and whatnot?"

"Don't be a prude, Virgil," fired Felix. "Stay hung up on the human body and you'll run in ever smaller circles throughout eternity. If servicing the physical is necessary, then it's done. I have no problem with my friends receiving—"

"Your friends?" I interrupted.

"Yes," said Felix. "My friends. We are all friends. Partners and confidants. And I have no problem with them giving or receiving physical pleasure... Born to die, what else? But stay hung up on that and you'll flail forever. Release the urge, you release the soul from its grip. Pen it up, obsess about it, and it rules you. I work for the cause, same as Laverna. No difference save for methodology: to free the mind, and move beyond."

"A true humanitarian," I said. "And I assume you're beyond the petty sexual realm yourself?"

"Not all dogs scratch the same flea," countered Felix. "But I can see you're locked tightly into past lessons. You've learned them well."

"Whatever, man. How about that girl you sent me last night? The girl with no name? Did she learn her lessons well, too?"

"She has a name," Felix answered sharply. "It simply hasn't been spoken yet."

"Oh, yeah? And when will it be spoken?"

He shook his head slowly. I was a dim pupil.

"You insist on focusing on a single drop of water while the waterfall crashes around you, Virgil. Her name will be spoken when she forwards the group in some way. She could go back to wherever she came from whenever she wants, and be called Judy or Sally or Linda or whoever she was there. Thus far, she chooses not to. So she will contribute with the rest of us. 'New' doesn't mean bad, Virgil. It only means new. You, of all people, should realize that."

What had started last night as an intriguing rap was beginning to make my skin crawl. The short hairs on my neck upended. Felix was a manipulator; a damn good one, too. If not for my cynicism and wariness, I might've even nibbled at his bait. As it was, it made me nauseous.

As he spoke, I saw his whole world unfurl: a battered child, powerless but intelligent, finds his way into life on the road, learns the ins and outs of travel and human influence, attaches himself to a band capable of luring impressionable young people in droves, and begins harvesting them for his own survival and amusement. Those were my speculations as Felix rapped on. What I didn't know could've filled a book.

"There's nothing wrong with depending on others, Virgil. Our country is built upon it. Majority leads, minority follows. My friends and I are as American as baseball, General Motors, the United States Senate. We're simply more powerless. The underdogs. The unloved and mistreated. So we band together to move ahead, to survive this world while contemplating one greater. No one is forced to accompany me if they don't want to."

I muttered the term that'd been bouncing around my head all day. "The American dream."

Felix waved a finger.

"Make no mistake, Virgil. The American dream is a lady in white, we are but the dirt beneath her soiled feet. Don't misjudge the power of the group. We live below the surface — underground, *di inferi*, subterranean — where we'll stay for now."

"And then what?"

He shrugged. "Why ask? Who knows? The important thing is that the search is underway. And my friends," he pointed over at the Lavernites, "they've simply joined the search party with me."

I'd had enough, more than I could take. I looked down at the table that separated us, and then back at Felix.

"So you want to buy a bumper sticker or what?"

Felix chuckled. He clapped his hands lightly before my face, bowed deeply, and moved off through the crowd; his mishmash of aphorisms, threats, capitalism, socialism, communalism, and whatever other -isms helped him gain control trailed after him.

I glanced over at the Lavernites, looking for her, the one. She was there, with the rest of them, standing in a cluster, talking seriously, bound together like a pack of unwanted kittens destined for a gunnysack at the bottom of a farm pond. I couldn't blame them. I'd grown up surrounded and supported by friends and loved ones. I didn't know who those people were, but something told me their stories were different. Maybe not. Either way, something must've gone wrong for Felix to be the one they now trusted.

Who was she? I kept wondering. *Where did she come from?*

I signed up a few more people for the mailing list. Sold two more bumper stickers, two t-shirts, one CD.

Who is she? Why is she with them?

Richard checked in, and was pleased with the sales and sign-ups. Papa came looking for Coolie. I suspect he wanted another sip of magic water.

Where does she come from? How did she get here?

Julius surfaced, lurking around the edge of the stage. Two girls spoke in quick, short bursts in front of him. His head bobbed and lifted, bobbed and lifted. Coolie slapped me on the back as he walked past, cruising like a mako shark through the crowd. He climbed onstage and nestled in behind the drums.

How can I meet her? Should I even try?

The rest of the band gathered onstage and picked up their instruments. Richard looked back at Coolie, then over at Papa: both grinning like stupid dogs. He checked Julius: head lolling in circles on his rubbery neck. Richard's mouth moved. I read his lips: "Motherfuckers."

He stepped up to the microphone, grabbed the stand. The crowd roared; tapers' decks spun. Richard dropped his guitar to his waist until it dangled by the strap. His eyes glowed fiercely, jaw set hard. He placed his mouth by the mike head and cut loose a minute-long primal scream that shook the bottles on the shelves and rattled up the backbone of every person in the club. Then he stepped back, checked the crowd, pleased with himself. A sharp grin appeared on his face.

"Take that, you sons of bitches!" he called out to no one in particular, thus everyone in attendance. "One, two, three, four," and then Laverna kicked into a pounding rendition of "Abandon the Gods."

Shake the trees, rattle the sky
Fake me, forsake me, make me cry
Abandon the gods, leave me to die

I felt a small tug at my elbow, then another. I turned. It was her. Mystery girl. She thrust a small folded piece of paper into my hand, then slipped away. I watched her, wanting to follow but holding back, somehow knowing that was best. Not now. Not now, not yet. I unfolded one corner of the note, then another, checking for spies, watchers, for Felix himself. I read: *Behind the movies. 3 a.m.*

Movies? What movies? Where? And then I remembered driving to the club, setting up, seeing it across the street, down a block, the glowing marquee, three Xs — XXX — lined up across the top. Papa's smirking remark regarding Albany's cultural center.

The movies? Could that be what she meant? But she was already gone.

My options seemed clear: follow a trail of breadcrumbs dropped by an alluring stranger I'd never spoken to, yet who was already taking hold of my romantic imagination, or let it go and forget her. I mean, why would she be different from any previous unrequited infatuations? The barista, the artist, the hygienist... even Kathy Baker, the original heartbreaker. If she really wanted to connect with me, she could have stayed and talked. Right?

My rational mind wisely responded: Yes, she could have stayed and talked. It's time to learn your lesson. Just let it go, Virgil.

The rest of me, as usual, answered: Rational mind? What's that?

As I stood at the table calculating my next move, Richard continued blazing through song after song. The rest of the band could've been semi-conscious, and it wouldn't have mattered. He took command of the stage, whipping his guitar through fierce solos, roaring out lines about ancient gods, Roman hedonism, and thieving worshippers begging for their children back.

Between songs, he spoke to the crowd, flirting with girls, challenging everyone to dance and cut loose, now and forever. It was the edgiest, most masterful performance I'd ever seen Richard give; fully committed artistry with the chops to back it up. He was a dangerous man hurling desperate notes into the yawning chasm of rock-n-roll mythology.

Richard finished the set with "Temples," a soulful tour of forgotten, crumbling centers of worship all over the world, then dropped his guitar and exited stage left into the little dressing room in back. The crowd went wild. It didn't matter. There would be no encore. Coolie, Papa, and Julius — finding themselves on stage without a front man — gave little bows and waved, and meekly followed Richard.

Suddenly the merch table was booming. People crowded each other out, elbowing, grabbing CDs, t-shirts, and stickers, thrusting money into my hands. Twice in five minutes, the mailing list pen got lost, but I produced new ones like a pro, happy to be of service. People tried talking to me, but I had no time. I was inspired, commandingly working my little sphere of influence, making things happen. At final tally, I'd sold forty CDs, fifty-five bumper stickers, eighteen t-shirts, and added seventy-nine names to the mailing list. An impressive night of grassroots merchandising to pay for gas, cigarettes, beer, pizza, and coffee to make it to the next town and do it all over again.

When I went backstage to tell the guys, my spirits soaring off sales and my impending rendezvous behind the movie theater, Richard was angrily berating the band. I stood in the doorway, half in, half out. Coolie, Julius, and Papa sat side by side on a small, tattered sofa while Richard paced in front of them like a furious general, gesturing a smoldering joint for emphasis.

"I'll tell you why I'm so pissed, Julius! I'm fucking pissed because my keyboard player's turning into a goddamn junkie, and you guys," he stared at Coolie especially, "my rhythm section, looked like fucking cartoon characters up there. Jesus Christ, I'm trying to bring everything down for 'Shepherd's Grove,' create a little ambience, get things mellow, and you guys are grinning like goddamn rubes on a tropical vacation. This isn't some fucking zydeco band, man. I'm out there busting my ass trying to make things perfect, and you guys are lost on Mars. You can't even wait a few hours to get fucked up?"

He took a hit off the joint to calm himself down.

"Christ knows I don't give a fuck if you party," he continued. Pointing at Julius, "Them, not you. I'm not down with partying like that. You gotta cut that shit out, man. I won't end up some VH1 footnote about coulda-beens. I thought you said you were out, anyway."

Julius's head went down in repentance. He waved a hand. "I'm out, that's it. That was the last of it."

Richard handed Coolie the joint. "Yeah, well, it better be." He blew out his hit. "Too many players have gone down that way, and I'm not about to hook my wagon to one of them. I swear to God, I will leave your ass on the road, Julius.

"And you two," he pointed between Coolie and Papa. "A few hours is all I ask. Just a few to play the gig straight, got it?"

Coolie, still smiling madly despite himself, handed Papa the joint.

"It's all good, Richard, man. It's all good. You know we're usually totally cool with this shit. I was just pumped for this gig, man. And we fucking wrecked the place! We blew it apart! Those people were going nuts, man! Fucking nuts!"

That got him. Richard finally cracked a smile.

"And buying everything on the table, too," I said, stepping all the way into the dank little room. "I must've sold fifty CDs at least. A bunch of t-shirts and bumper stickers, too. You guys killed out there, man! They couldn't get enough."

Richard patted my shoulder. "That's awesome, Virgil. Thanks for handling all that stuff, man. We could use the money, too. We didn't make as much at the Dark Star gig as I was planning, so this will help."

I handed over the small metal lock-box containing the revenues.

"I didn't want to leave it in the van. I didn't count it yet, but it's got to be at least a few hundred. I packed the rest of the stickers, shirts, and CDs and stuff in the van already."

Richard gave me a thumbs-up.

"Speaking of which," he cast a mischievous smile across the room, "since I carried your asses all night, you guys are gonna pack all the equipment without the benefit of my assistance." He grabbed the joint, took one last hit, then handed it to Papa. "Let's meet around noon tomorrow at that diner across the street from the pizza place we ate at today."

Coolie's eyes were shining bright. "What are you going to do?"

Richard tossed his answer back over his shoulder on the way out the door. "What do you think?"

Julius shook his head mournfully. "More like, who's he going to do," he muttered.

But no one seemed to care.

I kept an eye out for the mystery girl as we packed the equipment. The Lavernites were long gone, so I didn't really expect to see her. Still, you never know. The rest of the guys were heading to an after-hours party at Mr. X's nearby loft. It sounded tempting, but a glance at my watch — 2:45 a.m. — told me I had better things to do. For better or worse, my decision was made. I would play it out and follow her trail.

The vehicles packed, we stood in a semicircle on the curb outside the club.

"You got someone you gonna meet then?" asked Coolie, disappointed I wasn't going with them. "This party is gonna be totally happenin', man! My buddy's got all kinds of shit up there. And girls and stuff, too. It should be real cool. If you already got something lined up though…"

I nodded expectantly. "Yeah, man, I'm all set. This girl slipped me a note during the gig to meet her, so it's looking pretty good."

"No shit. She gave you her address?"

I hesitated. I realized it was strange to set up a meeting behind a porno theater. Saying it out loud would've only made it weirder. "Uh, yeah. She gave me her address. She's pretty cute, too. Listen, you guys mind if I take the Subaru and you take the van tonight?"

They looked at each other, exchanging indifferent shrugs.

"You sure you know where you're going?" asked Papa.

Julius was already climbing in behind the wheel of the van.

"Yeah, it's, uh," I glanced down the street toward the theater. "It's really close, I'll be fine." I patted Papa on the back, flashing Coolie a peace sign. "Take it easy on those girls there tonight, Iron Man. You may not know your own strength."

Coolie leapt up, smacked the top of the van, and climbed in back with the equipment. I shut him in, Papa took shotgun, and off they went. I glanced at my watch. 2:53 a.m.

The closer I got to the theater, the stupider the whole thing seemed. Somehow, in the heat and excitement of the moment, the gig, the crowd, the covert exchange with a pretty girl, I'd downplayed the underlying weirdness. Who meets behind a porno theater at 3 a.m.? Who even knew porno theaters still existed?

The illicit rendezvous spot, the covertness of the exchange... It must have been about eluding Felix. I just knew it. It had to be. Somehow Felix was to blame for this bizarre sequence of events. And I couldn't forget that this girl was a Lavernite, as much as I would like to. She was a part of Felix's twisted galaxy. That was important for me to remember.

I pulled in behind the theater to a narrow back street with one dim streetlight glowing green twenty yards away, and parked the car. Once again, the hair on my neck prickled and lifted. It was two minutes to three. As I sat, waiting, I made mental notes of my surroundings. When I got bored of that, I found some slips of paper and a ballpoint pen in the glove compartment and began jotting down actual notes. At least if I got knifed waiting, there would be a written record of my last minutes on earth.

3:08 a.m. – A mangy raccoon just waddled past, paused beside the Subaru, stared at me. I stared back. It licked its paws, shook its head, waddled away. Even it is disgusted.

3:11 a.m. – A pack of three teenagers who look far too young to be out so late just rode past on BMX bikes. They were wearing hooded sweatshirts and dark sweatpants. I locked my door and shrunk down in the driver's seat. I feel like a nervous substitute teacher.

3:16 a.m. – She's never gonna show. I should've known. She is too pretty, her world is too out there. I'm too square. Square? Who even says that anymore? This whole thing is probably just a gag. Probably Felix getting even with me for challenging his authority and mocking him. I can't believe how stupid I am.

3:22 a.m. – A middle-aged man and a woman with heavy makeup wearing a fluffy, feathered coat just swung around the side of the porno theater arm in arm. They were laughing. The man tugged the woman closer. She pulled him into a rear entrance and pushed his back to the door. He reached into his pocket, handed her some bills. She tucked them into her coat, unzipped his pants, and rolled a condom over his hard dick. He tried pushing her shoulders down, but she shook her head and sucked him standing up.

3:26 a.m. – The woman just stood up and arched her back as if it had stiffened. I'm sure it had. The man zipped up his pants, walked past her and back around the building. She removed a compact from her pocket and fixed her makeup. She looked over at the car but I'm crouching so low I'm barely visible above the steering wheel. The streetlights are flickering and buzzing in the alley. She dropped the compact into her pocket, shook her hair down, and followed the man's path back around the far side of the building.

3:32 a.m. – A good song just came on the radio. "Elderly Woman Behind the Counter in a Small Town" by Pearl Jam. It made me think of Richard, then my mother. I need to call her again soon. I should call her more often.

3:40 a.m. – A figure just approached, walking fast up the street.

My heart pounded. Was it her? She looked slightly taller than my girl though. Her body denser. When she passed under the streetlight, I realized it wasn't my girl at all. It was an older woman. Fifty, maybe older. My girl is early twenties. She looks that way anyway. This woman was wearing a dirty maroon windbreaker, royal blue pants, and a black baseball hat pulled tight over an unruly nest of hair. She was a homeless woman with the crazed gait of a crackhead. I really do need to call my mother more often.

3:55 a.m. – I'm half-asleep. I'm drifting, floating in that mystical zone before deep R.E.M. where all associations are fair game. I'm thinking about the girl, meeting her in the alley. The meeting just happened. Outside, it didn't. In my dream, it did. She was desperate to get me alone, asked me to save her, help her, rescue her, and take her away to my private home in the country. I had a private home in the country. She wore a white skirt, spun around to show me how it flared when she twirled. I wore a pastel linen suit and strolled in a dignified manner. I had a walking stick.

There was a sharp knock on my car window. It shook me back to consciousness. I flicked my eyes open and focused. A figure, a woman, was peering in. Her face was pressed so close to the glass that it seemed freakishly distorted: nose too large, eyes mismatched, mouth sloping at a disturbingly acute angle. But it wasn't the features so much as the accents around the features: the plastered rouge, scalding red lips, the deep blue coating extending over the eyes to the painted-on shards of black eyebrow. It wasn't my Lavernite at all. It was the hooker.

I rolled down my window.

She looked down at my crotch, then into my eyes. "You waiting for me, sweetie?"

I rubbed my watery eyes. "No. I'm just waiting."

"Yeah? You want some company while you wait?" She reached into her purse, pulled out a pack of Eve Lights, the lady's choice. She placed the smoke between the scarlet pillows of her lips, and leaned in for a light. "Well, you gonna just sit there or you gonna help me out?"

"Oh, yeah, sorry," I mumbled, pressing in the Subaru's lighter. I pulled out a smoke of my own, and waited with her.

"I think I fell asleep," I explained, though she hadn't asked. It's true, I had fallen asleep. But this wasn't a dream: I was in an alley behind a decrepit old porno theater in Albany, waiting for a cigarette lighter to pop, waiting to meet an attractive girl I'd never heard speak, waiting with a prostitute I just saw blow a man in a dark doorway, waiting for something better to come along.

We waited together. The lighter popped out. I extended it out the window, lit her cigarette, lit mine, and pushed it back into place. We smoked for a few seconds in silence.

"I thought I saw someone over here," she said, finally. "You're not a cop or something, huh?"

"No. Sorry about that." I shook my head earnestly. "I wasn't really expecting... I was just supposed to meet someone back here and..."

"Enough," she stopped me, waving her fake purple nails. "I don't need to know nothing I don't need to know."

"Yeah," I said. "Right." We smoked a few more seconds in silence. "Listen, I don't really have any money or anything, so..." I let the implication drift away.

"Don't sweat it, honey. Just taking a break. Can't smoke inside. I thought I saw you out here though. I knew I was right." She leaned on the door to take a better look at me. "You been out here a while." She scanned my eyes. "Think your friend's gonna show?"

I shook my head. "No. Actually, I don't."

"Actually, I don't," she repeated, mocking me. "A piece of advice." She exhaled and ground her Eve Light out beneath the toe of her three-inch stiletto shoe. "This ain't the place to spend the night. Even rats don't like this alley. Go find someplace else you wanna sleep. Fall asleep here, you wake up on the ground with no more car."

I knew she was right, but hadn't yet considered my options. I was alone, didn't know a soul to call, it was 4 a.m., my date hadn't shown. I realized she wasn't going to show either.

"Thanks for the tip," I said, snubbing out my smoke in the car ashtray. I started the Subaru, and put it into gear. "Take care."

She looked at me like I was insane. She was probably right.

I pulled out into the street, made a left at the side of the porno theater, and drove back onto the main road. I was so tired the streetlights became a soft white blur. I had to find someplace to stop soon or I was in serious danger of falling asleep at the wheel. I drove straight, passing one dark parking lot after another, dismissing them all as too sketchy. Finally, I found a neon-lit cheap motel, the E-Z Rest. I turned off my lights, pulled around back, and parked the Subaru between an F-150 pickup and a beige Bonneville. I climbed into the backseat and fell into an exhausted, uneasy sleep.

GOOD LUCK

I had three days between gigs to think about the way I'd been blown off. Three days to ruminate and plot my acid-tongued reproach next time I saw her. I planned all the ways I'd give her a proverbial piece of my mind, scold her for wasting my time and leaving me waiting in a seedy back alley alone all night. Or maybe I would use the cold shoulder approach. I'd pretend that I could barely even remember her face: women throw themselves at roadies like me who are close to the band all the time. How was I supposed to remember this one random babe?

Either way, revenge would be mine. That much was certain.

Papa had a friend with a cabin just outside of Kingston in Saugerties, NY. The guy was a biker originally from Papa's hometown. He would spend half the year working the oil fields in Texas, half the year holed up in Saugerties. Apparently the band had stayed at his cabin before. Although the biker had gone west already, Papa was welcome to stay anytime. He knew where the key was hidden. We cemented our plans over weak coffee and runny omelets at a diner in downtown Albany.

"Why don't you just come with us?" Richard urged Julius. "We could hang out for a few days and go over some new tunes I've been thinking about. It's cool up there, all quiet and secluded."

I took a sip of orange juice and stretched my neck. I'd used the door armrest in the back of the Subaru as a pillow and woke up with my neck cranked at an ungodly angle. I moved it around and massaged it with my hands as I ate French toast and listened to the band bicker.

Julius's plan was to take the Subaru straight to Kingston alone. A friend of his from the city had recently opened a small bed and breakfast just outside of town. Richard protested the plan under the pretense of wanting to work on a new song, but what I think really concerned him was Julius's increasing distance from the rest of the band. Things hadn't changed on the road as Richard had been counting on. Julius was just as moody and distant as he'd been in Burlington, maybe even worse. A constant tension hung between him and Richard especially. A tension everyone knew the root of, but no one discussed out loud.

"I told my friend I'd be coming, Richard. It's all arranged," argued Julius. "Besides, I can contact the club owner before you guys get there and make sure everything's set for the gig."

Julius looked from his eggs to Richard as he spoke, unwilling to focus on either one. It was uncomfortable, like watching a friend's parents argue in public. "Is it really a big deal? You guys can show me the tunes between the city and Scranton, or something. We can go over them then."

There were only a handful of other people in the restaurant. An old couple who looked to be in their eighties ate in resolute silence. A solitary man with a fedora on the seat beside him ate wheat toast and drank coffee at a counter stool. A young mother with bags under her eyes fed pieces of pancake into a hungry toddler's mouth while nursing a plate of home fries and scrambled eggs. Our waitress circulated, pouring warm-ups of coffee, eyeing pedestrians as they passed on the sidewalk, exchanging quick banter with the cook through the pick-up window.

Richard shook his head. "No, it's not a big deal, Julius. It'd just be nice to have everyone hang out together in a mellow setting for a change. It'd be nice to have some time to work without distraction."

Coolie stepped in. "Hey, Julius, can we stay with your friend when we get to Kingston then?" His eyes were large as he fed one last piece of extra crispy bacon into his mouth.

"I'm gonna check that out too," answered Julius, turning from Richard to address the rest of us now. "That's another reason why I want to get there early. I know there's only a few rooms at the bed-and-breakfast, but we can probably crash in the main living area, on the couches or something if we want. I've just got to scope it out and see."

"Whatever," huffed Richard. "Do whatever you want, Julius." He downed the last of his coffee. "Just don't start shooting dope again while you're there, alright? That's all I ask. We've got some big shows in the city. If you go in there all strung-out, we'll never pull them off."

"Fuck you, Richard."

"No, fuck you, Julius."

Papa waved at our waitress, motioning for the check. "Well, this has been a treat, kids, but I don't think we're getting anywhere with it all." He pulled out his wallet to retrieve the band credit card he'd been entrusted with. "Julius, I've got your friend's number." He glanced at the bill the waitress handed him, then handed it back to her with the credit card. "Have a good time in Kingston. We'll see you in a couple of days."

Julius shook his head, and shoved his plate to the middle of the table. It smacked into a glass saltshaker, knocking it over and spilling salt across the formica tabletop. "You'd better get off your goddamn high horse, Richard. It's getting really fucking old really fucking fast."

"Just stay off the hard stuff, Julius," Richard shot back, picking up the shaker. He gathered the stray grains of salt and tossed them over his shoulder.

"Just stay off the whores, Richard," hissed Julius, grabbing his coat off the seat. He turned to me. "Virgil, do you have the car keys?"

I fished them out of my front pocket and handed them over.

"Adieu," Julius said, waving goodbye. The bells on the door rang against the glass as he whipped it open and stormed out onto the sidewalk.

Tension was heavy; no one said a word. The only sound came from a television over the counter stools. A sculpted announcer in a dark blue blazer read the afternoon headlines: "The body of a young woman was found in a dumpster outside the Lamplight Hotel in downtown Albany this morning. Authorities say the girl was discovered naked with lacerations across her stomach and chest, but give the cause of death as strangulation. Her identity is unknown as yet. Police say she's between eighteen and twenty-five years old with long brown hair and a distinctive birthmark on the side of her neck. Anyone with information is asked to contact police officials immediately."

Yes, it was time to call my mother. I found a pay phone beside the bathroom at the back of the restaurant, punched in the digits, and listened for the ring. I read the graffiti on the wall as I waited, a selection of numbers to call for a good time. Men's scrawl.

"Hi, Mom. It's Virgil. How are you doing?"

"Virgil!" Her voice came through crisp and loud. "Oh, I'm so glad you called! How are you? Where are you?"

"I'm fine. Fine. How's Dad?"

"Where are you, honey?"

"I'm in Albany. We just ate breakfast, and we're about to head down to Saugerties for a few days. I just wanted to call before we left. We've got a few days off before the band plays again, so we're going to stay there."

"Is Richard with you?"

"Of course Richard's with me," I laughed. "He's in the band. It's his band. We're all here together."

She paused. "How is he?"

"He's fine. You know, he's Richard. He's really got a good thing going here though, Mom. The band is outstanding, really great."

"That's good, dear. I'm happy for you."

"It's Richard's band. He's the one you should be happy for, Mom," I said. "I'm just going along for the ride."

"And then what, Virgil?" she asked. Her voice grew more tentative. "Have you thought any more about what you're going to do next?"

I shook my head, leaning it against the gritty diner wall.

"I don't know, Mom. I really don't know yet." I massaged the knot on the sorest part of my neck. "I'm just gonna do this for a while until I figure it out."

She was quiet again. "I'm worried about you, Virgil." Her voice was soft, tentative. "So is your father. We both are."

"How's he doing?"

"He's fine. We're both fine. But don't change the subject."

I sighed. "You don't need to worry about me, Mom. I'm fine. I'm just a little backwards right now. I'm just trying to sort everything out." I paused, waited. "This trip is helping, Mom. It really is. I know that probably sounds weird, but it's true."

"Oh, Virgil." I pictured her gazing out the den window into the sparkling Sunny Valley Community pond. "I don't think it's weird. I really don't. I just worry about you, that's all. I'm your mother, that's what we do."

"I appreciate it, Mom. I really do. But I'm fine. Really. Things are going well with these guys, and it's fun to be a part of it for a while." I stood up straight and rolled my neck back and forth. "I'll figure out what to do next. It's just going to take a little time." I grinned. "I'm your son, this is what I do."

She laughed nervously.

"Well, just not for too long, Virgil, okay? I can't take it. Why don't you come down here if you need to figure things out anyway? You know we've got the extra room that never gets used. It's a shame to have you bouncing all over the state of New York while we have a perfectly good room for you here."

"But, Mom, I'm—"

"I know, I know," she cut me off. "You can't blame a mother for trying." She exhaled a long, audible sigh. "You know I want you to do what's best for you, Virgil. Whatever you need to do. But..." she hesitated. "You've always been so good to Richard... watching out for him, taking care of him. And, well, he hasn't always treated you as well in return. I just worry..."

"That's not true, Mom. Richard has treated me fine."

"I don't want to argue with you, Virgil," she said, firmly. "I'm just asking you to watch out for yourself, that's all. He's always had a way of influencing you. And not always for the best."

"I thought you liked Richard."

"I do like Richard," she answered quickly. "I've always liked Richard. But we both know that Richard has had a difficult life. I don't blame him for getting off-track sometimes. But that doesn't mean you do whatever you can for him without taking care of yourself, Virgil."

She waited. I didn't respond.

"You've always been one to put others before yourself. That's not a bad trait, Virgil. It's very admirable. But there are lots of people in this world who will take advantage of that."

"Richard's not like that, Mom. He's—"

"I hope not, Virgil," she cut me off. "I really hope not. Because I know how much you think of him. All I ask is that you take care of yourself right now. Put yourself first for a change. Richard can take care of himself. He always has."

I waited, but she was done. It was hard to hear, but it was also hard to argue with the truth.

"I better get going, Mom," I said. "I just wanted to call and check in."

"The rest of your trip from Ithaca was fine? No problems or anything? Your father was a little concerned about the truck having so many miles on it."

"The truck was fine. Tell Dad the truck was fine. Everything went really smooth. It was an easy drive."

"Good, honey. I'm glad to hear it."

"I should really get going, Mom. The guys are waiting for me outside." I kicked the wall molding, trying not to read the graffiti. "I'll give you a call in a week or so, probably when we get to New York."

I thought for a moment, smiled. "You want me to get you anything? One of those miniature Statues of Liberty or Empire State Buildings or something?"

"I want you to be safe, Virgil," she replied. "Safe and happy. That's all I want."

Her concern was familiar, comforting.

"I'm really fine, Mom. I swear. Don't worry about me. Tell Dad, too. Don't worry about me. I'll call in a week or so to check in again. I love you."

"We love you, too, Virgil."

LARRY'S CABIN

It didn't take long on the road to shake off the dark mood from the diner. We were all ready for a few days of solitude and nature — Richard especially. Ever since he'd discovered the restorative powers of nature beside the old blue water tower near my childhood home, he'd been using the outdoors as a shelter from the world. At that time, it was a retreat from his father's death and his mother's instability. Now it served as a retreat from life on the road and the rigors of rock-n-roll. Richard could've gone to any major city in America to play; most likely making his rise to fame easier and faster. But he didn't. He chose Burlington. A city couched on all sides by lush farmland and the verdant green hills of Vermont. He went to Burlington to build his following as a natural progression. To grow it organically. To stay close to the nature that had always welcomed him back.

Larry's cabin was tucked away in a sparse grove of pine trees about a mile off the nearest road. The dirt path we took to get there almost destroyed the van. We had to grab ahold of the equipment to anchor it and ourselves against the dips, ruts, and potholes. Coolie and Papa were whooping and hollering like bronco wranglers the whole time while Richard and I just held on and prayed our spleens wouldn't burst.

Once we arrived, I realized why Larry owned this place. There were no neighbors for miles in any direction and the cabin was tucked into a small clearing surrounded by dense forest. It was the perfect secluded hideaway. The key to the cabin was hidden underneath a shingle on the outdoor shed, but the most basic thief could've broken into it in a heartbeat. What was there to steal? A rickety wood-burning stove, some old pots and pans, a battered boom box, enough canned and dehydrated foodstuffs to survive a month-long sequestering, some dog-eared books (Bob Arnold, Gary Snyder, Hunter S. Thompson, Edward Abbey), a broom and dustpan, bedding supplies, cleaning supplies, odd bits of accumulated furniture, the random sock or t-shirt. It wasn't exactly the motherlode for a thief, but it was adequate for Larry's survival. And perfect for our retreat.

We drew straws for rooms. I ended up getting Larry's bed while the other guys divvied up a found air mattress (Coolie), and the van (Papa), leaving Richard to stack a couple of sleeping bags together and crash on the floor. Considering his role as leader of the band, I was a little surprised at how easily he allowed fate and democracy to call the shots. But after spending the previous night in the Subaru, I wasn't arguing either.

Those days at the cabin were my favorite times of the whole tour. Richard, Coolie, and Papa jammed all day and night, working on new material. Even though they stopped and started constantly, it was like having my own private acoustic concerts. I loved watching their creative process at work.

It was amazing to me how Laverna the band captured the spirit of Laverna the goddess. Through their music, they became avatars for all that she represented and also for those who had worshipped her. At their best, they channeled the energy of ancient Roman goddess worship into modern day meaning, and evoked spirits of devotion, abandon, and even antiquity. Because Laverna the goddess was a marginalized figure associated with thieves, mischief, and general deviancy, the band — Richard, in particular — had attached itself to energy sources buried deep inside the DNA of rock-n-roll. At live shows, their music unlocked those energies inside the audience and the whole crowd melded into a sea of dancing, swirling, sweaty devotees grooving in perfect synchronicity with the band. At those moments, it was hard to distinguish the audience from the players from the music being played. The whole environment seemed to elevate — even levitate — and shift to a higher plane. More than any concert I'd ever seen, Laverna shows felt — and looked — like a quasi-religious celebration. A ritual. A worshipful sacrifice. That energetic fluidity gave each performance its own unique flavor and also shaped the songs the band played on any given night. The band, the crowd, the room, the spirit of it all coming together determined what and how Laverna played. Each night was a new gathering, a new celebration. Thus each recording made by a taper became a unique artifact of an event that would never happen again. As such, it became a currency to the whole live music community. Especially the Lavernites.

I woke on the morning of our third day to hear the guys playing in the front room. I went to pee in the small bathroom beside Larry's tiny closet, then lay back down in bed, staring up at the ceiling, listening. I kept picturing some teenage kid — ten years in the future — squirming with envy as he imagined what it would be like staying in a secluded house with his favorite band as they played concerts that only he could hear. It was the true fan's ultimate fantasy and I was living it every day.

The music stopped and Papa made a loud announcement about making breakfast. The woodsy fresh air had been making us all ravenous, and Papa had been whipping up tremendous platters full of eggs, toast, and bacon from the supplies we'd bought in town.

I stretched out on the bed and rubbed my hands together like a squirrel, imagining the breakfast feast to come.

"Morning, bro." Richard popped in the door, acoustic guitar in hand. "Did we wake you up?" He seemed to be in a good mood. If he was, that would be his third day in a row. That fact alone was enough to make me happy, too.

"No, man, I've been up for a little while. Just hanging out, waiting for Papa to cook up some chow. "

Richard sat on the corner of the bed and started strumming his guitar. As some sick joke, he sang the first few bars of Billy Joel's "Just The Way You Are" until I kicked him into stopping. The smell of frying bacon and eggs came drifting in from the kitchen. It was perfect: Richard's good mood, our familiar banter, being awoken by soft acoustic music in a cabin in the woods on a beautiful sunny fall morning. Now I was hungry and the bass player was cooking my breakfast. What could be better?

"Here, man," Richard said, pulling out a joint from behind his ear. "Something to start the day right."

The day just got better.

"Thanks," I said, accepting the unlit joint and Richard's lighter. "Should we wait for Coolie and Papa though?"

"No." Richard continued strumming. "It's cool. They've got one of their own going for breakfast patrol. Spark it up."

So I did. And for ten minutes we passed the joint in silence. There was nothing to say. Richard strummed between hits. I leaned back against the wall just smoking and listening. There was nothing more that needed doing. Nothing at all.

How often do moments like that come along?

How long can they last?

"So we're back on the road tomorrow," I said, handing Richard the joint.

He nodded, took a hit, and snubbed the roach out on the sole of his green Doc Martin. "Yup. Down to Kingston, and then to the big NYC."

I cringed, dreading the transition. "Gonna be a culture shock after being here for three days."

"No doubt. Kingston's a good midway point though. It's pretty mellow there, too, but they've got a good younger crowd. A lot of people from the city live there. Some of them even commute back and forth. It's usually pretty cool."

"You guys still thinking about playing acoustic?"

After three days of practicing acoustically, they had started talking about playing half the Kingston show that way. It would undoubtedly make for a special event, for the Lavernites, in particular. However Julius still had to vote, and the consensus was that he was unlikely to go along with it.

Richard nodded. "Yeah, we're all into it. Playing one set acoustic and one electric. We haven't done that in a long time, but I think it'd be really cool." I voiced my agreement. "It's just a matter of what Julius will say." Richard rolled his eyes exhaustedly.

"What do you think he'll say?"

Richard mimicked Julius's slightly nasal voice. " 'What are we, the Allman Brothers or something?' That's what he'll say. 'What are we, Country Joe? Hootie and the Blowfish? Joan Baez?' " Richard shook his head and scoffed. "Julius can be a real tool sometimes."

I took my opening. "What's up with you guys anyway?"

"I don't know," Richard shrugged. "He's just weird."

I narrowed the field some. "Yeah, but he seems to have something special against you. What's up with that? Has he always been like that?"

Richard stopped strumming. He gave me a good, long look. I could tell that he was deciding what to divulge and what to keep hidden. How much I could handle. How much he felt like getting into right now. Fortunately, his good mood prevailed.

"Alright, man, I'll tell you. Just don't get all freaked out or anything." I shook my head no. Richard took a deep breath and then continued. "Okay, you know how we all went into the basement with those girls before we left for tour?" He checked my comprehension. "Remember those girls?"

"Yeah, I remember," I said, not wanting to let on what Coolie had already divulged. I wanted to hear Richard's version first. "What about them?"

"Well, that's something we've been doing for the last few tours. It's kind of a tradition now with Coolie, Julius, and me. It's no big deal really — nothing too weird or anything. We just have a little orgy for good luck. You know, a sex offering to Laverna." He snickered, hung up on his own bullshit. "Alright, it's about us getting off. But it's a damn good excuse!" I gave his honesty a half-hearted chuckle. "But the girls are down, we're all down with it. It's good all around, you know?" He checked to see if I did. I nodded him on — no big surprises so far. "Well, Julius has been dabbling more with gay stuff the past year or so. It's no big deal, we're all cool with it. And I know he's still into girls, too, 'cause he's told me flat out that he's bi. But he's been kind of strange about it a lot of the time. Really uncomfortable around us and stuff. I'm pretty sure that's why he's been keeping away from us in Burlington, too. That and the drugs. Unfortunately, the guys showing him around the gay scene are the same ones supplying his smack. It's a double shot, 'cause I think they're the only ones he feels comfortable around right now and they all use, too. He's got the hook both ways." Richard sighed loudly. "So I always just assumed those were Julius's big hang-ups, why he's been acting so weird and distant lately. But..." He paused. "I think there's a little more to it."

"Yeah," I said, letting Richard know I knew the gist. "I think so, too."

"So, the other day," he continued, "we've got our little group going in the basement and everything. The lights are off, we've got the candles going, the girls are into it, everything was going fine. Coolie was with one of the girls, I was with the other. And for a few minutes, I guess I just lost track of Julius." He looked into my eyes, took a breath. "That's when I felt the hand."

Papa stuck his head in the door. "Hey, breakfast is done! We're gonna eat outside by the van."

Richard nodded and Papa ducked back out the door. Richard stared down at the guitar on his lap, waiting, reflecting.

"The hand?" I said, urging him on.

"On my balls," he continued. "While I was, you know, back and forth."

"Julius?" I asked.

He nodded. "Yeah, Julius. I turned around and there he was, staring at me with this weird look in his eye. I mean, you know me, Virgil. I'm no prude, man. I'm down with just about everything. I probably wouldn't have even been that freaked out if I didn't know him so well. But Jesus, man — Julius is like my brother or something. I don't know, it was just too weird. And that look. I mean, you see how he's been treating me. It's like he's, I don't know —"

"In love with you?"

He nodded slowly. "Yeah, or something. And that's how he looked at me: all serious and everything, you know? Just a little too intense."

"So what did you do?"

Richard dropped his eyes. "I didn't handle it well," he muttered. "I really fucked up actually. It just surprised me though, you know? I didn't know what to do."

"What did you do?" I pressed.

"I freaked out," he blurted, staring straight ahead at the wall. "I lost it. I told him to take his hands off me, stay away from me, all that shit. I really don't know what I said. It's kind of a blur. Whatever it was, it wasn't what I should've said. Coolie, the girls... it freaked everybody out. Everybody just, like, froze. Halted mid-fuck, you know? I don't think anybody but Julius even knew what was going on though, which probably made it even weirder for everyone."

"What did the girls do?"

"They didn't know what was going on either. Like I said, everyone just sort of froze mid-stroke staring at me. I got my clothes and left without saying a word. Maybe those guys finished up, maybe they didn't. I don't even know. I was up the stairs and in the shower in less than two minutes."

"So what did Coolie say?"

Richard shook his head. "To tell you the truth, I still don't think he knows what happened. He probably just thinks I freaked out or something. I mean, it's been pretty obvious to everyone the past few days that something's up between Julius and me. But I don't think anyone but Julius and me — and now you — knows the whole deal."

"Wow," I grunted, unable to think of anything worth saying. "That's awkward, man. I mean, the whole thing — just really fucking awkward."

"Yeah, tell me about it," said Richard. "Coolie came up a few minutes after I got in the shower to ask what was up, but I didn't tell him anything. I just didn't want to get into it then, you know?"

"So Julius stayed in the basement with the girls?"

Richard thought for a moment. "Yeah, I guess he probably did. Coolie hopped in the shower right after me and I didn't see Julius again until we took off."

"Wow," I repeated, monosyllabic despite the hundred questions I had assaulting my mind. "So, who are these girls, anyway? Are they from Burlington, or what?"

Richard stood up off the bed, guitar in hand. He walked to the door, turned and waved me on. "After breakfast, man. Let's eat first, I'm hungry. And I need a break from the sex confessional before diving into that beehive."

I raised my eyebrows, intrigued. "Beehive?"

Richard dropped his hands to his side, momentarily exhausted with me. Apparently he still felt I was due some answers though. "You know the guy I sent you to stay with that first night in Saratoga Springs? Kind of the leader of those kids? What do you call them?" He chuckled, recalling my term. "Lavernites?"

"Yeah, what about them? You mean Felix?"

"Yeah, that's what he calls himself now. Felix. Let's just say the girls were a few friends of Felix. They were all, like you say, Lavernites."

"But why —"

"After breakfast," Richard said over his shoulder, heading for the door. "We'll take a walk after breakfast, okay? Just you and me. I'll tell you whatever you want to know."

At that point, I would've given up a month of breakfasts — lunches, too — to sink my teeth into the information Richard was dangling. But as long as he stayed in a good mood, I reasoned, the information would keep coming. A full stomach could only help my cause.

After a breakfast of bacon, eggs, and toast eaten while perched on the back bumper of the van, Richard and I set off on our hike while Coolie and Papa drove into town for fresh ice, food, and beer for our last night in the cabin. We had also decided to buy Larry a bottle of Jack Daniels (his drink of choice, Papa informed us) in thanks for letting us stay there.

Early afternoon light spilled through the scattered limbs above our heads as Richard and I hiked off down the vaguely defined path leading from the cabin to a small pond roughly a half-mile away. Picture a Father's Day card depicting the idyllic father-son stroll down to the old fishing hole, poles and tackle silhouetted against orange morning light, then swap father-son for musician-buddy and switch the typical birds-and-bees chat to talk of orgies, groupies, and drugged-out lifestyles of the young and debauched.

"So, how does it work that Felix gets these girls for you? I mean, what's up with him anyway? I've met him a couple times now and it's just… weird. The way those kids follow him and everything. I don't get it."

"First of all," began Richard, "his name's not Felix. When I met him, his name was Calvin Trill. To me, that's who he'll always be."

His response caught me off guard. "You've known him for a while?"

"Yeah." Richard picked up a pinecone and juggled it between two hands. "I've known Calvin since Oneonta. He used to come to our shows when I was playing with Exit and Orphan Bags. He was just a townie kid, you know? Most times he'd be the only one in the bar who wasn't a college student. I used to let him carry in equipment with the band when he couldn't get into shows 'cause he was underage. Shit, I was underage myself most of the time, but nobody was stopping me from playing. I felt bad for him, I guess. I don't know." Richard thought about this, then whipped the pinecone at a gnarled clump of roots. "That's when I met him anyway."

"What did he do? Follow you to Burlington or something?"

Richard shrugged. "It's not like he really lives there or anything… I don't really know though. I don't know what he did after Oneonta. I know he traveled for a while, spent a lot of time in the Southwest I think, but I don't know what he did there. Whatever he did, it changed him. Like I said, we weren't like buddies or anything in Oneonta. It's not like we hung out all the time. I'd get him into shows sometimes, he'd help carry equipment or whatever, but that was about it. He came to just about all our gigs though, that's for sure. He was always real interested in what I was doing, what I was playing and writing and stuff. But just like a younger kid interested in music, you know? Nothing too hung up or anything. Just into it."

"And when did all this Lavernite shit start?" I asked.

"We'd only been playing out for a couple months when he showed up in Burlington. We'd never even played out of town at that point. In fact, Julius wasn't even in the band yet." Richard reflected on this, organizing memories. "It's strange to think about that now. It seems like so long ago, but it's only been a couple of years. So much has happened..." he drifted off.

"Were you surprised to see him, or what?" I asked, nudging him back to the story. "I mean, after Oneonto it must've been weird to have him turn up in Burlington."

"Kind of," answered Richard. "But not really. Shit like that always happens, you know? That's just life. People come and go, pop up and disappear. Especially in a town like Burlington. It's just one of those places. Certain kinds of people want to check it out, on the East Coast anyway, and see what it's all about. So, no, I wasn't really surprised to see him. Calvin's the kind of guy you expect to pop up again and again. That's just the way he is — that wandering drifter type."

"He seems like a bit more than that," I huffed. "Those kids following him around don't just see him as a wandering drifter type."

"Yeah." Richard nodded. "But that all came later. When I first started seeing him again in Burlington, he'd appear at shows or around town. I didn't even realize who he was at first. He was so different. He'd become..." Richard thought for a moment. "I don't know what the right word is exactly. Worldly, maybe. Kind of worldly. Self-assured, you know? Like I said, when I met Calvin, he was just this skinny kind of kicked-puppy townie kid. His clothes were always ratty and dirty, like old hand-me-downs... shirt, shoes, everything. And he'd never look you in the eye. It was always like he was embarrassed or something. Like he had a secret he was afraid you'd find out."

"Well, he's not like that anymore," I said, thinking of Felix's booming bass voice and cocky swagger. "I think he's well past that awkward

149

phase."

"Yeah, I know he is," said Richard. "But that all happened some-time between Oneonta and when he showed up in Burlington. It's pretty amazing, I give him a lot of credit actually. It's like everything, I don't know, weak about him before has been completely reversed. In Oneonta, you could hardly even hear him when he talked. He had this little squeaky mouse voice, you know? Now his voice is the first thing you notice."

I nodded in agreement.

"But everything's like that: his walk, the way he carries himself, clothes, attitude. If he didn't tell me who he was that first night I saw him in Burlington, I don't think I would've recognized him. He's changed that much."

"For the better?"

Richard shrugged. "I guess that's a matter of taste. He's certainly more confident in himself now. He seems happier, more in control. So that's something."

"But what about those kids that follow him around?" I asked. "I mean, it's like they'll do whatever he tells them to. And it's all attached back to you somehow, too. Doesn't that make you feel uncomfortable at all?"

"Should it?"

I hadn't really thought that through. I just hadn't had the necessary information. Either way, Richard's opinion on this topic was more relevant than mine.

"I don't know, man. I'm still just trying to figure it all out. All I know is what I saw. This guy's got kids hanging on his every word. I mean, it all seems pretty over the top."

"Calvin is a drug dealer, Virgil," Richard blurted out. "He swings pounds of bud up and down the East Coast, sometimes ecstasy, acid, whatever he's got at the time. But always lots of good buds. And every one of those kids is involved in it somehow." He threw his hand into the air dismissively. "So you'll have to excuse me for not feeling too sorry for any of them. They're all part of an operation that easily makes more money than we do, and they have a damn fine time doing it."

"Well, see," I mumbled, taken aback. "I didn't know any of that."

"Why would you?" countered Richard. "It's not like he advertises or anything. He's got connections up and down the East Coast, sells only in large quantities to a handful of people, and maintains a very low profile. I'll tell you one thing though," he laughed. "You seem to like his bud well enough."

"You mean what we've been smoking?"

Richard nodded, grinning. "Shit, man, I haven't paid for pot since Calvin turned up in Burlington. Anytime we get low, he just lays a couple of ounces on us." He chuckled again. "With this crew, it saves us thousands of dollars a year."

"Huh," I muttered, taking it all in. "So what about the other kids, the Lavernites? And the girls and sex and everything?"

Richard shrugged. "That's Calvin's deal, man, not mine. I don't know exactly how he does what he does. He digs the band, our music, our vibe, plus we move up and down the coast at pretty regular intervals. So he's having a good time, digging the music, and he's got an excuse for traveling through the same cities so often, too. He's not asking to be a part of the band in any way or anything. We wouldn't want him to. I mean, shit," he huffed. "I probably talk to him a total of twenty minutes per tour. He's got his business, and we've got ours. We just happen to be on the same schedules. Think of it as salesmen covering the same territories."

"And the girls? Like from the basement?"

"Hey, man, give me some credit," Richard said, smiling. "Yeah, they're part of his crew, but that doesn't mean they don't dig us, too. I mean, I'm not saying there isn't a kind of symbiotic relationship between Calvin and the band, Virgil. I wouldn't go that far. He hooks us up with buds and introduces his cute workers to us; turns new kids on to our music and all that. I mean, he's definitely helped build up our whole scene. But that's really just a byproduct of everything else."

We rounded a corner in the path. The pond came into view thirty yards ahead.

"And what do you all do for him?"

"Like I said, we provide cover, entertainment. What's the point of swinging buds and living a partying lifestyle if you're not going to enjoy it? Calvin digs my music, always has, so it's a bonus for him to check out all our shows. Again, give us some credit, Virgil." Richard smacked his chest proudly. "We're a hot fucking band, man. People want to see us. More and more all the time."

"But do you think you guys are helping him recruit kids, too?" It was a question that wouldn't leave my mind. The answer was clearly more important to me than to Richard.

Richard shrugged. "Hey, man, I'm nobody's father. I don't know why those kids do what they do. I play my music and I want as many people as possible to hear it. That's what this is all about, nothing more. If those kids want to follow the band, get into the whole lifestyle and everything, then, yeah, maybe we're helping Calvin's cause. But like I say, that's only a byproduct. We play our music, he swings his goods, and at different points our goals overlap. That's all. Anything else you read into it is just talk-show babble bullshit." Richard was getting worked up. He started speaking louder and waved his hands to punctuate points. "I'm not saying this about you directly, Virgil, but I'm just saying: I'm so fucking sick of hypocritical middle-class American morality I could puke."

We reached the ridge overlooking the pond. We took seats on a large boulder that had been lodged in the same spot since the glaciers receded. I felt a Richard Payne Knight lecture coming on.

"Oh, but that's not directed at me at all, Richard. Why should that offend me?" I asked, playfully sarcastic. Richard knew I could handle it. I lit a smoke and loosely focused my gaze on the spangles of sunlight dancing on top of the water.

"I'm serious, man. I mean, think about it. We're a fucking rock-n-roll band. We drink, take drugs, fuck good-looking women, and tear out our hearts on stage every goddam night. And millions of people in this country would be offended by that. I just don't get it. What the hell do they want from their rock stars? Do they really want Mick Jagger to act like an accountant? Wear business suits on stage instead of feather boas? Stop banging models on the side? I mean, Jesus, who would make their nipples hard in the supermarket checkout line if it weren't for celebrities acting bad in the tabloids? And then, not only do they feign shock and dismay at this lack of moral fiber, but they act like it all started once these guys became stars!" Richard shook his head. "I mean, maybe that's true for some. Maybe they got a taste of fame and fortune, and suddenly felt license to do everything society says is wrong. I don't know." He shrugged. "All I know is, I've been on a rock-n-roll path since I was born. I want to play music, straddle the world, and do a double shot of tequila while suburban daughters drool over my poster on their bedroom walls." Richard laughed at this image. "And I'm not slowing down for anyone!"

He looked into my eyes. I smiled back at him, took another drag on my cigarette.

"So, to answer your question," he continued. "No, I don't feel bad at all, even if we are helping Calvin lure kids into a life of sex, drugs, and rock-n-roll. Fucking great! I think those are the three best things this fucked-up world has to offer. I don't feel bad about having sex with his girls, smoking his weed, and I don't give a shit if he's using the band as a vehicle for his work. Truthfully? I hope he plants a joint and a Laverna CD in every household in America. And that the housekeepers find them, turn the kids on, and they all end up naked, smoking pot, and screwing each other to our music. You know what I'm saying, Virgil? You know where I'm at?" His voice was pitched, insistent. "I'm not out in the world on a whim, and I'm sure as hell not running anybody else's program. You tried that in Ithaca, and look what happened to you." He looked at me for confirmation. "I mean, what did it do for you?"

I shook my head, puffing out smoke rings. "Nothing."

"Absolutely!" he agreed. "It did nothing. I saw that coming a mile away. I knew you'd be on tour with us by New Year's Eve, man. I swear to God. It was just a matter of time."

"Come on!" I cocked my head in disbelief. "What do you mean you knew I'd end up here?"

Richard nodded confidently. "Shit, man, I knew it all along. It's destiny. You and me." He tapped my chest. "Right here, right now, sitting dead in the middle of a big-ass pile of destiny."

For the moment, I was willing to go along with that. "And if your destiny's making music and screwing groupies, where do I fit in?"

"Same way you have since we were kids, man. Same way we talked about in the van. Shit, you know me better than anyone, Virgil." He motioned back toward the cabin. "These guys — Coolie, Papa, Julius, and everyone — they don't know shit about me, about my life. They don't know where I come from. What I was like before." He looked me dead in the eye, tapped my chest again. "It's you, Virgil. You and me. The writer and the musician. You heard my first song ever, man!" He said this loud enough for the pond basin to echo it. "You saw my first gig, my first girl, my first everything. You know how fucked up everything was for me growing up. Damn, Virgil, if it weren't for you I wouldn't even be here, man." His sincerity glowed through his passion. "I get hung up on my music and all my own bullshit, but I never forget for a second how many times you pulled my ass out of bad situations. I mean that completely, Virgil. I wouldn't be here if it wasn't for you, man."

I felt genuinely moved. "I've never heard you say that before."

"I know." He nodded. "But I've always thought it."

I stared at him for a few more seconds before continuing. "I still don't get it though, Richard," I said, searching for the final, true answer. "I'm still not clear what I'm supposed to do with all..." I gestured at the sky to symbolize everything beneath it. "All of this."

"You're the keeper of the stories, man," said Richard. "You're the ancient scribe. My life, the story of the music, the band, our life together — you can record the whole mission. Write it down so it lasts a thousand years."

I didn't feel the same feelings of manipulation as when Richard had talked about such things on the way to Saratoga Springs. This felt different. More equal, more honest.

"And what mission is that?" I asked. "I guess if I'm writing the story, I should at least know that key part, huh?"

"That's right," Richard smiled, patting my arm. "Now you're getting it." He waved his arm across the expanse of water and trees. "I'm out to spread my music across the world, man. I use Laverna because she's a badass pagan anarchist goddess who screwed with societal norms. A symbol of deviance and hedonism, but also redemption. Laverna was there when the screw-ups needed her most." He picked up a pinecone and tossed it toward the water. "I tell you one thing, Virgil. I wasn't put on this earth to cower. I was put here to play music that'll tear chunks out of all the bullshit shields we construct to live in the world. Maybe I'm just a small part of that process. Maybe it's been going on since some caveman shocked the tribe by painting the bloody reality of the hunt on the side of the community cave." He shook his head. "I don't claim to know how it all works, Virgil. All I know is, I was put here to do my part until I drop. And I know in my head that you're a large part of that mission, too. It's been going on since we were kids, man. It's just finally starting to pick up steam now."

Richard's speech fired bullets through the confusion I'd felt the past several months. It tore holes through my despondency, spackling it over with a new sense of purpose. I never doubted Richard's drive, but it turns out I didn't need to fully believe in his mission to play my role in his scheme either. I simply had to take some of the most poignant memories of my life and write about them: the very thing I'd always secretly felt I was meant to do.

Could it all be so easy? So clear cut? Sitting on the lip of the pond that day, the answer seemed to be yes. And it was the first easy answer I'd had in months, maybe years.

"I don't know what to say, man." I felt unable to articulate much in the face of Richard's powerful oration. "That's a lot to swallow all at once."

"I know," said Richard, nodding. "But you get it, too. It's all a part of it, Virgil. All of this is just a part of it."

My mind jumped back to Felix. "So what about Felix, Calvin, or whoever? Is he a part of this, too?"

Richard shrugged. "If he forwards the message he is. To me, everything else is bullshit. And right now, he's helping spread the word as much as, if not more than, anyone in the band. So, yeah, I guess you could say he's a part of it."

I nodded, absorbing this last bit.

Richard's voice became solemn. "But that doesn't mean I think he's a good guy, Virgil." He was serious, focused on this point. "I don't care what he tells people. Calvin is only out for himself. I saw that kid when he was a scruffy street punk down on the balls of his ass. Once you live those days, you don't forget them. No matter what he says, he's in it for himself, man. And those kids, the Lavernites? They're all a part of that trip for him, too." Richard looked me straight in the eye. "When I said I talk to him about twenty minutes per tour, I wasn't kidding, Virgil. He'll send girls our way, hook us up with bags of weed — usually through someone else — but that's about it, man. I don't deal with Calvin directly, and I don't think you should either. All said and done, I don't really know where his head is at. I don't really care to. I've got enough problems dealing with my own."

I waited, but Richard was done. It'd been an honest and revealing discussion, but this last part stuck in my throat. "So why did you send me to stay with them that night if you think he's fucked up?" The idea pissed me off. "That seems pretty screwed up, Richard."

He nodded. "Yeah, it is screwed up. Trust me, I've thought about it a lot since then. I still don't know if that was a good idea. At the time it seemed pretty clear-cut, but… I'm not so sure now."

"Why'd you do it?"

"I told you, man. It's not always pretty or nice, but the mission is the mission, and like it or not, Calvin's a part of that. I knew you'd see him at every show. The other kids, the Lavernites, come and go. They pop up at different places. I don't pay too much attention. He sends them off on runs and stuff, picking up and dropping off shit all over the country. Most of them don't stick around for long anyway. But Calvin's at just about every show, and I knew you'd notice that quick. I just wanted to get you into the full experience right off the bat."

"That's fucked up, Richard." I said, still pissed. "Not okay."

"I know, man," he nodded. "You're right. In hindsight, it is fucked up. I just had a full head of steam going, and you being here seemed to put it all in play. I just wanted it all rolling right away, you know?"

I stared back. No, I didn't know.

"I told him to be cool to you," he insisted. "That you were writing the story of the band." He paused, faltering. "I'm really sorry, man. From now on, you're in on everything right from the start. No more bullshit, I promise."

I paused, waiting, measuring circumstances. Finally I cracked a smile, reached over and shook his hand. "Alright, man. It's a deal." We both looked out over the pond for a few seconds, mulling it all over. "I was pretty pissed at you on the way down to Saratoga though, you know. You were acting so weird. Hinting at all this stuff, but never really saying anything."

"I know," Richard bobbed his head. "I could tell. I'm serious though, man. That stuff with Julius really twisted me up. It just caught me off guard, you know?" He shook his head at his own hypocrisy. "Here I am going on about society's Puritan values and I'm all flipped out about some guy grabbing my nuts. Pretty weak, huh?"

I nodded. "Yeah, kind of."

"It's not really about gay or straight or bi or whatever though, man. It's about trust and friendship. I just didn't see it coming, you know? It just caught me off guard. I'm cool with it now." He picked up a stone and threw it into the pond; the recurring ripples reached for shore. "I just hope Julius can get cool with it. I really don't want to see this screw up the band."

"Have you talked to him about it since then?" I asked.

Richard shook his head bashfully.

"Probably time to do that, huh?"

He nodded, still keeping his eyes lowered.

"And, hey," I said, making sure he was looking at me now. "No more bullshit with me either. We've known each other too long to hide this stuff. It doesn't work. It just comes out all fucked up. Cool?"

"Cool," Richard said, extending a hand.

BED AND BREAKFAST

We arrived in Kingston three hours before the show, but couldn't get in to set up right away. The bar was closed, nobody around. I felt like eating pizza, but Coolie loved the burritos at Pepe's, the taqueria in town, so we went there instead. It was a Wednesday before 6:30 p.m., so we couldn't park for free on the street yet. The guys had gotten a ticket on that same street the last time they were there. I waited with the van while Coolie, Papa, and Richard went into Pepe's to order and get change for the meter. What had been an overcast day was slowly shifting to a cool, breezy evening. It was one of those evocative western New York autumnal moments that almost make up for the humid summers, brutal winters, and too-fleeting springtimes. Two girls with dyed green hair walked arm-in-arm out of the record store across the street singing Duran Duran's "Rio" at the top of their lungs. Their enthusiasm was shocking. I couldn't help but stare.

"Alright, man," Richard said, handing me the change. I pried my eyes away from the singing girls. "Put enough in the meter for an hour-and-a-half just to be safe. We can just carry the equipment in from here anyway. They've got a pretty decent PA, so we just gotta bring in the amps and instruments. It turns free soon, but last time we got a ticket here, and, of course, we never paid it. So it's best not to attract attention now."

I started feeding the meter. "Did you talk to Julius?"

"Papa's calling him right now. Hopefully he can hook us up with a place to stay tonight. I don't want to fuck around too much here. We've got a lot coming up in New York. I just want to play the gig and get down there as soon as possible. I'm reining in everybody tonight." He followed my eyes to the girls singing down the street. I couldn't help myself. Richard nudged my shoulder, chuckling. "Virgil, I said 'everybody.' "

I'd be lying if I said I wasn't hoping to see the mystery girl from Albany at the Kingston gig. I was still angry, trying to stay tough, but somewhere inside I was itching to see her, too. I wondered if I'd find anything worthwhile in her the second time around, or if I'd just want to kick myself in the teeth, wondering how I could've spent the night in a seedy porno theater alley just to meet her.

For better or worse, she never showed up in Kingston. None of the Lavernites did. Not even Felix. It was the only gig they were entirely absent from all tour.

Truth be told, it was a boring gig, too. Maybe they saw that coming. The crowd wasn't bad, they were into the show, but they were sparse. Part of the problem was that the venue was a bar, not a club. That meant it was a 21-and-over show. Depending on the spot, that could suck up a large part of Laverna's fan base. Another problem was that it was a Wednesday. People over 21 had to work in the morning.

All things considered, Kingston wasn't a total washout. We made some money, sold a couple CDs and a t-shirt, signed a few people to the mailing list. But when Julius vetoed the acoustic set, he siphoned off the last hope of making it an outstanding gig in any way.

In fairness, Julius hadn't been part of the woodsy ambience that had spawned the acoustic idea. Hadn't savored the sounds of hand percussion and tangy acoustic guitars under a canopy of fragrant pines, whistling birds and crisp fresh air. But still, most of the rejection was out of spite, an opportunity to be contrary. Julius's bitter wounds were still moist and fresh. Only Richard, if anyone, could make them right.

The one big surprise Kingston offered came after the gig in the form of Julius's friend. Perhaps it was unfair, but after everything that'd happened, all I'd discussed with Richard, I had some pre-existing ideas of who this friend might be: a gay man, stylish, young, enthralled with the idea of running a quaint bed and breakfast in a small town; or perhaps a dignified older man, wise with years, come to the country to escape the urban neck-slashing corporate battlefields; or maybe a domestic young man, singularly happy at finally finding his niche cooking crepes and dousing strawberries with cream for visiting New Yorkers out to rekindle the romance of a flagging thirty-year relationship. In short, I was slotting the friend into a preset stereotypical framework I had developed in my mind.

But Julius's friend was none of these things. Nothing reminiscent of my talk with Richard. Instead, I found myself revisiting the talk I'd had with Coolie on the way from Burlington to Saratoga Springs. For the first time, I saw glimpses of who Julius must have been at one time. A time before dope, Laverna, and a spooky candle-lit room in the basement of a trashy rock-n-roll house.

Julius drove the Subaru back to the bed-and-breakfast after the gig to tell his friend we were on our way. The rest of us stayed to pack up and settle with the manager. Luckily we got our $300 guarantee for that gig as opposed to a take of the door, which definitely worked out in the band's favor. Three hundred dollars is better than nothing. About an hour later, following Julius's directions, I wheeled the van up a crushed gravel driveway towards a quaint, well-maintained Adirondack-style house. A single window was illuminated along the side. We got out of the van and headed for the door beside the light.

The kitchen we entered was the one pictured in home magazines; the kitchen conjured in wholesome American minds when one says the words, "Grandma's Kitchen." It smelled like cookies, cakes, fresh baked pies, and brewed coffee. It was warm. Warmer than outside, so the change rippled my skin with contentment. We stepped inside, one after the other, and paused on the threshold to take in the scene. Julius's friend wasn't a gay man, young or old. (I suspect our collective hesitation revealed that I wasn't the only one who'd made that presumption.)

Julius's friend was a woman in her seventies wearing a heavy red night-coat, weathered terry cloth slippers, and a brown scarf over large yellow curlers. She stood at the stove stirring a wooden spoon through a copper pot, chatting calmly with Julius who was seated at the kitchen table. Above her head, around the burners, dangled an array of scrubbed and shining pots, pans, strainers, graters, and other cooking accouterments.

She greeted us with a warm hello, beckoning us to join Julius at the table, and offered to make us sandwiches or soup. Richard, Papa and I graciously declined. Coolie requested a ham and cheese on toast, if she had it. She did, of course. She gladly made him the sandwich. Before doing so, however, she placed a mug of warm milk in front of Julius and urged him to drink. She said it helped him sleep.

Far from merely a friend, this was the woman who had raised Julius: scrubbing his feet, washing his clothes, cutting the crusts off his peanut butter and jelly sandwiches, and tucking him in at night when his parents were off at one gala fundraiser or another. She was Julius's nanny, the closest thing to a traditional mother (well, as I understood a traditional mother to be, anyway) he'd had. She was sweet, pleasant, as wholesome as fresh baked bread, and willing to put us all up for the night, no questions asked.

Julius averted his eyes, sipping the warm milk. We grinned and winked at him and one another in various stages of amusement, surprise, enchantment, and envy. It was a rare glimpse into Julius's shadowy background; a soothing foreground to the cold opulence we'd encounter the next day at his parents' vast Manhattan apartment. Her name was Nanny Madeline, and her farewell breakfast of pancakes and sausage the next morning was the closest thing to love I'd tasted in months. As we piled our filled bellies into the van and car bound for New York City, I couldn't resist asking her a single question for the record: "What was Julius like as a child?"

Nanny Madeline's voice was thick, gentle, forgiving. Her answer was brief. "Good. He was a good boy."

TISSUE PAPER KING

I have never liked New York City. The noise, crowds, the giant awful squash of humanity scraping heavy heels over lurking bridges, cracking concrete, and all forms of colossal structure. My first experience with New York was in eleventh grade, visiting my cousin Sam in Scarsdale. We drove his hand-me-down Volvo to the edge of the city to buy booze, parked on the edge of some looming housing project, and eventually allowed a twitchy man into the car, giving him our money so that he'd buy us beer at the liquor store across the street. He got out of the car and immediately disappeared into the housing project's shadows with our money. Apparently, the twenty bucks offered in payment wasn't comparable to the twenty-five dollars he was holding, even if we did offer our smiling teenage gratitude as a bonus. So New York City had never done me right, and although I'd known we were coming here, I hadn't really dealt with that reality until we were smack in the center of buildings, smog, and traffic.

"Man, I can't stand this place!"

Papa looked at me in disbelief. "A writer who hates New York City? What good are you?"

I nodded in agreement. "Not much good at all, I guess. I can't help it though." I shivered. "Every time I get here, I just want to peel off my skin and start over."

Papa laughed. "I think that's the whole idea."

"I know," I said mournfully. "And the problem, too."

After ardently refusing to navigate either vehicle through NYC traffic, I slouched down in the rear of the Subaru to pout and ride. Eventually I knew we'd be somewhere, inside, where I could close the drapes and forget where we were. After all the stories I'd heard about Julius's parents' place, I figured that was as good a hideout as any.

As we rode along, I couldn't help but mimic the nauseatingly trendy, oft repeated, New York location we were bound for. "Uppah West Side."

"What?" Papa leaned over the seat. "What did you say?"

"Nothing." I looked away, out the side window.

"Come on," Papa urged. "What did you say?"

I couldn't help but laugh at myself despite my disgust. I tried on the voice of a middle-aged, born and bred, lifelong New Yorker. "I saa-aid, 'Uppah Wesside.'" Papa and I both laughed at the sorry imitation. I tapped Richard's shoulder, "Driiivahh, Uppah Wesside!"

Richard was not amused. Between the stress of the upcoming gigs and nudging his way past indifferent cabbies and erratic commuters, his nerves were cooked. He preyed on my fear of the streets. "Settle down," he threatened. "Or I'll make you walk to Julius's." He found my eyes in the rearview mirror. "You'll have to ask real New Yorkers for directions and everything. How'd you like that?"

I glowered in the back seat, hunkering down lower, fixing my eyes on the floor mat.

That wasn't funny. It was not a joking matter.

The elevator up to the 22nd floor was as mirrored, gilded, and as gleaming as the apartment itself; though even calling it an apartment is misleading. In my experience, apartments are small, cramped, dingy places controlled by manipulative landlords. This palace was expansive, airy, wide open. Our vehicles and gear stored safely underground, we were welcomed like dignitaries by doormen, elevator operators, and burly, uniformed security guards.

"My parents are in Paris for a few weeks. They go there every fall," explained Julius on the elevator ride up. While my eyes took in every stunning ornament from lobby to twenty-second floor, Coolie nudged me, throwing elbows and winks, as taken with the whole scene as I was. They'd all been there before — Richard and Papa seemed far less impressed — but Coolie absorbed it all as if for the first time. I appreciated his comradeship. "They offered to leave Eleanor and Aggie, our cook and maid, while we were here, but I didn't think that was a good idea."

"Good choice," muttered Richard.

Julius nodded. "Yes, I thought so, too."

He keyed in, opened the apartment, and allowed us past. I followed just behind Coolie; both of us stopped cold on the white marble and crystal chandelier threshold while the others shoved past into the living room. Coolie elbowed me vigorously; we both rotated our heads inspecting the enormous black vases filled with long stemmed alien-looking flowers, a wall-length gilt-edged mirror, and the marble topped entry table upon which Julius carelessly tossed his keys. A full minute later, Coolie and I finally entered the apartment proper. Coolie joined Julius, Papa, and Richard already in the living room discussing plans for tonight's gig. But I couldn't stop gawking.

I tapped Julius's arm and pointed into the next room. "You mind if I —?"

Julius waved me on, unconcerned. "Go ahead. Try the view, too," he added. "I think you'll appreciate that."

"Right," I mumbled.

I tottered off in a daze.

I felt like a hick, but I didn't care. I'd honestly never seen anything like it. It was a home straight out of the movies, an expanse only a snooty English accent could do justice to. If I could dazzle you with the proper names for the elegant tables and chairs, the artists who painted the originals in each room; if I could recount the origins of the antiques, the continents which spawned the baubles, the cut of the crystal, the original owners of the end tables and the palaces they'd no doubt come from, the royal brandy snifters they'd supported, I would do so. I cannot. I believe you will find that writer living somewhere in New York City. As it stands, I am from Utica, New York, and all I can say is: it was fucking incredible. Each piece reminded me of something out of a museum, something too expensive to touch, under glass or out of reach behind a velvet rope. But there they were, out in the open. I could sit in the chairs, run my fingers over the original artists' paint, remove crystal stoppers, guzzle auburn liquor, and replace the lids willy-nilly if I wanted. I could've run and leapt horizontally onto an emerald velvet loveseat that looked as if it had once supported the plump royal ass of any number of Queen Elizabeths. But I didn't.

As it was, I'd been trained well in the 'look but don't touch' school of discipline. I walked with hands at my sides, leaning over to inspect the more interesting pieces, but never lifting a finger in curiosity. The mere thought was enough to make me sweat.

I pushed open the tall glass double doors in the dining room leading out to the spacious balcony overlooking Central Park, pulled a lounge chair up to the railing, and lit a smoke. Julius was right: the view was gorgeous, and I did appreciate it. I exhaled, feeling, momentarily, like a proper king.

Two glorious hours of pampered luxury. Two hours of experiencing life at the pinnacle of the American Dream food chain. It was remarkable to me that people actually lived that way. What passed for rich in Utica wouldn't have bought a cot in the boiler room of the Edson's building. As I looked out over the balcony, I knew that somewhere, down there, past the gargoyle downspouts and chauffeured cars, there were people rattling along inside the subway trains: people headed for minimum wage jobs, or hoping desperately to land minimum wage jobs; public school teachers juggling laps full of papers and pockets full of unpaid bills; mentally-ill indigents pleading for a few spare coins; hungry children staring at ceilings with dreams they would never express. I knew that those people existed. I knew they were down there. But high above it all, reclining my limbs in ultra-exclusive luxury, it was hard to picture their faces. It was hard to think about their lives. It was hard to imagine their concerns. They felt so far away that, in some ways, it seemed pointless to think about them at all.

Until I had to become one of them again.

Richard used the toe of his boot to prod me out the door. "Go," he said, pushing his green Doc Martin into my ass. "Now!"

I allowed myself to be pushed out into the hallway, then grudgingly rode the elevator down, and skulked into the backseat of the Subaru. It was time for the next gig. I ducked my head as we drove away from the isolated privilege of the Upper West Side. It had only been two hours, but I already resented any activity that took me away from those posh surroundings. Especially work.

Our first NYC gig was at Copper's, a small club in the West Village. Saturday, we were opening for the Doctors at Swampland, and then Sunday, it was back for a last show with the NYU crowd at the Bingo Parlor. They were all good gigs in their own way: different crowds, different exposure. But everyone was most hopped-up about the Swampland gig.

The Doctors had been huge seven or eight years earlier, and then fell off the face of the earth. Now they were in the midst of making their comeback. Industry people were bound to be in attendance at the gig. After playing a series of opening slots for smaller, lesser known bands at Swampland, and a few headline shows on off-nights, Richard had deftly talked his way into getting Laverna the opening slot for The Doctors. He wanted the show to be flawless. Independent or not, it couldn't hurt to have the labels see you coming.

"This place doesn't have shit, Virgil," Richard said, leaning over the Subaru's front seat. "That means we've got to set up the PA, sound check ourselves, and everything. It's a small place, so it shouldn't be a big problem — but we've got to do it right." He cracked a small, nervous smile. "That means you're going to have to run the soundboard, too, man."

I felt a queasiness flutter through my guts. "So, what do I have to do?"

"It's really no big deal," reassured Richard. "You're not going to be running the table at all tonight. We're not even going to worry about that. So, all you've got to do is sit with the board and make sure nobody fucks with it. We'll set up, do a sound check so all the levels are right, and after that you shouldn't need to touch a thing. If something sounds off to you during the show, or if one of us asks for more vocals, or monitor, or instrument volume or whatever, you'll have everything labeled with masking tape right on the board. All you've got to do is find who needs more of what, and tweak it up a touch." Richard saw the hesitation in my eyes, interpreted the fear screwing up my face. "Wait till we set up before you sweat this, man," he comforted. "It's really much easier than you think."

I nodded, but didn't say a word. Richard patted my forearm, then turned back around in the front seat to help Papa navigate the streets.

I looked out the window disgustedly. "Hate this place," I grumbled. Richard whipped around. "What?"

"Nothing," I said, too quiet for him to hear. He cocked his ear intently.

"Nothing," I repeated loudly enough for both of them to hear this time. Papa turned his profile, and for a moment they both glared at me. Then they looked at each other and snickered.

"Hate this place," I muttered a second time.

They both laughed again, but no one bothered looking back.

A dark little club is a dark little club whether you're in Detroit, Wisconsin or New York, New York. Once we got inside, it really wasn't as bad as I'd imagined. After we set up, the owner — a friendly little Italian man with a wicked comb-over — allowed us to park in his fenced-off parking space down the street. We were home for the night.

We set up just like always, except this time Papa and I hooked up the band's PA. In a way, I was happy to finally be using it. Between the board in its large steel case, and the bulky twin speakers and stands, the PA took up a lot of room in the van. I figured if we were going to haul it all over the place, we might as well use it. Plus it gave me something different to do for the night. Job variety.

"Alright, man," Papa said motioning to the mass of knobs, dials, and green and red graphs spread like shrapnel across the board's face. "Everything's labeled, see? That one's for Richard's vocals, that one's mine, that's Coolie, and that's Julius. Same with the instruments." He pointed. "Labeled right below the volume." He caught me scanning all the other gizmos on the board. "Don't even worry about those, Virgil. Those will all be pre-set. All you've got to do is, if you see one of us motioning, or we ask for a little more of something, you bump it up a tiny bit until we give you a thumbs up. Got it?"

I got it, but I didn't like it. "What if..." I searched my mind for scenarios. "What if it feeds back, or something? I mean, what if it all just cuts out?"

"It won't," reassured Papa. "In all the gigs I've played, I think the sound has cut out maybe twice. And both times it was for stupid reasons we're not going to have." I looked at him doubtfully. "I'm telling you, Virgil, unless this city blacks out —"

"It's happened before," I burst out.

Papa sighed. "I know it has, Virgil, but it won't tonight. I promise. And we're going to do a soundcheck right now to make sure nothing feeds back." He waved to Richard, Julius, and Coolie who were milling around onstage. A few early birds were drinking at the bar, waitresses and bartenders were preparing for the Friday night crush, but we pretty much had the place to ourselves.

"Alright, guys, let's try a check," he called out to the band. "Just do it without me, and then I'll come up and Virgil can set my levels." He looked at me and winked. "It's all good, just make sure you can hear me in the mix."

I nodded bravely.

All things considered, the night actually went smoothly. Once we sound checked the rest of the band, Papa hopped onstage and played his bass. I boosted him until he blended into the mix — he asked for some more monitor, which I gave him — and that was it. Once during the night, Julius asked for more bass in the monitors, and Richard immediately wanted more vocals, but that was about it. Two songs into the gig I simply kicked back and enjoyed the scene.

The crowd was a mix of younger college kids and older bohemian-type village dwellers. I spotted Argute, Fecunde, and a few more Laver-nites across the bar a few songs into the night, but there was no sign of Felix or my Albany girl. Their absence added to my relaxation. I simply kicked back on my stool three-quarters of the way back in the bar, and pretended to be important to the night's proceedings. Something about the soundboard kept everyone at a distance, too. Nobody wanted to be responsible for screwing up everybody's fun. At least not until the annoying man at 11:35 p.m.

"Hey, man, it sounds good," the guy slurred. I nailed him immediately as the dreaded buddy-buddy drunken convert fan. Not a favorite of mine. He wore a cheap rumpled sport coat over a black t-shirt, Nike running sneakers, and plastic prescription glasses with thick lenses. He swayed back and forth as he spoke. "I never saw these guys before, they're really good."

"Yeah, thanks, man," I answered. "I'm glad you like them." I quickly leaned over the soundboard, pretending to monitor something.

He didn't back off. "Have they..." He wiped his nose. "Have you guys been around long?"

"A couple of years now," I said looking up, then down again. "They're out of Burlington though, so they're only here every few months."

"Are you always with them?"

I didn't feel like running down my employment history with a guy who'd forget it immediately, so I took the easy way out. "Yeah. Always."

"No, you're not," he replied. His words were blunt, his tone so altered that it didn't register at first. I looked over slowly, confused by the switch. He suddenly appeared totally sober; feet planted firmly in place, not swaying. His eyes looked lucid and intelligent. He focused on me and said it again. "No, you're not."

I didn't know how to respond. He was playing some kind of game with me, but I didn't know what it was.

"I'm not?" I asked. He shook his head slowly, dead serious. "And how would you know that?"

He leaned in close to my ear. I leaned away and looked into his eyes, waiting patiently, gauging his intentions. I took a chance and came a bit closer. There was no alcohol on his breath as he spoke. "'Cause we've been watching."

"Me?"

He nodded again, motioning towards the stage. "All of you."

I was dumbfounded. His tone, his transformation: it seemed almost surreal. I tried to make sense of it. "What are you, with a record label or something?" He shook his head, said nothing. "So what, then?" I was starting to feel agitated. I waited, but he said nothing. That really pissed me off. "Actually, just forget it," I said angrily. "I don't even want to know. Just get away from me, man. You're creeping me out."

He smiled a small phony grin. I stared him down, waiting for him to leave.

"She never met you last week did she?"

"Who?" I demanded, truly angry now. "Who didn't meet me? What the fuck are you talking about, man?"

"In Albany, the girl, she never met you when she was supposed to."

That did it. I was convinced the guy was some weird Lavernite head-fuck sent by Felix to mess with me. And that pissed me off. I searched the crowd, fully expecting to spot Felix in the corner laughing his head off. But I didn't. All I saw was a sea of unfamiliar faces turned toward the stage.

"Just get away from me, man." I said, pushing his arm away. "I don't have time for this bullshit." I looked down at the board, studying it.

"It's no game, Virgil Frey," he said ominously. "We'll be in touch."

He disappeared into the crowd and was gone.

That was my limit. I'd had enough. Enough of Felix and the Lavernites. Enough of feeling like an amoeba under their sick microscope. I abandoned my post, stormed over to Argute, gripped his arm, and spun him away from the stage. "Where is he?" I demanded. Argute merely stared back, puzzled and obviously stoned. "Where is he, Argot, Wingnut, or whatever your name is? Where is he? Where's Felix?" The other Lavernites stopped dancing and fanned out around him. "All of you fuckers — someone's got to know where he is? Where the hell's Felix?" They were blank-faced, stupid, pissing me off. Argute cracked a shitty little smile.

"You know what?" I was filled to the lid with angry poison. "I don't give a fuck where he is. You just tell him and that little bitch next time you see them that I'm done with their stupid fucking games! I don't care what you do, I don't care what he's up to, or what the hell her game is — I just want to be left the fuck alone." I tapped Argute on the side of the head. "You think you can remember that, drone? Huh? Or is that too much for your programmed little brain to handle?" He moved toward me, ready to retaliate, but Fecunde held him back. "You just tell them that, Wingnut. And while you're at it, stay the hell away from me, too." I motioned to all of them standing in a semicircle around me now. "All of you, stay the fuck away from me!"

"What's the problem, Virgil?" A voice came from behind. "Are these kids giving you trouble?"

I turned to find Tony, the club owner, standing beside two mountainous bouncers. It was my turn to smile the shitty smile. "Yeah, Tony, they are actually. I'm trying to run the soundboard over there, and these assholes keep giving me a hard time. I finally had to say something to them."

Tony looked into the faces of the gathered Lavernites. He clapped the flanking bouncers on their flaring lateral muscles. "Get 'em out of here," he commanded.

Tony put an arm around my shoulder and escorted me back to the soundboard while the hulking bouncers cleared the resistant Lavernites out of the bar. "What are you doing trying to handle this yourself?" he asked, motioning a thumb backwards. "That's what I pay them for." I took my stool, feeling flustered despite my petty victory. "From now on, you handle this." He motioned to the board. "And let us handle the bozos. You just come straight to me if anyone else gives you a hard time, got it?"

I nodded thankfully, feeling protected. "Alright, Tony. Thanks, I appreciate it."

"It's nothing," he said, turning to leave. "I'll have Dana bring you over a drink."

Tony asked what I was drinking. True to his word, a double Jack Daniels and Coke arrived on Dana's tray only minutes later. I took a heavy pull, glancing above the rim for errant Lavernites or the strange drunk/sober man. All clear. I tapped Dana's shoulder as she turned to leave.

"Do me a favor?" She nodded, waiting. "Keep 'em coming."

Dana did her job, and I did mine. By the end of the gig, she'd brought and removed a dizzying number of glasses while I kicked back on my stool, eyed the occasional board level, and drank on as the crowd got wild. I'll give NYC one thing: they got Laverna right away. The match fit surprisingly well, considering all the lyrical references to fields, gods and goddesses, orchards, and the natural world. Maybe that was the key though. Maybe New Yorkers were desperate for music that didn't sound like jackhammers and subway lines; instead, wanting music that helped them forget being surrounded by five hundred trillion cubed tons of concrete, glass, and steel. Whatever the cause, by the end of the night, people were filtering out of Coppers sweaty and smiling, whooping their way into the streets and back to their tiny hovels.

"Hey, nice job," greeted Papa, first off the stage. "See? It wasn't too tough running the board, was it?"

"Nope," I answered, a little too abruptly. Papa looked down at me; I grinned dumbly back at him.

"Jesus, you're wrecked!" I shook my head no, spilling some drink down the crotch of my jeans. "You are!" he exclaimed, slapping his leg. "I can't believe it!" He turned and waved the other guys over. "Hey, check out Virgil!" He pointed at me swaying on the stool. They gathered around the soundboard. "He's trashed!"

I had little to do but try and keep a straight face.

Julius was the first to comment. "No wonder he didn't screw it up. He was too busy drinking to touch anything." He shook his head, and went back to the stage to pack up his keyboard.

"Shit, Virgil, how'd you get so drunk out here?" asked Richard.

Coolie stepped in, bobbing amusedly. "Were you drinking with some hot chicks or what, man?"

I shook my head, bracing myself against the edge of the stool. "Nope, just me. Me and Dana."

"I knew it!" exclaimed Coolie.

"Who's Dana?" asked Richard. "Where is she now?"

I pointed over to my sweet angel waitress emptying glasses into a gray plastic bin.

"You mean her?" he asked in disbelief. "The waitress?"

I nodded, and flashed that idiot grin. Coolie guffawed, slapping my knee, and left to break down his drums. Richard motioned for Papa to go handle his bass gear.

"Man, Virgil," he said, once we were alone. "You're kind of making me look like an asshole here. I gave those guys so much shit over getting screwed up in Albany, and now here you are, my boy, trashed when you're supposed to be watching the board."

"Sorry, man," I said, trying to keep a straight face. "Sorry, Richard. It just kind of happened."

"That's alright," he said, hesitantly. "But I'll tell you the same thing I told those guys. We've got more time to get fucked up than we could ever possibly use, and a few hours a week to actually work. We'll all come out looking a lot better if we don't mix them up."

I saluted, perhaps too arrogantly. "Won't happen again, man. My apologize."

"Right," muttered Richard. "Your apologize." He shook his head, looking me up and down. "Well, listen, man, you're no good to us now. Why don't you just hang out while we pack up? We'll grab you when we're ready to split."

"You know I hate this place," I offered as some sort of explanation or defense.

"New York Shitty."

"I know, man," Richard said, clapping my back. "Just hang out. We should take about twenty minutes."

I stood up off my stool, toppling a little, then regained my balance, and meandered over to the bar to wait.

But why wait empty-handed? I waved at Dana.

However much the alcohol had soothed my anger and frazzled nerves at Coppers, it did me no such favors Saturday morning. I awoke in an enormous canopy bed surrounded by looming portraits of serious-looking men in suits of armor, my brain screaming out for liquids, aspirin, or cyanide. The way I felt, it wouldn't have troubled me at all if one of those portraits had come to life, leapt off the canvas, and ran a sword through my bloody heart. I knew that surviving the day would be a feat of endurance.

Coolie pushed into my bedroom carrying a tall glass of orange juice and a bottle of pills. He sat on the corner of the bed as I drained half the glass in one gulp. I burped.

"Coolie," I said, wiping my mouth. "You're my fucking hero, man. I've been trying to will liquids in here for over an hour, man."

"I caught your vibe, man," nodded Coolie. "You use the force well, young Jedi."

He shook out a couple small white pills, and dumped them into my outstretched palm.

I turned them over searching for a brand name. "Aspirin?"

Coolie shook his head, grinning. "These people are loaded, man. Rich people don't eat aspirin — that's way common."

I gave them a closer look, but didn't recognize the marking. "So what are they?"

"Just take them," reassured Coolie, helping me tip the glass to my lips. "They're Julius's mother's Vicodin. She's got a whole bottle of them." He rattled the small brown plastic container. "I'm telling you, you'd need a medical degree just to find your way around in that bathroom. She's got more prescriptions in there than a pharmacy counter."

"Wow, man," I mumbled, swallowing two pills and the last of the juice. "What time is it anyway?"

"I'll say, wow man!" laughed Coolie. "It's almost eleven. You were trashed last night." I gave him a you're-telling-me look. "Richard, Julius, and Papa are going back to the village to check out record stores, and buy some strings and stuff. They wanted me to see if you want to go."

I shuddered at the idea of merging into New York's pedestrian traffic while my brain screamed out for hari-kari. It was bad enough sober. "Shit, no," I said, shivering.

"What are you gonna do?"

Coolie brandished the pills, rattling them around. "We're in the king's palace, and those guys want to mix with the peasants?" Coolie shook his head. "I don't think so. We've got good bud, a bathroom full of pills, food in the fridge, and a big ass TV." He laughed, slapping my leg. "I think I'll be just fine right here."

I felt saved. The first rays of light shined through the morning. "Have I told you you're my hero yet, Coolie?"

He took my glass, and made for the door. "I know I am, Virgil."

To a band on the way up (or, in the Doctors' case, the way back up) playing Swampland was a benchmark. The better the schedule, the higher the mark. Laverna's first gigs there were on Monday or Tuesday nights; they were definitely on the calendar, but playing to tamer, smaller audiences. After that, they played a few opening gigs on Thursdays, and a couple of Friday nights — better crowd, but not with the headlining bands that draw major attention. So, for Laverna, the Saturday night gig opening for the Doctors at their first major comeback show was a very high mark. Not headlining on a Saturday night yet, but one step away.

The guys were pumped and ready for the gig. Swampland was packed with hipsters, hippies, hotties, groovers, musicians, straights, freaks, and A&R people waiting in the wings to see if the Doctors could cut it a second time. And, by the way, who was this opening band everyone was talking about?

Richard, Julius, Coolie, and Papa knew what they had to do. I had the merch table set up in the entryway as they took the stage, greeted by a full house of nearly 800 screaming music aficionados. Richard kept it short and sweet. "Stand back. We're Laverna." And then cut into a riveting version of "Welcome the Gods."

No need for introductions, you know who I am
Snuck in through the middle, fell straight into your hands
Welcome the Gods, the sinning world is ours to command

It sucked being out in the entryway. I couldn't see what was happening on stage, but by the sound of it, the guys were working their magic to full effect. A few smokers and struggling couples trying to make a love connection lingered in the hallway, but for the most part, when the music started, everyone crammed inside the ballroom leaving me alone. "Welcome the Gods" ended, and the crowd roared their unanimous approval. Without missing a beat, Richard kicked the band into a stellar rendition of "No Thieves."

"I hear you gave my friends a hard time last night." I turned away from the doorway, already recognizing the deep voice. "Life on the road getting you down, Virgil?"

"I'll tell you what I told them, Felix" I said, looking him straight in the eye. "Leave me the fuck alone."

Felix shook his head amusedly. He was dressed in a loose white cotton shirt and billowy black pants; a single beaded dreadlock hung over his left eye. "Tsk, tsk, tsk, Virgil. Is that any way to talk to your friend's number one fan?"

"Richard's got plenty of fans, Felix. I don't think he'd miss you any."

"Perhaps not," he speculated. "But what about the others I bring to the table? I've been known to fill out what would've been an otherwise empty room."

I looked around his side. "Where are your little followers anyway? I'm surprised your two main goons aren't with you."

"Actually, it's fortunate for you that they aren't. Believe me, Argute and Fecunde wanted to come. But I thought it better that they find alternative amusement tonight."

"Oh, I'm sure they will," I jabbed. "And, of course, they do whatever you tell them to."

Felix raised his eyebrows, shifting the dreadlock aside. "You'd better hope it stays that way, Virgil. They're none too happy about your unwarranted attack last night. I kept them away in your best interest tonight."

"Unwarranted!" I huffed. "Who's shitting who here, Felix? Or should I say — Calvin?"

"Felix will do just fine," he responded calmly.

"Fine. Felix, then," I continued. "Ever since I joined these guys, you've been trying to fuck with my head. First, feeding me all that bullshit back in Saratoga, running your weird programmed followers around in front of me just to freak me out. Then sending your girl over to lead me on and ditch me in Albany. And now the guy in the sport coat at Coppers last night." Felix cocked his head curiously, but didn't interrupt. "So, I'll tell you again as nicely as I can: leave me the hell alone. You go your way, and I'll go mine. It's obvious we're traveling in the same circles, but that doesn't mean we have to interact. I won't mess with your thing, no matter how fucked up I think it is, and you don't mess with mine."

"And I suppose you don't want to meet any more of my female friends either then?" he asked, oozing superiority.

"Hey, man, whatever deal you have with Richard and those guys is your business. Like I said, just leave me out of it. To tell you the truth, your whole scene, including the hook-ups, creeps me out. Your followers, your stupid little code-names — all of it. I don't need any of it. Besides, your girl from Albany was lesson enough."

Felix looked puzzled. "Who's this girl from Albany you keep talking about? And the man from last night?" He shook his head. "Frankly, Virgil, I think you're becoming a bit paranoid."

"And I think you're a total asshole, Calvin." I couldn't help letting him know I wasn't completely in the dark about his past. "But that shouldn't make a difference, should it? Richard told me what's up with you, and your business is your business. Just don't make it mine, and we'll get along fine. Understand?"

"We're ships that pass in the night, Virgil." Felix winked. "From now on, consider us visions, specters, shadows on the wall of as little consequence to you as a stranger's passing exhalations."

"Yeah, right. Whatever. Just keep your goons, Fetid and Wingnut, away from me, too. All of you. Put out the order. Do whatever you do." I waved my hands. "Keep away from Virgil."

"Goodbye then, Virgil." Felix said, bowing.

He turned and danced his way into the main ballroom.

I knew that getting rid of Felix and the Lavernites wouldn't be that easy, but at least my message was conveyed. At the time I had no idea of the true sickness lurking behind Felix's cool exterior. I sensed there was more to it than just controlling a vast weed empire though. The Lavernites were too obedient to simply be his workers. At the very least, he was head-fucking them into submission to control his illicit business. I was pretty sure he was head-fucking them for more twisted purposes than that, though. Either way, I wanted nothing to do with any of it. I didn't like Richard or Laverna being involved with them either, but that was their decision. For better or worse.

BACKSTAGE PASS

After Swampland, the labels saw Laverna coming. It's hard to ignore a tight band with great songs, talent, chops, and a visionary front
man oozing charisma from the stage. By night's end, there was a buzz
through the crowd about a Doctors comeback. But there was another
buzz, too — about Laverna.

Richard approached my table after the Doctors' two sets. I'd sold
thirty-six CDs, eighteen bumper stickers, twelve shirts, and signed up
eighty-seven people to the list. But he didn't care about any of that. Neither did anyone else in the band. They were soaring.

"How many discs do we have left?" Richard asked, practically vibrating with nervous energy. Seeing Richard so excited fired me up. I
knew what this gig meant to them, and, after a short taste of self-man-
aged life on the road, I knew why.

People were lingering in the hall and ballroom, but the Swampland
crowd was beginning to thin out. Sweaty club-goers strolled casually
out the doors, arm-in-arm, euphorically buoyed on an ocean of good
music, high energy, an aura of sex, and plenty of booze.

"I don't know, I sold a bunch, hang on." I rifled through the box un-
der the table, quickly counting CDs. We'd brought a thousand out from
Burlington, but I generally carried only seventy-five into a gig at once.
The numbers were dwindling fast, a great sign. As I counted, people ex-

iting offered Richard kudos and encouragement on their way past: You guys are sick, man! Totally mind-melting! When are you playing here again? Killer set, man, killer! Amazing tunes, bro, really hot! Richard took it all in stride, returning thanks and shaking hands with the fluid moves of a seasoned politician. This, too, was Richard's domain.

I popped up from under the table. "I've got about thirty-five left in the box."

Richard held out his hand, energized. "Good, give them to me."

"All of them?" He'd never asked for more than one or two comps at a time. "What's up?"

"This," he said, holding out a hand filled with paper. I leaned over the table to inspect the squares; each one a business card with a different music label's logo in the corner. He nodded animatedly. "Time for Laverna to meet corporate America, man. Hand them over, Virgil." I turned the box of CDs over to Richard. He made a kind of whooping sound, spun away, and started for the ballroom entrance. He turned back on the threshold. "Hey, Virgil, man! Pack up and put that shit away! The workday's over, man, we rocked it! Stow that stuff and come on backstage, we're partying with the Doctors!" And with that, Richard disappeared into the main ballroom to hand-out discs, shake hands, disseminate band statistics, and give the suits a chance to salivate over his own cosmic brand of old school rock-star flavor.

Being backstage after a high energy gig at a high profile club with two hard-partying bands is something like waking up from a dream you don't want to end, then willing yourself back into it; barely controlling your actions while gladly being swept along, momentarily grabbing ahold of solid images to gain perspective, then letting go, releasing, and being swept back into the stream of events without concern; just coasting, floating, riding it out while all along you maintain the subliminal awareness that none of this is really real.

Backstage at Swampland, not only was I confronted at every turn by the surreal image of guys who had been famous for years — the Doctors — smoking pot, snorting coke, and generally getting crazy; I was surrounded by music executives passing joints to roadies, club owners making deals about plans and plans about deals, a group of bikers attacking the cold cut platter with animalistic vigor, some older lady with green hair circulating Ecstasy tablets to Swampland waitresses and bartenders, and the guys from Laverna mixed up in it all, soaring skyward on their breakthrough gig, the true rock-n-roll high life, and glowing with the promise of more to come.

I made my way through the frenetic party and took a seat on a sofa in the corner, dropping down beside Julius and Richard locked in an intense conversation. Neither batted an eyelash at my entrance. I leaned my head back against the cushions to take it all in. I tilted my head slightly, cueing in on Julius and Richard's conversation.

"I'm not saying that. That's not what I'm saying at all, Julius."

"Well, it certainly sounds like it to me, Richard. And that's what comes through in your actions, too."

"Hey, man. I love you. You know that, dude. You're the fucking one, man. I couldn't — we couldn't — do any of this without you. You're the glue. You pull us all together out there. Shit, man. I got no problem however you want to live your life. Do whatever you want — I trust your judgment. Who are any of us to point fingers anyway? I mean, really. Think about it."

"All I'm saying is, I need to be myself, Richard," said Julius. "Especially with you guys. I've carried around too many faces for too long, and I just won't do it anymore. I will not do it. So you and Coolie and Papa all need to accept that before this goes any further."

"What are you talking about? We all love you, Julius. We're a unit: what one does all of us do. Who do you think doesn't accept you? Coolie? Papa?" Pause. "What? Me? Oh, man! Why?" Pause, pause. "What? Because of that stuff... back in Burlington? Hey, I fucked up, Julius. I'm the first to admit that. I overreacted, lost my shit, freaked out. All of it." Richard leaned back, and exhaled up at the ceiling. "It was totally my problem. I care about you screwing around with needles — that's what I care about. I've said that a hundred times, and I'll keep saying it: I don't want to see you doing it. I think it'll take you nowhere, and I think it'll fuck up the band. I'll say it again and again: I don't accept you using that shit. But as far as the other stuff, you being into guys and whatever else, I'm cool with whatever's gonna make you feel right. We all are."

He placed his elbows on his thighs, and moved closer to Julius. "I mean, I'm not saying you didn't freak me out a little when you grabbed me. You did." He tapped Julius good-naturedly on the shoulder. "I wasn't ready for it. I didn't expect it, and that's not what I'm personally into. I'll say that flat out: that's just not my thing, Julius. But what I am into is you doing whatever you need to do to feel comfortable — with yourself and in this band." Pause, pause. "I really mean that, Julius. And I hope you believe that, too, because I'm completely serious when I say we can't do this without you. I mean, look around you, man. None of this can happen without you."

The next pause was long. Even through my outsider status and shut eyes, it felt pregnant with portent. I opened them, turned my head. Julius and Richard were hugging, side by side on the couch. They broke; Julius pecked Richard's cheek. "I know you mean it, Richard. I really hope you do, because, to be completely honest, this band means more to me than you know. It's... Let's just say, I haven't had a lot of closeness in my life. Not many meaningful relationships. This band, you guys, are the closest thing to family I've ever had. Without you all..." The emotion cracked in Julius's voice. "It's because of you guys that I'm finally feeling... comfortable with myself. Maybe I'm the only one who's not accepting that. I don't know. Maybe it's been coming out all screwed up in different ways." Pause. "I'm still just trying to figure this all out too, you know? I don't know. Maybe that's what all of this has really been about. All I know for sure is, things are changing for me, and I need... I just need to know I have all your support, you know? I just..."

"We're here, man," soothed Richard. He put his hand on Julius's shoulder. "We're all behind you, brother."

And that was it. They hugged and didn't break for two minutes, three minutes, four minutes... I stood up and walked away. This was their moment.

As I made my way over to the cold-cut buffet I saw Coolie slamming a glass of syrupy black fluid while bouncing a waitress on each knee. In another corner, Papa was hunched over a mirror covered with white powder, a biker with a razor blade on one side, a man in khakis and a blue blazer patting his back and talking ninety miles an hour into his ear on the other. I opened my mouth to insert a slice of salami, but before I could close it, the lady with the E pills tossed one into my mouth. I smiled at her, and swallowed.

OUT OF TUNE

Coolie and I had plenty of company in the apartment Sunday. Everybody's spirits were still high, but nobody was in any condition to go anywhere. Coolie and I popped some codeine tablets from Mrs. Edson's stash, and told Papa to pick out something nice for himself. He selected an amusing little Darvon. Nice choice. We thought it best not to say anything to Richard or Julius about our stash invasion though. Julius surely knew the stash was there if he wanted it. If we told Richard, he might start asking about when we found them, and eventually stumble into Coolie and I taking pills before the gig. Pot was one thing. But Richard would most likely consider mixing Valium and pot a breach of his no partying pre-gig golden rule.

Whatever partying had gone on at Swampland the night before, some reconciling had happened there, too. There was an ease in interaction between Julius and Richard that I hadn't seen before. Between Julius and everyone really. Like he'd pulled up anchor in the Swamplands and was finally drifting free, unfettered. I wouldn't go so far as to say Julius was a changed man, but — simply put — he was nicer, easier to be with.

We lounged on loveseats and stuffed chairs in various degrees of rumpledness in the Edsons' television room. The room was a modest concession to human comfort in an otherwise foreboding decor. It was still uptight for a den, but you could kick your feet up almost anywhere without displacing ancient artifacts. Out of curiosity, I'd poked my head into Julius's bedroom on Saturday afternoon while they were gone: no posters, no pictures, no trophies or diplomas, no sign that a boy had once grown up there. It didn't surprise me really; he'd been gone for a while. Still, I couldn't shake the feeling that a similar sterility had stalked Julius throughout childhood.

"Oww," moaned Coolie. His feet were kicked up over the back of a loveseat, his head dipping near the ground. His pain was felt by us all. "Riiiiccccchhhard," he moaned. "Call the Bingo Parlor and tell them we can't play." He paused, allowing his eyes to roll back in his head. "I think I'm dyyyyiiiinnngggg."

"Shut up, Coolie," chided Richard. "We're all dying. Suck it up."

"Suck this, boss," retorted Coolie, grabbing his crotch. He stayed there for a while, hand on his crotch, head hanging down. Images of past Simpsons episodes flickered soundlessly on the large-screen TV in front of us. "Hey, Julius, man. Is that a DVD player beneath the TV? You guys got any movies for it?"

Julius slowly hobbled over to a small closet, opened it, and fished past some coats into the black depths. He came back out with a stack of discs. He held them above his head as we ooohhed and ahhhed.

"I bought these at a flea market last Christmas for just such an occasion." He lowered the first disc down to face us; on the front was an image ingrained into the brain of every American male born since 1976: Luke Skywalker with raised lightsaber, Princess Lea at his side with laser pistol drawn, droids beside them; in the background floated the faces of Hans, Chewie, Darth, and Obi-wan. "Gentlemen," announced Julius dramatically. "For your viewing pleasure, may I present the *Star Wars* trilogy on DVD? A truly mind-numbing experience."

"Too late," moaned Papa. "My mind's already numb." The Darvon was no doubt kicking in for him. "And dumb."

"You're probably still numb from all that coke you snorted with those bikers," jabbed Richard. "Every time I looked over, you were leaning over that mirror again: snorting, chopping, rubbing it all over your mouth and gums. Jesus, you were practically bathing in the shit. I'm surprised you slept at all last night."

Coolie, Papa, and I looked at each other and tried not to laugh. We wanted to, but it would've hurt too much.

"Who said anything about sleep?" mumbled Papa.

It was true. Between Papa's coke, my Ecstasy, and whatever Coolie had in him, none of us slept more than an hour or two. Even Julius and Richard couldn't have gotten more than a few paltry hours: we didn't get back to the apartment until almost 5 a.m. After that, Papa, Coolie and I had sat out on the patio, looking out over the park, slowly deflating our buzzes, smoking cigarettes and pot, and dipping into Mrs. Edson's pill collection to even us out.

As the original *Star Wars* began, our eyes drooped collectively. By the time Darth Vader made his entrance, we were all asleep.

We made it to the Bingo Parlor for Sunday's gig, but just barely. It was the loosest show all tour. The guys played every song like a meandering space-rock jam; allowing one note to bring itself to another, never quite sure where or when the next turn would arrive. Every so often, Richard would step up to the mike and add vocals. Their eyes were small slits, hair (even Julius's) sticking up at odds all over their heads, clothes wrinkled, greasy, sagging.

Forty-five minutes before the gig, Richard had awoken, realized the time, and scrambled everyone up and out the door. We rolled in under the glare of the on-duty manager, Vanessa, set up in record time and, without a soundcheck, the guys started playing. I stood at the merch table glowering at anyone who dared come close. Not many braved it. The band's music made no converts that night either; too loose, too spacey, too experimental, for most listeners. The only ones who seemed to dig it were the Lavernites. They ate it up, noodling around the dance floor, flapping their arms and rolling their heads like acid-drenched flower children.

For the first time since Albany, I saw the mystery girl that night. It was not a joyous reunion. Felix, Argute, and Fecunde were there, too, along with ten more Lavernites. Some familiar looking, some not. Felix winked at me across the room, but never approached. Maybe my demands worked after all. Every once in a while my Albany girl would shoot me a look, a glance, but I always turned away quickly. She was just as pretty as I remembered: long brown hair, a single red and green hair wrap dangling down her back, petite compact figure, unassuming yet independent air, and liquid brown eyes I was careful not to fall too deeply into. I'd hoped that seeing her again would turn my stomach. But there was no such luck. She pulled me right back in.

At one point it looked like she was coming my way; something about her stride told me she approached with a purpose. But Fecunde caught her arm, and she turned back. It was only at night's end, as they all filtered past my table and out the door, that she made contact. True to Felix's word and command, no Lavernite said a word to me. Not even Argute or Fecunde. Only my Albany girl ventured a communication. Last in line out the door, she dropped a small piece of paper on the table in front of me as she passed. I waited until she looked back at me and then crumpled it dramatically and tossed it into the garbage as if to say: "Now who's the fool?"

Once again, I was.

Our next gig wasn't until Wednesday in New Paltz. The band used the time and the Edsons' spacious apartment to rehearse new songs (Julius using the baby grand he'd played while growing up), recover, and prepare for the second half of the tour. We all needed the break. Coolie, Papa, and I stayed dreamily sedated much of the time; the pills even giving me enough buffer to venture out for short stints to bookstores, restaurants, music shops, a stroll through the park, and a stumbling tour of Chinatown.

I didn't want to admit it, but I was beginning to see what all the New York City fuss was about. It did have more to offer than, say, Utica. Of course, having a million-dollar apartment and vanity full of pills to return to each day helped soften the noise, crowds, and pollution I despised. Still, by the time we rolled out of town on Wednesday morning, I was actually a little sad to bid New York City farewell.

TAKE IT TO THE BRIDGE

Until Rochester, the only other time I saw Albany girl was in Cortland. In addition to seeing her there, being in Cortland brought back a slew of memories. I remembered driving there with Richard to see Hot Tuna play at the Haunted House, the same club Laverna was now headlining. We were sixteen years old. Richard was obsessed with electric blues, and had stolen his mother's car to make the trip. Who knows what happened to him because of that? I don't even want to think about it. I'd rather remember the way we talked the bouncer into believing we were eighteen. Telling him we'd come all the way from Utica for the show, holding up the line until he let us in. I'd rather remember the wild music: Jorma, the sweet devil with the guitar, and Jack Casady, his face popping like hundred-degree soup, running through cosmic blues covers and swampy originals with ferocious power. I'd rather remember Richard and I shaking Jorma's hand before he slipped into the backstage room along the side wall; the way he'd smiled that devious smile. The way it made us both, Richard especially, buzz and grin. It was my first real taste of live rock-n-roll.

As Laverna played, I couldn't help looking around and wondering if there was a kid like that somewhere in the club. A kid who'd snuck past the bouncers just to taste his first live music. I wondered if Richard, wailing away on-stage, was thinking the same thing. And I wanted that kid to be there. I wanted Laverna to be his first. I wanted to pat the kid on the back, tell him to enjoy it, that this was a moment he would remember forever.

Albany girl arrived that night dressed all in white with small purple flowers laced through her long brown hair. She came in with the rest of the Lavernites while Jabez Stone, the opening band, was playing their set. I tried not to look, but I couldn't help myself. Throughout the night, I glanced back and forth between her and the stage, but we never caught each other's eye. I figured that was for the best. I also felt vaguely guilty about tossing away her note without reading it. I'd thrown it out right in front of her. Now I stood at the table wondering: What did it say? What did she want? Why wouldn't she simply come up and talk to me? I swear I could feel her looking at me, too, but she was dancing on the edge of the tapers, on the fringe of the Lavernites, and neither one of us was risking contact. Why won't she say something? Why won't I say something?

I knew the answer to all of my questions: Felix.

For all his creepiness, I had to admit that Felix was a man of his word. Argute, Fecunde, and the rest of the Lavernites scarcely looked my way, and Felix did nothing more than nod politely.

After the Haunted House gig, the band ended up at a Cortland frat house party. I don't know which one, but it seemed to matter to them because they all wore hats and t-shirts emblazoned with the same Greek letters. The "brothers" were totally into the show. They insisted we party with them back at "the house." They kept saying "the house" and "brothers" while slapping each other's arms and readjusting their baseball hats: "the house, the house, gotta come back to the house, party with the brothers at the house." So despite my dislike of being surrounded by testosterone-swollen men with baseball hats, we did. I partied with them for a while; even made out with a cute girl in a Cortland sweatshirt until her roommate pulled her away. Richard disappeared fast. I saw the girl he slipped away with and couldn't blame him. She was gorgeous, tall with long, tanned, tapering legs. After a while, I slipped into an empty bedroom and curled up on a well-worn futon in the corner. As I tried to fall asleep, I could hear Coolie yell every few minutes, no doubt giving the biggest house partiers a run for their money. Papa found my hiding spot and passed out on the floor next to my feet. Before he lost consciousness, he sneaked a call to Julie on the frat kid's phone. Lovestruck bastard, I thought.

We played a second Haunted House show, then there were three days off, and then it was on to Ithaca. While Ithaca wasn't technically a hometown gig, it still felt like returning to a place I needed to reconcile with. There were ghosts there; there was closure that needed to happen. Ithaca's Town Theater was built in 1915. It was originally a vaudeville theater, then converted into a movie theater in the 1930s. At some point, it was divided up: half the space rented out to small shops, the other half dedicated to live music. During my brief tenure as an MFA student, I'd seen a few shows there and was always impressed at how the old-timey vibe was sustained, even while a sonic electric guitar assault was underway. Despite the fact that I was only a roadie and merch monkey, I still felt like I was making a semi-triumphant return to Ithaca. At least I wasn't slinking back there with my tail between my legs. The Town Theater was a prestigious venue for groups at Laverna's level, and I was riding the wave of an excellent band on the crest of a big breakthrough tour.

That's what I told myself anyway.

After soundcheck, I peeled away from the band to wander downtown. I'd considered contacting some people from my old program — the guys in the band encouraged it in order to pump up attendance — or maybe my old roommates, but I also knew that my tiny room had already been sub-sublet, and there was no one I really knew well enough to call. It was over for me in Ithaca. I simply hadn't stayed long enough to make any significant attachments. Still, it was good to be back there. Much like Burlington, Ithaca is a classic East Coast college town with a liberal history of music and counterculture. As a result, bands take their gigs there seriously. In 1977, the Grateful Dead played a concert in Ithaca that was considered to be one of their best shows ever; no small feat given how many shows they played. Bruce Springsteen, Red Hot Chili Peppers, Faith No More, Santana, Bob Dylan... For a small town, Ithaca's musical history was long, storied, and illustrious. Now Laverna was joining those ranks.

I found my favorite little sandwich shop off Aurora Street and swung inside. I placed my traditional order — chicken salad on rye bread — and carried it to a secluded table in back. I nudged my chair closer to the pay phone on the wall. It was time to check in with my mother again.

"Virgil, it's about time!" She answered the phone on the second ring. Her gentle chastisement felt as nourishing as the chicken salad. "Where are you now?"

I swallowed my bite. "Well, don't get excited, but I'm in Ithaca."

"Oh, that's so wonderful!" she exclaimed. "You're back in school!"

"No," I said, prepared for her disappointment. "Sorry, Mom. I was afraid you'd think that. But no, I'm just here for a gig. Laverna is playing here tonight."

"Oh." Her sigh sounded like air rushing out of a balloon. "Right. Of course, of course. My mistake." She recovered quickly. "Well, that's nice. Nice for Richard. Nice for you, too, I suppose."

"Yeah, Mom" I said, putting a good face on it all. "It's a great venue. I'm really happy they're playing it. It's nice to be back here, too."

She brightened again. "Do you think you might want to go back? Have you run into any of your professors?"

"No, I haven't." I turned my sandwich over, absentmindedly studying the caraway seeds in the rye bread. "I don't know, Mom. I've thought about it, but..." I let the thought drift away.

There was a few seconds of silence, then she spoke. "It's okay, Virgil." Her response took me off guard. It actually sounded like she meant it. "There's no rush. You have time."

"Yeah?" I asked. "You mean it?"

"Sure," she answered. "Why not? You're young, traveling, spending time with your friend, enjoying your life. This is the time to do that." She laughed. "Besides, it's not as if getting a fiction degree is a solid career track. Who knows? Maybe this is all for the best."

I had to laugh. Of course, she was right.

"Do you know that the other night we were playing Bridge and your father was telling people that you were working in the music industry? Isn't that a hoot? He was proud of it!" Her voice softened. "We're both proud of you, Virgil. You know that. Your father just has a harder time expressing it sometimes, but we're both very proud of you. Whatever you decide to do. We just want you to be safe and happy." She paused, allowing that to float between us. "So are you?" she asked.

"Am I what, Mom?"

She paused again. "Are you safe and happy, Virgil?"

Throughout the rest of the night I kept hearing that question in my head: "Are you safe and happy, Virgil?"

I hung up the phone, threw out my uneaten pickle spear, and slid my tray back over the counter ("Are you safe and happy, Virgil?"), walked back to the Town Theater, and settled in behind the merch table ("Are you safe and happy, Virgil?").

I even stumbled through an awkward conversation with a drunken group from my former writing program: "Did you really drop out to roadie for Laverna, man? That's wild, dude, wild! We heard that, but figured it was just a rumor! Good for you, bro!"

Through it all, my mother's voice looped endlessly through my thoughts. "Are you safe and happy, Virgil?"

Am I safe and happy? As the question swirled, I kept returning to the image of Richard and Julius sitting together at Swampland. The intimacy of their conversation. The closeness and acceptance I had witnessed in that moment. Julius asking for support and understanding. Richard offering it to him. The gratitude they both felt for each other, their relationship, as this raw human need — acceptance — was exposed for both to embrace or reject. As I worked the table, making up deals (buy a CD and t-shirt, get a free bumper sticker), I wondered if the connection I had witnessed between them was the essence of "safe and happy." Perhaps the answer I was looking for was buried in the brotherhood I had stepped into with Laverna. Perhaps I was on the trail of "safe and happy" after all.

Unfortunately, my good feelings were short-lived. As we pulled out of Ithaca, I could sense Richard growing tense the closer we got to Rochester. It was the last stop before Utica, and the specter of seeing his mother again clearly had Richard on edge.

Although Mrs. Knight had been crazy for as long as I'd known her — basically, my whole life — it had taken a dramatic public episode to finally get her hospitalized for good. Considering the bruises and general malaise Richard carried through school, it's sad that no educators had bothered to probe deeper into his home life. Even a shallow dig may have gotten Richard taken away from her until he was no longer a minor. But then — even for me and my parents — bruises can be safer to ignore than to deal with; bad family situations can be attributed to a father's death, a mother's stress, a child's misbehavior. Making the decision to intervene can seem like a dangerous leap into the unknown, never knowing if it would be for better or worse in the end.

Still, the decision should have been made. Someone should have intervened. It would have been for the better.

As the story goes, Mrs. Knight made away with 27 crucifixes before she was caught. Her Plymouth Duster was filled with silver and gold crosses, large and small, gathered from every church within a 30-mile radius. It wasn't until the St. Christopher's heist that police apprehended her. She was shakily making her way down the stone front steps, a 50-pound crucifix pulled down from the altar slung across her back, spewing a rambling diatribe of prayer, blasphemy, tongues, and family complaints.

Once the police spotted her, Mrs. Knight merely added them to her spewed shit-list, moving steadily towards the Duster. She tossed the crucifix into the trunk with the others, seemingly oblivious to the officers' commands of "Freeze! Halt!," and began reviewing a scrambled list of over one hundred local-area churches she intended to pillage. The police approached, their weapons drawn, while Mrs. Knight remained oblivious to their presence. Finally, one touched her shoulder. She whipped around and drove a pair of scissors through his forearm, cutting through muscle, past bone, and out the other side. The cops tackled her and that was it: she'd been a resident of the Utica Psychiatric Center ever since.

So I didn't blame Richard for being more tense than usual. He had a lot on his mind. On top of it all, he'd been put off by two record companies' A&R men who'd finally agreed to take his call with variations of "It's not the right time for your kind of music." Two others were still unreachable after several tries, and a fifth still hadn't listened to the CD yet: he'd be in touch real soon. As we hit Rochester, I could sense that Richard's tension was high and tight. He was coiled, taut.

II

If I told you all that went down
it would burn off both of your ears

—Robert Hunter, "Deal"

GOODNIGHT, ROCHESTER

Coolie found us a place to stay in Rochester. He set us up with some guys he'd met on Laverna's last trip through town. The apartment we crammed into was basically a crash pad for weed-smoking teenagers, coke heads, and young dope users needing a place to get off. I never did figure out who actually lived there and who was just passing through. Everyone seemed equally at home sprawled across the couches, floor, beds, chairs, watching whatever was on TV, listening to whatever music was playing — usually dictated by the coke heads. We were on Alliance Street, just off of Monroe Avenue, downtown Rochester's main hipster scene: punks, hippies, street people, skate rats, goths, and weirdos of all stripes mixed there to eye each other and exchange goods and services. Despite the fact that our time in that apartment was minimal, whatever time we spent there was too much. Those two days in Rochester pushed Richard over the edge. And he took the rest of the band with him.

Laverna was booked Friday and Saturday night at the Warehouse. The Warehouse was the top venue available to an unsigned, indie band like Laverna, but also hosted radio-friendly one-hit-wonder bands, as well as touring war-horses like George Clinton, Bela Fleck and the Flecktones, and Max Creek. The place was appropriately named: an old, drafty, cavernous, former flour warehouse had been converted by a long side bar and a decent stage and sound system into Rochester's best midsize music venue. The gigs there were good ones, noteworthy. Laverna had worked their way up, playing smaller bars in town, and opening gigs there first. This was to be their first full weekend.

Friday's show went well. The turnout was outstanding. Rochester was another city to pick up on Laverna's sound early, and the all-ages crowd was energized and enthusiastic. The band rocked hard, mixing up the set list, adding plenty of texture, even playing a new tune tentatively titled "Mediterranean Mistress" that they'd worked on in New York City.

Unfortunately, Friday night was as successful as Saturday night's gig was disastrous.

It all began careening downhill at 3 a.m. Saturday morning. The first thing to go was Julius's heroin sobriety. In all fairness, you'd never ask a drunk with one-week sobriety to spend all night in a bar full of drunks. Not exactly an AA recipe for success. Heroin was the most covertly used substance in the apartment, but that didn't matter. Julius sussed it out immediately. Before any of us even realized it was available, Julius was hidden away in a back bedroom spiking his arm. Unfortunately, it was Richard, already drunk and ornery, who found him there. I heard the yelling down the hall and went to investigate. None of the other twenty or so people still partying hard at 3 a.m., including Papa and Coolie, even noticed. To them, the yelling was just more scrambled noise above the already muddled sonic mix of Jane's Addiction, Brady Bunch reruns, and wasted, meandering conversation.

I poked my head around the edge of a dangling purple tapestry. Julius was seated on the far corner of the bed, legs pulled tight against his chest, works neatly arranged on the nightstand beside him. A scrawny long-haired boy, eighteen at most, was reclined across the bed in front of him; at his side was a cardboard box of fresh needles sealed in industrial plastic. Led Zeppelin was playing on a boombox in the corner. I stayed put where I was.

"So this is the way it's gonna be?" Richard slurred drunkenly. "This is how it is, huh? You're gonna be a junkie and keep using and fuck up the band and wreck the whole deal?" Julius stared up at Richard, expressionless. "Fine, man! That's just mother-fucking fine, Julius. You do what you need to do." He collapsed on the opposite mattress corner, nearly bouncing the skinny kid off. The kid rearranged himself and looked over, as if seeing Richard for the first time. Richard looked the kid up and down, wheels turning. "You know what?" he finally said. "Shoot me up, too, man." Richard reached into the box and took out a fresh needle. He nudged the kid's thigh. "Come on, kid, shoot me up. I've got the money." He reached into his pocket and pulled out a crumpled wad of cash. "Look — advance money for the gigs, the owner gave me some tonight." He looked over at Julius. "What do you say, Julius? If we're going to do it, let's do it right! Let's take all the band's money and shoot it right into our fucking veins! We'll go out just like dumb-ass rock star cliches! But without the contracts or albums. Why not? It's all going to fucking hell anyway!"

I stepped around the curtain toward Richard. He whipped around and pointed at me. "Get the fuck out of here, Virgil! Get the fuck out right now! I don't need you babysitting me tonight!"

"Hey, Richard, man," I said, raising my hands in peace. "I'm not here to babysit you. Just stop for a minute, and look at what you're about to do." I pointed down at the needle in his hand. The whole band had already been drinking heavily since the end of the gig, doing lines of coke, and smoking pot, too. But Richard was about to take it to a different level. I tried talking him down, but my own buzz got in the way. "All I'm saying is, don't do it. It's stupid, man. Leave these guys here." I pointed to the two inanimate human objects sitting motionless behind him. "Come back to the party. We're all waiting for you."

Richard pointed at the door. "I'm not gonna say it again, Virgil. Get the fuck out of here, man. I know what I'm doing. This is between me and Julius! This has nothing to do with you!"

"But, Richar—"

"VIRGIL FREY!" He shrieked like a lunatic. "YOU GET THE FUCK OUT OF HERE BEFORE I TAKE YOU THE FUCK OUT!"

I was stunned, dazed. Pissed off. "Fuck you, too, Richard Payne

Knight," I spat back, feeling oddly calm in that moment. "It's your life, asshole."

I turned and left. The lock clicked shut behind me.

All the weird energy and intense partying continued through the night and into the next morning. It was like the stopper had been pulled out, and all the tension from the road, the band, the strain of trying to make dreams into reality spewed out across that nasty apartment, soaking us all in its bitter juices and seeping into our veins in the form of powder, pot, and alcoholic rage. Come dawn, Coolie, Papa, and I were stumbling down Monroe Avenue looking for a place to eat, swearing at restaurant Closed signs, and shielding our eyes from passing vehicles and pedestrians.

Julius and Richard had been holed up in the back bedroom all night. The skinny kid, too. Coolie and Papa asked about them a couple times, but I blew off the queries with mumbled excuses and rolled bloodshot eyes. Now it was Saturday morning. A new day.

We finally found an open diner, Gitsis, and seated ourselves. Apparently we ordered food, too, because we all ate some. The conversation was stilted, scattershot.

We laughed, mumbled, and we somehow ate and somehow paid the bill and somehow found our way back to the apartment and finally passed out.

The day only got worse from there.

Richard and Julius finally emerged from the back bedroom a couple of hours before Saturday's show. I was asleep on the couch, Coolie and Papa passed out on loungers across the front room, when the sounds of a toilet flush and muted voices down the hall rousted me awake. I considered that they might be Richard, and fell immediately back to sleep. Even if it was, fuck him. My brain was Swiss cheese, and Richard had crossed a line. Stress or no stress, he was on his own.

The scene I finally woke up to was a cold reality slap across the face.

"Come on, man," Richard whispered eerily. "Everybody wake up. It's time to play, man. It's time to party."

I opened my eyes; Richard was inches from my face. His pupils were tiny, laser-like dots. In one night, he seemed to have aged ten years. His face was pale, lined, the bags slung under his eyes reached down his cheeks, his hair was matted and greasy. The mirror he held to my face trembled in his hands. But worst of all was that voice: the raspy whisper of a psychotic, coolly recounting a gruesome triple murder.

I blinked, hoping the face would disappear. It didn't. He nudged my shoulder again.

"Come on, Virgil. This is it, man. It's time. The gig of gigs. Rock stardom, paranoid delusion, effortless nirvana … It all begins today."

I looked over at Papa. He was stretched out on a recliner chair, wrapped in a nasty old blanket, his eyes barely peeking out the top. He seemed frightened, too. I searched the room for Coolie and found him drinking Jack Daniels at the kitchen table with Julius.

It was getting worse.

"What the hell are you doing?" I finally asked. My voice had been scraped raw by booze and dozens of cigarettes the night before. I felt like an exhumed corpse. "What time is it?"

"It's time to gig, Virgil. Time to get down." He pushed the mirror, covered in fat white rails of coke, into my face. "We're going to try a little experiment tonight. What have we got to lose? Instead of playing sober, we're going to get as fucked up as we possibly can and see what happens next. Shit, man," he cooed. "The other way hasn't gotten us dick. Might as well try this for a change."

Richard was trampling his only solid rule: play sober. Despite all the craziness the guys regularly drummed up, this is the one law they'd tried sticking to. Especially under Richard's watchful eye. And now here he was desecrating that law, spitting in its face, and trampling its once-sacred ashes. It was horrifying.

"Jesus, Richard," I said, managing to swing my legs off the couch. "Have you even slept yet?" I found a clock on the wall: 7:30 p.m. "Man, you guys are going on in a couple hours and look at you. You're all a fucking mess."

Richard waved a finger in my face, smiling eerily. "Au contraire, young Virgil. We are simply visiting a new area of musicality. The full-force fucked-up jam. I've slept a million sleeps in a thousand feather beds. Tonight is the night to destroy all that. I am rested and ready."

"Fuck," I muttered, taking it all in. "Fuck. Fuck. Fuck." I felt like shit, my brain sluicing around loose in my skull. Even Papa was taking his first hit off a joint pinched between Julius's fingers. "I don't know what to say." Every fiber of my being told me to get out now, skip the gig, and wait the night out somewhere safe. No good can come of this, looped ceaselessly through my mind. "I've got to piss."

Richard shoved the mirror at me harder. "Snort now, piss later. We go as a band tonight, or we don't go at all. All for one — that's it."

I looked at the kitchen table: Coolie was tilting the JD to his mouth. Julius and Papa passed the joint. They were all waiting to see what I would do. Richard winked, and pushed the mirror at me.

"Hey, Virgil," I heard Coolie say from the kitchen nook. "Could you feel any worse than you already do?"

Just then the skinny kid emerged naked from the hallway, scratching his bald testicles and rubbing his eyes. He looked me dead in the eye and burped.

I was the fish against the river, the knot amongst the grain: I stayed sober for the gig. I convinced Richard that I'd be more effective for the experiment if I stayed lucid and chronicled it all. If they wanted to try this out, fine, that was their call. But if it was truly an experiment, why not have an impartial party — the scribe — recording the results?

Even through his drug-addled stupor, Richard saw the benefits of this. So I sat back and watched them drink, snort, and smoke themselves into oblivion before the gig. Soon the partying moved from the apartment — where they were soon joined by other partiers emerging from hidden bedrooms and other nooks to see what was happening — to backstage at the Warehouse. The small brick room was immediately filled with pot smoke and obnoxious kids of all ages, wasted out of their minds, urging Laverna head-on into their chemical experiment. I couldn't look. Despite Richard's insistence that I forget the table for the night — "Fuck everything!" were his exact words — I drifted out as soon as I could, and set up the merch table towards the back of the room.

The Warehouse was filled to their 850-person capacity; a crowd of mixed-ages, fired up for Saturday night music and raring to party. At 9:15, Laverna took the stage.

"I just wanna say," Richard began as the band took their places. His voice was cool and even, words only slightly slurred. He rocked a little as he spoke, gripping the mike stand and his guitar neck for balance. "I just wanna say, I've had some great times in Rochester and it's good to be back with you all. You guys know how to fucking party."

The crowd responded with whistles and catcalls, truly pleased.

"I just..." he tried to continue. "My fuckin'..." he stuttered again. "My fucking mother is..." I held my breath, sensing a bad turn. "She's in the fucking mental ward."

The crowd applauded wildly, thinking this was all a part of the show.

"A fucking mental ward," he repeated. "At Utica Psychiatric Center."

Again, the crowd broke into wild applause.

"So I just wanna..." He turned, appraising the band, all in place, waiting with bloodshot eyes. "We just wanna..."

He stopped to catch his breath. He looked out over the crowd and caught my eye in the back of the room. A sudden fortitude seemed to grip him. He reached down, turned the volume up on his guitar, and brought down a power chord that rattled my teeth. The feedback reverberated through the room as Richard said one more thing: "Mom, this song is for you!" And then he kicked the band into a tearing, angry version of "Welcome the Gods."

I felt a pull at my elbow and turned. It was her. Albany girl.

"I know who you are, Virgil."

I looked into her eyes; she was lucid, intelligent, carrying a message.

"I can't explain now. I'm not what you think. Meet me in the alley behind the club during set break."

"But..." I started to protest. I was ready to question, to bring up

Albany, our last scheduled meeting, her dedication to Felix's strange world.

"Here they come," she interrupted, flashing a quick glance past my shoulder. I turned and saw Argute approach with another Lavernite male I'd never seen. "Just do it, Virgil. It's important." And then she was gone. Argute was on us quickly, stalking past my table, throwing me a bitter glance. He moved fast in the direction of Albany girl.

I looked at where Argute had been standing with a handful of other Lavernites, including Felix, dancing on the edge of the taper section. There seemed to be fewer of them in the audience. Felix turned, his face stern, expression flat. He turned back. I looked left, a taper caught my eye: he'd been watching me, there was no mistaking it. He made eye contact, nodding sharply, and turned back.

I was surrounded by strange, foreboding faces.

I'd never felt so alone in my life.

The truth is, until that night, I had no awareness at all of the murders that were taking place. Killings that involved Richard, Felix, the Lavernites, and implicated the entire band, including myself, to some degree. Simply put, I was completely clueless; an ignorant bystander right up until the moment I nearly saw one occur only inches from my hiding spot in the alley behind the Warehouse. A spot I was squished into beside my one and only Albany girl — our first, and last, date. It was at that moment I understood that nothing was as I assumed it to be.

It was set break, and the band had somehow made it through the first set. Even more incredible, the crowd didn't even seem to notice how wasted they were. After seeing multiple Laverna shows over the past three weeks, I knew they sounded like shit: missing changes, flubbing lyrics, botching solos. But it seemed I was the only one who noticed. The crowd loved it; they applauded and danced like they'd finally found the musical oasis they'd been crawling over hot desert sands to reach. Luckily for the band, the crowd was as collectively wasted as they were.

Coolie approached the merch table as I made my break for the alley. "What's up, Virgil? Where you going, man?" He could barely stand still, arms and legs rubbery and trembling. I needed to get away fast to meet my Albany girl.

"I've gotta meet someone," I said, knowing the quick way to Coolie's heart. "I've got this girl waiting outside in the alley. She told me to meet her out there between sets. Watch the table and take people's money, okay? I'll be back in ten."

Coolie grinned broadly; it seemed this time the truth worked best.

"Where's Richard and the other guys?" I asked.

Coolie shrugged. "I dunno where Julius and Papa are. Fucking Richard kicked everyone out of backstage and took a couple..." He paused, searching for the word.

"Fuckin'... Fuckin'..." He pointed over towards the tapers. A handful of Lavernites were seated on the ground behind them. He looked into my eyes, pleading for help.

"Lavernites?" I offered.

"Yeah," he said, hiccuping loudly. "He took a couple Lavernite chicks backstage and kicked everyone else out. I don't even wanna..." He paused, burped. "I don't even wanna know what he's doing back there. He's in weird Richard mode. I don't even..." He tapered off.

"So he just kicked everyone out?" I was torn between this new development and meeting the girl. "Even you guys?"

Coolie nodded excessively. "Yup, kicked us all out. Fuckin' Felix and those guys walked the girls right over. Richard opened the door, the girls went in, and that was it. He just shut it on all of us." He shook his head knowingly. "He's wasted, man. Just leave him there, Virgil."

I had no intention of interrupting anyway. "Did Felix go in, too?"

Coolie shook his head. "Nope. Just the..." He hiccuped again. "Just the girls."

"Alright, man," I said, nudging the box of extra CDs, shirts, and stickers under the table, just out of sight. "I've got to meet this girl. Do me a favor: stay put for a couple of minutes and make sure no one steals anything. Just take people's money if they want to buy something, okay? The prices are next to the goods. Cash box is under the table."

Coolie saluted, and I raced off through the crowd.

"Good luck, Virgil!" I heard him yell. "Go get her, man!"

I raced past the bouncers, out the front door, and down a narrow side alley toward the small back street running behind the club. Just as I was about to emerge into the street, a hand reached out from the shadows and grabbed my shirt. It yanked me forcefully into a blackened doorway. "Shhh."

It was Albany girl.

"What's going on? Who are you?"

She put her fingers to my lips, silencing me. Still dressed in hippie gear, her long brown hair dribbling in tiny braids down her back, she reached down the neck of her peasant shirt and pulled out an FBI badge.

"What the—?" I stammered, but she silenced me again. She turned my head and pointed across the street: I saw the taper who'd been watching me inside. He was crouched behind a green VW camper, pistol drawn. She pointed higher, and I saw two more men crouched with rifles on a darkened fire escape. I heard voices; she pushed me back against the door, deeper into the shadows. The voices came closer, then their bodies came into view beside the backstage entrance. It was Felix and Argute.

"Where the hell did she go?" asked Felix.

"I don't know," pleaded Argute. "I told her the situation, that she was to complete her final task tonight before receiving her name. She knew what to do. She knew where to go. I pointed out the backstage door and everything. She knows who Richard is. But then she just... disappeared."

"And whose fault is that?" spat Felix.

"She's been so good up until now," pleaded Argute. "Perfect. She's done everything we've asked her to: made exchanges, carried product, everything. Why would I expect her to screw up this last little task?"

"I don't know," insisted Felix. "That's your job, not mine. If I wanted to do everything myself, I wouldn't keep you and that other idiot around. I'd bury you along with her. Now I've had to substitute a girl I wasn't planning on using for months. Richard requested two this time."

"Well, do you have to kill her?"

A loud slap sounded through the alley. "Say that out loud again and I swear to God I will bury you. What I do with these girls is my business. Whatever I decide to do with them. Do I take care of everything and everyone?" He waited. "Well, do I?"

"Yeah," Argute answered, sounding wounded. "You do."

"And what do I ask in return?" He repeated it again quickly, loudly. "What do I ask for?"

"Nothing," stammered Argute. "You don't ask for anything."

"Wrong," corrected Felix. "I ask for this one thing. I want the girls after he has had them. That's all. You and Fecunde can do whatever you want with them, whenever you want, as long as it doesn't interfere with business. I don't want any of that, and I don't say anything about it. All I ask is to have the girls when he's done with them. Is that too much to ask?"

"No," conceded Argute. "It's not. All I'm saying is, if you don't want to waste the other one, maybe you don't have to go all the way this time."

"All the way? And what is 'all the way'?" demanded Felix. "How do you presume to know what my going 'all the way' entails?"

"I don't, Felix, but—"

"No, you don't," he finished. "So let's keep it that way. We'll handle this the same as any other. The girls know what to do. They'll come out this entrance when they're finished, just as instructed, and you collect them and bring them to the van. After that, you locate the missing one and find out what happened. And I want to talk to her when she turns up. I should've trusted my judgement about her from the start."

I turned my head slightly left, saw a man creeping along the far wall, keeping low and in the shadows. For an instant, I saw his face. It was familiar. Suddenly it registered: the drunk/sober man from Coppers. He gave Albany girl a signal, then the taper behind the Volkswagen. The backstage doors opened and two Lavernite girls emerged. The FBI converged on them from all over the alley. Albany girl pushed me back against the door.

"Stay here," she commanded. She raced off toward the Lavernite leaders.

Felix and Argute were stunned. Albany girl — Special Agent Renee Edwards — spearheaded a 360-degree assault that had them on their bellies and handcuffed within seconds. While Felix and Argute were facedown on the concrete, the two Lavernite girls were being hand-cuffed beside the van. All the while, Taper Agent's knee was lodged se-curely into the pit of Felix's lower back.

Suddenly I felt a hard poke at the back of my head. Then another. I turned and found myself staring into the dark barrel of a .45 caliber pistol pointed directly at my left eye. The command was simple.

"Walk," said Fecunde, gesturing me forward with the gun.

Once my eyes were able to focus beyond the pistol I saw Richard standing beside Fecunde. My brain struggled for purchase: What was Richard doing? Was he a part of this? Was he going along with Fecunde?

Then Fecunde turned the gun on Richard and ordered us both out of the alley in front of him.

We stepped out of the shadows, fingers laced behind our heads as instructed.

"Let them go!" Fecunde shouted from behind us. For a minute, it was as if nothing had happened. The arrests continued: two more La-vernites were brought out the back door of the Warehouse.

He shouted again. "Let them go! Now!" But this time he fired a shot into the air to punctuate his demand.

It worked. The FBI agents froze in their spots, heads turned instinc-tively toward the sound of the gunshot. They glanced at one another, calculating, making life and death decisions with every breath.

"Release those two," Fecunde yelled, pointing at Felix and Argute. They were still on the ground, hands cuffed behind them. "Let them go!"

The taper agent looked over at Agent Renee Edwards. She nodded. He removed his knee from Felix's back and stood up. The agents pulled both men to their feet.

"Take the cuffs off," commanded Fecunde.

Again, Agent Edwards instructed the agents to follow the command.

"Now back off!"

Fecunde must've spotted the agents on the fire escape. He grabbed me around the neck and pulled me against his chest. "Tell them not to shoot!"

I could hear the panic in his voice. His breath was hot against my neck, his forearm pressing hard against my windpipe.

"Up there on the fire escape! Tell them to drop the guns. Now!"

Agent Edwards motioned up to the men. They set down their rifles and stepped back. She looked at Fecunde.

"Take it easy, Fecunde. We've done everything that you've asked. Nobody's going to shoot anyone. Just let Virgil go, and we can work this all out." She raised her arms slowly, calmly. "Nobody's going to hurt anyone here. We just need to talk. Everyone just needs to sit down and talk to one another."

"Fuck you!" snarled Fecunde. He pointed his gun at Richard's head, then back at mine. "Faithless lying bitch."

"That's right, Fecunde," encouraged Felix. "Now bring them over here."

Fecunde poked the gun into the back of my head and ordered both of us to walk.

"Keep all of them back against the wall," Fecunde yelled to Agent Edwards. "Or I swear I'll shoot them both."

He kept me tight against his chest as we walked, a human bulletproof vest in case the agents on the fire escape decided to test their aim. We made our way in front of the line of agents, over to Felix and Argute who were standing beside the van.

"Where the hell do you think you're going, Felix?" yelled Agent Edwards. "We've got police and agents covering every exit out of here. There's no way you'll make it." Her voice softened. "Just let Richard and Virgil go, Felix, and we can talk about this. That's all we want to do. We just need to talk."

Felix took the gun now. He grabbed me in a stranglehold and motioned Argute, Fecunde, and Richard into the van. Once again, I felt the cold gun barrel press against my skull.

"I knew there was something wrong with you," Felix said to Agent Edwards. "I should've trusted my instincts." A hint of amusement crept into his voice. "Who knew an FBI agent could be so obedient though?" He laughed at this, digging the gun deep into my neck now. "Tell them to let us through." He raised the gun so that they could all see it, and then nestled the barrel tight inside my right ear. "I will kill him. He's nothing to me. If anyone tries to stop us, I'll shoot him." He studied Agent Edwards. "And you know I'll do it, don't you?" She didn't make a move. His voice exploded, hard and low. "Do it now!" He dug the barrel deeper.

Agent Edwards gestured for a walkie-talkie. We were too far away to hear what she said, but Felix loosened his chokehold and called for Argute to start the van. She took the walkie-talkie away from her mouth.

"Where are you going to go, Felix?" she asked quickly. "There's nowhere. Even if you get out of here, there's no place you can hide anymore. We will find you. Don't make this worse than it already is. We can still talk about this, work something out. Don't blow it, Felix."

"I'm not the one who blew it," railed Felix. "You couldn't just leave us alone, could you? You had to get involved with something you understand nothing about. You had to—"

"Leave Virgil," she interrupted. "He's not a part of this, and you know it. He's innocent. Just leave him here."

"Nobody's innocent!" hammered Felix. And with that, he pulled me inside the van and slammed the side door. I saw Richard laid out cold on the floor of the van. I leaned over to check him. Was he breathing?

That's when everything went dark.

THE LAST OF THE LAVERNITES

Time collapsed. I don't know how long I was unconscious for, but based on the distance we traveled, it had to be hours. When I finally regained consciousness, I feared that I'd been blinded by the blow. My entire skull pulsated, pain radiating out from a large bulbous knot on the back of my head. I couldn't see a thing. I was blindfolded, my hands tied behind my back. My body was pitched up into the air and slammed back down against the floor of the van. Again and again. And then I felt another body slam into mine — we were both thrown right and then left, bodies crashing against each other, legs tangling and slapping together. Despite the blindfold, it only took a few seconds to figure out who was bashing up against me: Richard Payne Knight. If my hands were tied, I assumed his were, too, leaving us both helpless against the violent lurching of the van.

"Richard," I whispered. But there was no reply. I said his name again, risking a bit more volume this time.

"Richard," I rasped. "Are you okay, man? Richard?"

Still nothing. I pictured his body laid out on the floor of the van, the last sight I saw before they knocked me out. Fear gripped my stomach and bile squeezed up into my throat. Was Richard dead? Had they killed him? As questions assaulted my mind, the van hit a bump sending us both sailing a foot into the air. I braced myself for a crash landing, but instead came down soft against what I assume was Richard's left thigh. That did it.

"Ow!" he yelled out. The response from up front was immediate.

"Shut up back there!" ordered Felix.

"Fuck you," rallied Richard. But Felix only laughed.

"Hey, Richard," I whispered. "You alright, man?"

"Virgil?" He lowered his voice. "Shit, Virgil, is that you?"

"You alright?" I said again. I still hadn't shaken the idea that he might be dead.

"Yeah, yeah, I'm okay, man. I'm okay."

We hit another bump that threw us hard right, slamming me up against Richard, and Richard against the wall of the van.

"Where the hell are we?" I asked, as soon as we had recovered.

"I don't know." I felt his body wince beside me. "But my ass is broken." His body tensed again. "And my head feels caved in."

"Yeah. Mine, too. They knocked us out. I..."

The van lurched to a halt, throwing us both forward and back again. The engine stopped. I heard doors open up front.

"What should we do with them?" I recognized the voice as Argute's.

"Nothing," answered Felix. "Leave them here for now. We've gotta check out inside first. The others will be here soon."

The van doors slammed shut. We waited a few seconds, but nothing happened. My breath was short and fast in anticipation of what might come next. Finally, we both settled down enough to talk.

"Can you see anything?" asked Richard.

"No. You?"

"No."

We both sat quietly, hoping for a sound that would clue us in to our surroundings.

"It's fucking quiet," I said finally.

"Really fucking quiet," answered Richard.

Again, we waited. The only sound was our bodies adjusting and re-adjusting, trying to find a spot on our asses that wasn't sore and bruised. Slowly we both settled into positions that we could hold: our shoulders resting against each other, arms still tied behind our backs, heads resting against the side wall of the van.

"Should we…" I struggled for ideas. "Do you think we can work these things off our wrists?"

"What am I, Batman?" shot Richard, his words slurred just enough to remind me how wasted he'd been at the gig. Between the hours we'd spent unconscious and the intensity of the situation, he'd clearly sobered up some — but not entirely. "You think I've got a utility belt with cutters or something? These are the plastic cuffs cops use. We're not getting them off until they cut them off."

I thought about this. There was nothing we could do. Nothing left to say. So I said the only thing I could think of: "You're no Batman. Not even close."

There was a pause, and then we both started laughing. Low and guarded, but still a laugh.

Richard turned serious. "Hey, Virgil, I'm…" He paused. "I'm sorry, man. I don't know what to say."

"That's a start," I said, nudging my shoulder into his. We both waited, listening again to hear any outside noises, a clue. I couldn't take the silence. It was obvious we'd be in the dark, literally, until Felix decided otherwise. "Hey, Richard…"

"Shhh," hissed Richard. "Someone's coming."

He was right. The van door opened and we were both pulled out.

"Where are you taking us?" yelled Richard.

"Shut up, asshole," answered a voice I didn't recognize. "You'll know soon enough."

Richard and I were shoved forward. We stumbled across uneven terrain. At one point I almost tripped, but the hand on my arm wrenched me back up. Eventually we were ushered onto steadier ground somewhere inside, and a hand pushed against my chest sending me backward. I tumbled into blackness, landing against a wall. I heard a door slam shut in front of me.

"Richard?" I whispered. But I knew I was alone. I moved forward, put my ear to the door. I heard scuffling, Richard swearing, and then another door slam shut. And then silence. I waited, nothing. Nothing. It was quiet. Too quiet. I was alone.

This was a ceremony. The other scenes I had witnessed — the basement rituals, the stage show — they had all been pretend. This was real. A sacrifice. But this sacrifice was not for the goddess Laverna. This was for Felix.

The first thing I heard when the door opened was Richard's guitar. His voice joined in a few seconds later. I didn't recognize the song, but Richard's sound was unmistakable. His voice was pitched higher with nerves and stress, but it was him.

Now is the time, the search is done
We've come so far, but there are always things left undone
We have built them together, these fields we have sown
Let's walk now together, through these fields we have grown

I was pushed forward, still blindfolded and bound. I had been cramped up on the floor of the closet for hours. My legs were stiff, moving like foreign objects beneath me. I felt the surface beneath my feet turn from smooth to uneven again. The air turned colder; the smells changed, and I felt a cool breeze. Richard's playing grew louder, clearer. His voice quivered with every phrase.

It's not so far we have to go, it all seems just a moment away
Eternity is a star shining overhead, this time is ours today
Let us walk past this dream, the time has come to be gone
By the morning they will sing our names in song

I could hear activity: people moving, groaning. My back was placed against a hard surface. Two hands held my chest firmly in place while another set of hands pulled my arms back. I reached with my fingers, felt the surface beneath them: rough, wood, bark.

My blindfold was pulled off. I blinked hard; a sudden temperature drop swept across my eyelids. I opened my eyes, tried to focus and look around. It was night again. I was tied to a tree ten feet away from where Richard played. He looked at me, but never stopped playing. He was seated on a stool, a music stand with sheet music placed in front of him. It took me a minute to register where we were. The cabin, Saugerties. Larry's cabin in the woods. They must've known all along that Laverna used this cabin. But never like this.

All around the front of the cabin, a crowd of Lavernites gently flowed, smiling and dancing together and apart in various stages of undress while a bonfire burned in the middle. The soundtrack to it all was Richard's guitar and voice, singing a song written specifically for this occasion by Felix himself. Richard played it now as if his life — all our lives — depended on it. For all we knew, they did.

Once we wandered in skies alone
Down here we cry, but up there we shone
They can have this world, we have built our own

I spotted Felix through the mass motion of sweaty bodies. He appeared on one side of the bonfire, disappeared behind it, and then reappeared on the other side carrying a small plastic dropper bottle filled with liquid. Two Lavernites stopped moving long enough to open their mouths and each receive a dropper dose in the firelight. Felix smiled widely as he moved back behind the fire. Then Fecunde appeared also carrying a small plastic dropper bottle. Then Argute and Felix again, dispensing doses into the mouths of various Lavernites around the bonfire. The Lavernites smiled at each lovingly, expectantly. They swayed, sweated, and danced with closed eyes.

And then, one by one, their knees buckling beneath them, they fell to the ground, and silently died.

By the time the Lavernites realized the doses were fast poison and not one of their usual mind-expanding drugs, it was too late. They were dead and dying on the ground around the bonfire. Richard stopped playing as soon as he realized what was happening, but Felix quickly appeared at his side and placed a gun to his head. He ordered Richard to keep playing. A young woman, no more than eighteen, had curled up into a fetal position and died three feet away from Richard's feet.

Richard's face blanched sickly pale. He stared at the dead girl on the ground. His entire body spasmed as he leaned over and threw up, spattering his shoes and the battered guitar.

Felix's eyes glowed wildly in the firelight. "Play for them as they die," he ordered Richard. "Send them home with your music."

Richard hesitated for a moment, then looked over at me, wiping his mouth with the back of his hand. In an instant, Felix was at my side holding the gun to my head now.

"I said, 'Play!'" commanded Felix. "If you won't play for your life, then do it for your friend's." His voice was a growl. "This is about commitment, Richard. Always remember that. It is about loyalty, faith, and commitment."

Richard opened his mouth, but Felix pressed the gun harder against my temple. I could feel the steel, the rough rope cutting into my wrists, my body trembling against the solid tree trunk.

Richard played on. He had no choice. He played Felix's song over and over until every Lavernite around the bonfire had stopped moving, stopped breathing. They were dead. All of them.

Argute and Fecunde came and stood beside the fire. The last of the Lavernites. As Richard finished the final verses of the final song, as the last notes rang out and faded away, Felix walked over and shot Argute point-blank. A strange sneeer crossed his face as he did the same to Fecunde. Then he looked at me, looked at Richard, put the gun in his own mouth and pulled the trigger. His body slammed backwards and came down limp, heavy, covered with sweat and blood, on the ground between Richard and me. We both were splattered everywhere with droplets of blood.

In the silence that followed, the only movement was the dance of the bonfire flames as the cold wind blew them back and forth.

NO ENCORE

I stared out the office window at a tall building jutting out from the Rochester skyline, topped by a statue of fleet-footed Mercury, contemporary to Laverna, god of commerce, travel, thievery — messenger of the gods. "How did you know I wasn't involved?" I asked. "I mean, why contact me?"

Special Agent Renee Edwards, transformed from waif-like braided girl to blue-suited government employee, was seated in a chair across from me. Except for the eyes, she may as well have been a completely different person. Albany girl was gone for good.

"We held off for a little while," she said. "Because I was certain you were a bystander. I infiltrated Felix's organization three months ago, joining at the end of the band's last tour, brought in by a member turned informant that we had busted with ten pounds of pot at Grand Central Station. She agreed to give up Felix in turn for a lighter sentence. That's what put us onto him."

She glanced at the manila folder on the desk in front of her, then back at me.

"After hearing about his operation, we decided it demanded a closer look. The things she was telling us — the names, the sex trafficking, the recruiting methods — were a red flag that this was more than just marijuana distribution." She shook her head, as amazed at the truth as

217

anyone. "Turns out we were right. For all intents and purposes, Felix made Charles Manson look like a scoutmaster."

She opened the folder; a photo of Felix sat on top. "He and Manson had the same charisma, like all cult leaders. Jim Jones, of the Jonestown Guyana massacre, was another one. That's how he got all those kids, runaways mostly, to join his ranks. The ones you saw at the concerts were only a part of Felix's organization. The entire operation was much larger and very self-sufficient. They made good profits selling drugs, and kept a low profile and low overhead by staying constantly in motion." Agent Edwards sighed. "The difference between Manson and Felix is that Felix killed his followers, like Jim Jones."

Fifty-one Lavernites died that night in Saugerties — thirty-one, when you count Felix, Argute, and Fecunde. Felix had already ordered all the Lavernites who weren't in Rochester to meet at the cabin that weekend. Whether it for mass murder or not, he was planning something for them. Unfortunately, anyone who would've known his rationale was dead. Another four girls were murdered along the fall tour. Nobody was certain how many others died before them.

"But why? Why would he kill the people who were following him?"

Agent Edwards leaned back in her office chair, looked out the window. "Why does any serial killer do what they do?"

The term fluttered my pulse: Serial Killer. I pictured Gacey in his clown outfit, Son of Sam stalking the streets of New York, gun drawn. Now Calvin 'Felix' Trill would join their bloody ranks.

"Our psychologists are still trying to put together a profile on him, but we've already got a pretty good picture. For whatever reason, Felix saw Richard as a beacon of some kind, an almost unconscious messenger of Felix's own destiny. Whatever messages your friend was intentionally writing into his songs, Felix was taking ten times the meaning out of them, twisting them around, and fashioning some kind of life purpose out of them. It's not that he even saw Richard as dictating the message necessarily. In fact, he might've even resented Richard's role in the process. Hated him for it. We're still trying to figure that out. But even when he took you two hostage, we had a pretty good idea that he'd never harm Richard. As you witnessed, he would rather kill himself than see anything happen to Richard."

"And me?"

Agent Edwards glanced at me, out the window, and then back again. "We had no choice, Virgil. We had to let the van go at the Warehouse in order to save you." She looked down. "But we fouled up. Lost them, lost you, we—"

She paused, composed herself, then resumed her professional duties. "According to what Richard told us, Felix started attaching to him in Oneonta. It seems at one point, after Richard's move to Burlington, Felix might've tried to break away to regain control over himself. Whatever he tried to do though, it didn't work. In fact, the time away seemed only to reaffirm his belief that Richard was the only one who could give his life meaning. Perhaps that's where the killings came from: his anger, his sense of helplessness and dependency on Richard. But killing Richard would mean killing his personal beacon, his messenger — it would never happen. If he killed the girls Richard slept with though, girls he himself delivered, then perhaps he could, in some way, control his own life."

"So that's why he did it? That's why he killed those girls?"

"Could be," nodded Agent Edwards. "Like I said, we're still trying to put it all together. It took us three months to figure out how the operation itself worked. It'll take much longer than that to figure out how Felix's sick mind operated. If we're ever able to figure it out at all."

I laced my fingers and locked them behind my head, shaking it gently. I sensed that Agent Edwards knew more than she was telling me, but nothing else she was willing to give up yet. The entire week since Richard and I had rolled wordlessly out of Saugerties and back to Rochester in the Lavernites' van — never even discussing our destination, just driving in shock, with the silence punctuated by an occasional whispered "Holy shit!" — had been a series of one horrifying revelation after another. And the flow had yet to cease.

"So, what was the operation?" I asked. "How exactly did it work?"

Agent Edwards walked to the window and opened it a crack. A

slight breeze seeped in, ruffling my unwashed hair. She took a seat on the ledge, crossing her legs at the ankle.

"You know the basics already," she began, measuring her words. "Felix was the leader; Argute, his second-in-command; and Reginald Hall, or Fecunde, just under him. It looks like Fecunde understood little of how the organization actually functioned. He was still mainly just a follower. A... What was your term again?"

I shook my head, chagrined that the term was sticking. "Lavernite," I answered grudgingly.

"Right," she sighed. "Lavernite. Well, Fecunde was still mainly just a Lavernite under Argute's direction. And the rest of the Lavernites arrived in different ways: once a few were in, new members seemed to join much easier. To some, it was the attraction of adventure, partying, hook-ups, or simply having your needs taken care of by the group. Others seemed to be drifting along and just found themselves there. The rules were simple: you do for the group and the group does for you. Right off the bat, they were stripped of their names. To get a name, you had to earn it. And to earn it, you had to prove loyalty by smuggling drugs, helping out on deals, bringing in new members, and engaging in the kind of sexual activity you witnessed, and..." She lowered her eyes. "Took part in."

I protested, humiliated. "I told you, I had no idea what the —"

Agent Edwards raised her hands. "I know that, Virgil," she said, trying to calm me. "We've known that all along. That's why I contacted you originally. Once I started to put together the holes in Felix and Argute's explanations for where the girls were disappearing to, we began realizing the operation may be something different than we'd thought. That's when we started watching everyone more closely, including the band. We knew that you were new, what your relationship to Richard was, your past. It was apparent that you were a bystander in all of this. That's when we decided to contact you. We needed an inside link to the band to better understand their involvement. But each time I tried contacting you, the group interfered in some way. By the time we connected the body in Albany to the Lavernites, it was too late to bother with an inside track. We needed to act immediately. If we hadn't, those two girls at the Warehouse would most likely be dead right now, too. Along with..."

She shook her head to clear the memory. All those dead bodies. She returned to her seat across the room.

"It's taken a little longer with the rest of the band, but we suspected they were unaware of Felix's motives. We're satisfied now that's the case. In truth, the only ones who fully realized the implications of their actions were Felix and Argute."

"So, what about us then?" Although we hadn't exactly been under arrest, the entire band was kept separated under the FBI's watchful eye for the past week. "Does that mean we can go?"

Agent Edwards stood and came across the room. "Yes, you're all free to go," she said. "But we do ask that you keep us informed of your whereabouts so that we can contact you if and when we need to. The others have been given the same instructions."

She reached out a hand. I stood up and shook it.

"So, where will you be going next, Virgil?"

PROMISE

By the time we left Rochester, the "Cult of Laverna Murders" was national news. Our faces glared back at us from newspaper headlines and magazine covers; our names were repeated by network news anchors, witnesses, fans, and every cult deprogrammer and serial killing expert they could drag in front of the cameras.

In one of the sick twists of fate and tragedy, Laverna was now getting lucrative offers from recording labels. Their music was being played on modern rock stations across the country, and Rolling Stone was preparing a long article on the history of the band, including details about the murders and a side-bar with reviews of Laverna's demo recordings: a nightmare wrapped in a dream wrapped in a nightmare. It was more than any of us could take.

After our release by the FBI, Coolie and Papa fled Rochester in the middle of the night. They floored the Subaru non-stop all the way back to Burlington. Papa decided that he would move in with Julie right away. Coolie would sequester himself in the band's house until it could be sublet or until the news crews decamped from out front. Julius flew directly to New York City where anonymity would be easier, but sobriety harder.

Despite their newfound fame, the fate of the band was uncertain. It was an issue none of them were ready to address.

I still had one more promise to fulfill.

Richard eased the van onto the exit ramp just inside Utica city limits.

"After all that's happened, you sure you still want to do this?" I asked.

"Yeah." Richard's voice was barely a whisper. He was focused intensely on the road in front of him. "Especially after all that's happened, I need to do this." He looked over. "Thanks, man. For being here, for going through with this."

I reached over, patting his shoulder. "Don't sweat it, brother."

Richard smiled. "So what about you? You gonna lay low in Florida for a while?"

"Yeah. A little while, anyway." I spotted the Dairy Queen our little league coach used to take us to after each win. "I just need to get away, you know? Process all this shit. Figure out my next move."

"Those agents," Richard said, negotiating the turn across from our old school, Theall Elementary. "They said the media is going to make our lives even crazier for months, maybe years."

I nodded my head knowingly.

"I can't imagine what that means." He blew out a puff of air. "What could be crazier than all this?"

I lit a smoke, dropped my head back against the passenger seat. "They don't know shit," I answered calmly. "Nothing's crazier than what we just went through." I shook my head slowly. "Nothing."

Richard made a left onto Blossom Road. The Utica Psychiatric Center loomed large before us. He pulled into the parking garage, took a ticket, and parked on level two. We both sat in the car for a few more minutes, staring at the dashboard. I needed to finish my smoke. We both needed to steel our nerves.

After a few minutes, I stubbed my cigarette in the ashtray and looked over at Richard.

"Ready?"

"Yeah," he nodded, exhaling deeply. "Let's do this."

We climbed out of the van and locked the doors behind us. Level two of the Utica Psychiatric Center parking garage was linked to the facility by a glass breezeway. We crossed it slowly, looking out at the city surrounding us. The Center was only two miles from where we'd grown up: we'd traveled these same streets daily, going about our lives in ways that, only now, seemed so simple. Just before we entered the building, Richard touched my shoulder. He pointed at the blue water tower looming like a giant in the distance. A huge red beacon flashed on top.

We took the elevator up to the third floor and approached the main desk. A nurse in a starched white uniform appraised us over her black-framed glasses. "Can I help you?"

"I'm here to visit my mother," Richard said, glancing quickly at me. "Ginny Knight."

The nurse looked surprised. She glanced from Richard to me, and back again. "Do the doctors know you're coming?"

Richard shook his head. "No, I..." he paused, searching for the right explanation. "It's unexpected. I didn't realize I'd be in town."

She looked over at me. "Are you a relation also?"

I shook my head, edging slightly behind Richard. "No, I'm not."

Without a word, the nurse picked up the phone and turned her back on us. She spoke to someone, presumably some higher-up, re-counting the situation, occasionally glancing over her shoulder at us, then turning back. She hung up and spun around.

"You can go ahead," she said to Richard. She pointed at me. "But he has to stay. Family only."

I nodded; we both realized that'd probably be the case. I walked over to the small waiting area in the corner.

The nurse pointed out some double doors up the yellow corridor. "Right through there," she said to Richard. "I'll buzz you in, and Doctor Galba will meet you on the other side. He wants to talk to you before your visit."

Richard turned and started for the doors.

"Good luck, man," I whispered, but I was too quiet for him to hear.

Richard turned back and looked at me anyway. He took a deep breath, and continued down the hall.

I took a seat in the corner, flicking idly through the magazines fanned out across the waiting room table. I heard a small buzzing sound as Richard was admitted. Minutes later the nurse approached me, nervously waving a clipboard in front of her chest.

"I wasn't informed of this visit," she said, apparently explaining something. "All visitors are required to sign in." She looked down at me expectantly; I didn't know what to say.

"Your friend," she said, pointing down the hallway. "He didn't sign in. I needed him to sign in first."

I was still unsure how this affected me. I took a guess. "You want me to sign in for him?"

The nurse glanced down the hallway and back, then quickly slipped me the clipboard.

I wrote fast, sensing her impatience. She took the clipboard back, bending over to inspect the signature.

"I can't make this out," she said, eyeing me over her glasses. "What's your friend's name?"

"My friend's name," I answered clearly, "is Richard Payne Knight."

THE BUTTERFLY EFFECT

It's fair to consider what I would have done differently. I once had a quasi-sadistic philosophy professor who posed the classic question: If you had a time machine and could travel back in time and kill Hitler as a baby, would you do it? Would you kill a tiny baby to head off the coming war and Holocaust?

It's kind of a sick headfuck of a question to ask. But interesting, too.

As expected, some in the class felt the answer was clear: Yes, absolutely, murdering one human to save millions is always worth the brutality of the action. To others, the idea of killing a child for any reason at all was unthinkable. To them, there were issues of fate, destiny, karma, God, not to mention the butterfly effect of unexpected consequences related to changing the arc of history, for example, a butterfly flapping its wings in Rio de Janeiro might change the weather in Chicago. No one could know. Once you start screwing with time and history, the outcomes are totally up for grabs.

Personally, I come down more on the side of the butterfly effect, but my larger response is: Until someone invents a time machine, who gives a shit?

I guess what I'm saying is, what's the point in speculating about what I would've done differently? I didn't do anything differently. I did exactly what I did. I didn't know what I didn't know: that girls were being murdered. I didn't know that Laverna's cult following was an actual cult.

One of the girls was only 17 years old. What am I supposed to do with that? They found her decomposing body washed up on the shores of Lake Ontario — her throat slashed wide open. What is the butterfly effect of such brutal murder? What of her parents, siblings, friends, future?

Would I have prevented those murders if I knew what was happening? Of course. I would've saved every one of those girls if I could have. But I didn't. I couldn't. I can't. I have no time machine, and the girls are dead, and even having so-called "justice served" doesn't diminish the horror I feel at having played any kind of obtuse minor part in their deaths, even if indirectly and unknowingly.

There is no reset button on history, no time machine, and speculation about possible alternative paths feels like pointless philosophical masturbation. There is no way to change what happened. It unfolded in the only way it could: exactly the way it did.

PURGATORY

After the short visit to the psychiatric unit in Utica where Mrs. Knight was so heavily sedated she didn't recognize Richard or know who he was, we drove back to Burlington in contemplative silence. Although Richard shared a few impressions of the predictably disappointing encounter with his mother, a series of college radio stations filled the conversational void as we passed through town after town. Richard was clearly drained. We both were. He also needed to sort out the band house situation, pay whatever bills needed to be paid, and figure out his next move. Once we got to Burlington, we spent the night at Tara's apartment to avoid dealing with the reporters that were camped out at the band house.

The next morning, we grabbed a quick breakfast together at a diner outside of town, and then I got on the road. For now, there was nothing left to say. I pointed my trusty old beater truck south and began twenty-eight hours of mindless driving from Burlington to Fort Meyers, Florida, powered by strong coffee, bad cold cut sandwiches, endless loops of painful recent memories, and one very long power-nap at the Fort Bragg Travel Center rest area in North Carolina.

Once I arrived and parked in the small visitor's area near my parents' condo, I rarely left the property. To their credit, my parents — even my dad — gave me plenty of space, too. I slept late, picked at the food my mother constantly placed in front of me, sat with my father while he stared at whatever sports game was on TV, and spent hours alone on their lanai after they went to bed early every night, gazing into the placid surface of the little blue swimming pool, jotting down thoughts in the black cloth-covered journal that had become my confidante and trusted therapist.

At some point, I would have to move on. Make some decisions. Next steps. I couldn't stay in purgatory forever. But at that moment even the non-weather there felt just about right, too. I picked up my journal.

It's 9:15 p.m. and Fort Meyers is quieter than a tomb. Why must all my thoughts include death?

Here is what I've learned: I am, at heart, a coward. I'm repulsed by violence. The reality of seeing those dead bloody bodies scattered around the bonfire will never leave me. But I'm not alone in that. Richard is there with me. Only a psychopath would feel differently. Maybe I have PTSD. My mother has spoken about soldiers returning from war and survivors of different atrocities. I haven't told her about my nightmares, cold sweats, the constant feelings of being watched, stalked, hunted. She probably knows.

Do I have PTSD? Of course I do. After talking on the phone a couple of times with the guys in the band, it's clear that we all do. We're just dealing with it in different ways. I only wish I could help them, like rescuing Coolie from the bottle he's drowning in. When we've spoken, he is always babbling, barely able to form sentences, wandering alone through that big empty house in Burlington. I worry that he won't make it. But I also know that he won't accept help.

Julius sounds better, but I'm worried that his courage comes from pills. He seems glad to be back in New York City, so at least that's something.

Papa has Julie, and that's been a blessing for him, for them both. I know they'll be okay.

As for me, I'm glad I came down to Florida. It's been calming to be with my parents, who have been surprisingly mellow since I got here. It's been soothing to be surrounded by regular people, civilians going about their ordinary lives at a glacial pace. The media vultures have moved on quickly to new titillating stories.

I still worry about Richard. But then, I've always worried about Richard. As I've been sitting on this lanai for what seems like eternities, I've been pondering the meaning of friendship, thinking especially hard about why Julius, Felix, and myself were so drawn to Richard. What is it about him that evokes such fierce devotion, protectiveness, envy, adoration? There are the finest of lines between romantic love, brotherhood, and obsession, and Richard dances on tightropes across them all.

Is love in any form just a cult? A cult of two: the adored and the adorer, the worshipper and the worshipped? Is it possible for those positions to ever change? Maybe love is only the passionate pursuit of changing roles: the adored to the adoring, the adoring to the adored?

I left school and went on the road with Laverna to find answers. In addition to the horrors discovered, I did find some.

Here's the truth: I still want to be a writer. I've decided to go back to school next semester. Well, maybe. Okay, probably. Yeah, I will. I want to work on arranging words, telling stories, illuminating shared experiences. To say things in a far less cheesy way than I just did. But now it's become clear that I want to write because I have questions, not because I have answers. I want to write because I need to better understand the nature of friendship, love, terror, desire, surrender, and death. I want to come to terms with what I have already lived through. And it's true, I'm almost ready to live again.

But until I am fully prepared to get back out there in the world, I'm content to sit here in limbo with a pen and a head full of heavy thoughts. I'll check in occasionally with my friends. I'll always try be polite to my parents. I'll eat the food I am given with gratitude and watch whoever's playing whatever game my father turns on. I will force a smile until someday, maybe, my face will smile again on its own. And once I have processed more of what the hell just happened, once I can make the words dance and shimmer on the page, I'll write the story of Laverna, and this whole bloody, fucked-up experience — the history of it all.

ACKNOWLEDGMENTS

Thank you to the following individuals for their help and encouragement in the writing of this book: Stephen Robinson, Patrick Kavaney, Todd Weiner, Linda Roghaar, Michael McGandy, the Conners family, the Senise family, the BOA family, and the Neem Karoli Baba and Recovery Dharma satsangs. Tremendous thanks to Jennifer Joseph for believing in this book, providing outstanding editorial guidance, and for founding the legendary Manic D Press. With love to Whitman, Max, Kane, and Little Max, and special thanks to Aimée.